JOHNNY TOO BAD

ALSO BY JOHN DUFRESNE

The Way That Water Enters Stone

Louisiana Power & Light

Love Warps the Mind a Little

Deep in the Shade of Paradise

The Lie That Tells a Truth

Johnny Too Bad

STORIES

JOHN DUFRESNE

W. W. NORTON & COMPANY

NEW YORK LONDON

For information about permission to reproduce selections from this
book, write to Permissions, W. W. Norton & Company, Inc., 500 Fifth
Avenue, New York, NY 10110

Manufacturing by The Courier Companies, Inc.
Book design by Barbara M. Bachman
Production manager: Amanda Morrison

LIBRARY OF CONGRESS CATALOGING-IN-PUBLICATION DATA

Dufresne, John.
Johnny too bad : stories / John Dufresne.— 1st ed.
p. cm.
ISBN 0-393-05789-5
1. United States—Social life and customs—Fiction. I. Title.
PS3554.U325J64 2005
813'.54—dc22

2004022794

W. W. Norton & Company, Inc.
500 Fifth Avenue, New York, N.Y. 10110
www.wwnorton.com

W. W. Norton & Company Ltd.
Castle House, 75/76 Wells Street, London W1T 3QT

1 2 3 4 5 6 7 8 9 0

For Lefty and Tristan

and in memory of Jim Whitehead

Please, consider me a dream.

—FRANZ KAFKA

CONTENTS

. . .

ACKNOWLEDGMENTS

. . .

THIS BOOK WOULD NOT HAVE HAPPENED WITH-out the encouragement and support of Cindy Chinelly, Dick McDonough, and Jill Bialosky. I also want to thank my writing pals David Beaty and Donald Papy for all their good cheer and conversation, our dear friends John Bond and Jeannie Deininger for great food and travels, and thank as well the Friday night writers, our Gang of Ten, and all my people.

Many of these stories appeared elsewhere, some in different versions: "Who Are They Who are Like Clouds?" in the *Mississippi Review*; "Lemonade and Paris Buns" and "You're at Macy's, Killing Time, When It Hits You," in *Tropic (Miami Herald)*; "Close By Me Forever," in the South Florida *Sun-Sentinel*; "Electric Limits of Our Widest Senses," in *Mangrove*; "I Will Eat a Piece of the Roof and You Can Eat the Window," in the *Sycamore Review* and as a limited edition chapbook, *Midnight Paper Sales*; "Based on a True Story," in *turnrow*; "The Dead of Night," in *Triquarterly*; "Johnny Too Bad," in

Triquarterly and *New Stories from the South: 2003, The Year's Best*; "Around the World," in *Rattapallax*; "Lefty" and "Breaking It Down for You," in *Shenandoah*; "Squeeze the Feeling," in the *Alaska Quarterly Review*; "Died and Gone to Heaven" in *Gargoyle*; and "Epithalamion" in *River City*.

J O H N N Y   T O O   B A D

LEMONADE AND
PARIS BUNS

I CALLED THE CLINIC AND MADE AN APPOINT-
ment for a cholesterol test. I ticked that off my list. I called
Dentaland at the Aventura Mall. They told me Dr. Shimkoski
was no longer affiliated with their practice. Well, what was I supposed to do then? I've got this temporary crown here. I thought
I heard someone outside talking to Spot. We can set you up with
Dr. Perez. Fine, I said. Wednesday, noon. I dumped the whites
into the washer, poured in the Tide, set the timer. I walked to the
window to check on the voice.

Four children sat on the ground near Spot patting him,
talking to him. Spot, I could tell, was loving the attention. I
went out to the deck and introduced myself. I said, I'm the
dog's—and I was going to say "master" until I heard the word
in my head and realized how absurd it was—I'm the dog's
dad, I said. I take care of him.

"What you dog name?" the oldest-looking child said.

"Spot. And yours?"

They were brothers, I learned, named Smith. The oldest,
Trayvien, probably ten, introduced me to Demetrius, Everett,
and Kendrick.

Spot rolled on his back with his legs in the air like quotation
marks. Everett stroked Spot's belly. I asked them where they

lived. Trayvien pointed across the backyard. I asked them if they'd like a snack. They would. So we had brunch on the deck.

Trayvien helped me set the table and led us in grace before we ate—his idea. We had lemonade and Paris buns. That's what I called them for the occasion. They were crescent rolls, actually, from Pastry Lane. Kendrick, the tiny one, sat on my lap and rubbed the hair on my arm back and forth. Trayvien was like the father. He poured lemonade for his brothers, wiped their faces with napkins. He asked me what I did for a job. I told him I write stories. He said that's what he did, too. I asked him to tell me a story. Trayvien told me the one he called, "The Wolf, the Bear, the Lion, and the Man." The four characters are friends, and they don't have enough money to buy ice cream. The Lion wants to eat the bank to get some. The Man says they should go to work and earn the money. The Bear is sure they can find some dollars in the street. The Wolf says we could just ask nice. And the Wolf is right.

As I scooped out the chocolate ice cream, I asked Trayvien did he have any stories with vegetables in them. No, he didn't. I told them all they should come by more often. Spot and I would enjoy their company. Trayvien said where they were living—he pointed across the yard again—was a frosted home, and they didn't know how long they'd be here. Foster home? I said. That's it, Trayvien said. Everett asked me, "Where you daddy?"

"Louisiana," I said. "Way far away."

I found out that their momma lived with a man named Walter. Their granny took care of them for a while. Now they're here. What are your foster parents' names? I said.

Trayvien said, We don't know yet. You think they might be worried where you are? Trayvien shrugged. I said, Well, let's go find them, okay? We all washed up at the kitchen sink. We put Spot on his leash and paraded down the street. We waved to Mr. Lesperence next door. Everett walked beside Spot. Spot kept licking Everett's face. Demetrius held the leash. Trayvien held Kendrick's hand. I held Trayvien's. Trayvien was sure it was a blue house. We made a couple of lefts and rights, but nothing looked familiar. Demetrius told me that Spot pees a lot.

"Here it is," Trayvien said.

I wanted to ring the bell, let the people know we were back, but Trayvien wouldn't let me. "They napping."

The boys hugged Spot. They stood in the driveway and waved good-bye until we turned the corner. This all happened a year and a half ago. I've never seen them again.

For a while, Spot and I took our walks by the blue house. One evening a man in a T-shirt and shorts stood there in the front yard, watering a Manila palm. He must have thought I was crazy. No kids ever lived here, he said. I looked around. This was the house. Spot slurped water from the hose. The man said, Shoo. Spot woofed at him. So you're not a foster parent? I said. He made a face. Spot sniffed around the side-walk. Evidently, the children's volatile molecules lingered here, though the children did not. I called the Welfare. No one there would tell me anything—confidentiality, the woman said. I said, What kind of world is this? Four babies wandering the streets. You shouldn't worry, she said.

My cholesterol is in the stratosphere, it turns out. So I drink red wine now with my Paris buns. I brunch on the deck with Spot, imagine Trayvien telling me a story with a happy ending. Like maybe he says, The Lion wants his friends back, but the Man says forget about it. The Bear is sure it was all a dream anyway. But the Wolf says what he believes is you meet everyone twice before you die.

The Lost Boys

AFTER MY FATHER DIED WHEN I WAS TWELVE,
my mother married Harvey Fahlstrom. When Mother died
five years later, she left Harvey to me, and then I lost him for
twenty-six years. Mother was the unhappiest person I've ever
known. She seems to have had the meekest of dreams—
wealth—and when even that did not come to pass, she
became insular and bitter, retreating to her bedroom with television and puzzles. My father was an unambitious man who
wanted a simple life free of mortgages, lines of credit,
lawyers, and all of that. He enjoyed a drink and loved to tell a
story. He tended bar at Uncle Charlie's Tavern until the night
he drove his drunken self through the guardrail, onto the ice,
and into the waters of Lake Quinsigamond.

At the funeral Mother seemed radiant, abloom with
resolve and expectation. She told her sister Alice that of
course she was heartbroken, but now she could make something of her life after all. Back at the house, at the reception
for the mourners, I sat on the sofa, ate Vienna rolls stuffed

with tuna and egg salad, and suffered the condolences and embraces of uncles, aunts, and strangers. Dad's buddies drank, toasted, reminisced about the time Dad did one crazy thing or another. Many of their stories involved cars and bottles, good luck and charm. And while they laughed and drank, they were able, I suppose, to forget that they, too, were dying.

Mother sold the house and moved us to Florida. She went to dances at the American Legion Hall in Dania and brought home a succession of inconspicuous gentlemen, who were shrewdly solicitous of me, who laughed too loudly, and who spoke to Mother in whispers. One man, Randy McSomething, spent every weekend at our house for three months. He bought me a yo-yo, took us to Pirates World, and finally confessed that he was already married and had a boy exactly my age, named Derek Jerome. Randy showed us the photo in his wallet, and then he left. When Mother learned two months later that Randy had lied, that he was a bachelor, she was bereft and hysterical. Then she married Harvey, having known him for two weeks. Perhaps she mistook his lunacy for eccentricity, his delusions for enterprise. Anyway, Harvey was crazy in a sweet and harmless way.

The first time I spoke with Harvey, he told me he was sensitive to information the rest of us were unaware of. Nuclear information. He and I were eating pancakes. Mother was back in her room working on a jigsaw puzzle of Monet's *Waterlilies*. Harvey told me that 100 million neutrinos passed through his body every second, that his organs crackled with their penetration. He told me he could feel the pull of the magnetic North Pole, and that it made his nose bleed. I said I'd better get going or I'd be late for school. He said he could feel the trill of gamma rays from supernovas, could pick up old radio and TV shows with his internal antennae. "They're in my teeth. The molars. Government implants." He said, "I just want you to know who you're dealing with."

A month after Mother died (aneurysm), the week before my high school graduation, Harvey packed his duffel bag with his notebooks, said he had to see a man in St. Petersburg, and walked away. And I didn't see him again until last week. I was folding the laundry when I heard a knock at the door. I opened it, and there he was, duffel bag and all. He'd put on a pound or two, his hair, which had been gray, was now glossy black. I made us bacon, eggs, and grits, brewed some coffee. I said, "Tell me what the hell you've been doing, Harvey." He said that these days he could see the entire color spectrum from infrared to ultraviolet, so just looking around keeps him pretty busy. Said he could predict earthquakes and volcanoes, that he was in harmony with the Big Bang through 3,000-degree microwaves, and could feel low-frequency sounds from the core of the earth. Keeps him up at night.

He said, "You seem to be alone here."

"I have a dog. He's out roaming somewhere."

Harvey plucked his eyebrows with his fingernails. "So what do you do?"

"I teach. I write stories."

That cracked him up. "You?" He laughed. "You never had any imagination to speak of. I pictured you in retail sales."

"No need to be mean."

"I'm sorry. But you thought neutrinos were a healthy breakfast cereal." He looked puzzled. "Stories?"

I cleared the table. He said, "Okay, Johnny, tell me a

story." He pushed himself away from the table, leaned back in his chair.

I told him about the four little boys—brothers—who walked into my life one day. I heard them from the kitchen. They were out in the backyard talking to Spot, giving him big hugs and pets. I introduced myself and we all had a snack on the deck, and we made up animal stories. Then we had ice cream. They were foster kids. I walked them around the block to their house. They said good-bye. I told them to come on back any old time to play with Spot the Wonderdog. They waved. Spot woofed. I never did see them again because they did not live in that house. Can you believe it? Four little kids wandering the streets. What's going on in our world?

Harvey said, "Now I'll tell you a true story." He closed his eyes, cleared his throat. He spoke as if he were reciting a script from memory. "By the time their handsome son, Barry Junior, had died—not from AIDS, as his friends had feared, not from the tumor he imagined was spreading through his brain, and not from the dozen or so ailments that had befallen him in his forty-nine years (Crohn's disease, asthma, gout, hepatitis), but from simple heart failure, exacerbated by a daily regimen of Seldane D and Prozac—by the time their baby's rotting corpse was discovered dissolving into the living room couch with the television still droning and flickering (their darling Barry, who played accordion at seven, starred in his high school's production of *Finian's Rainbow*, who scored a perfect 100 on the postal exam), by that time his parents, Barry Senior and Dee, were unable to comprehend his passing." Harvey opened his eyes, sipped his coffee, looked at me.

"Dee did not attend her older boy's wake or funeral. She stayed in her room at the Parkside Manor, staring at her knees and hands, all her past having fled from her—her childhood in Dorchester, sneaking cigarettes behind Lusignan's Candy Store, the prom out at the Totem Pole, the wedding at the Italian-American Club, the three children, the twenty-five years in the front office at Donnelly Advertising, the summer weekends in Maine, the boyfriend, Harvey, who had dated her for twenty years—an open secret—and who still comes to see her at the home, still takes her to early bird dinners at Tropical Acres, feeds her, tells her once again who he is—all of it, all of them, gone.

"Dee's husband, Barry Cozzolino, her sweetheart in seventh grade, sat in his wheelchair at the funeral home, not intoxicated, but drunk from forty years of constant whiskey, his leg in a cast—he'd fallen down flights of stairs four times in the last year—and told his pals, whose names he couldn't remember, told them how his older boy Barry wanted to act in summer stock but made the right decision and took a job with the post office. You can't beat government work. Acting's no career for a guy. He'll be able to retire in thirty years with a full pension."

The Boyfriend

She said, "So what happened to Harvey?"

I said, "He stayed for two days, sort of rummaged around the house—looking for traces of himself, I imagine. He walked around with a stemmed goblet in his hands, said he could feel the vibrations of people speaking through it.

People from the past. Said he heard my mother say, 'This is a lesson every saint has to learn: *You are not better than anyone.*' He told me he needed to take Dee to supper the next day, said, 'It's a long haul back to Tampa.' I dropped him at the bus station."

A half hour earlier, I had been sitting at the bar in the King's Head pub, nursing a draft and reading a neurology textbook. I must have been entranced because I heard her voice before I saw her sitting beside me. She said, "I've never seen anyone with a little book light in a bar."

I said, "It gets dark in here."

She smiled.

"I know what you're thinking—why come to a bar to read?"

"Must be good."

"I'm reading about Charles Bonnet Syndrome."

"What's that?"

"Some people with forms of blindness experience intense and vivid visual hallucinations. Like I might look at you and see horns on your head, or a group of well-dressed monkeys with briefcases might walk up the wall. But I'm not crazy because I know they're hallucinations."

"Are you a doctor?"

"No."

"Going blind or something?"

"Nope."

"You will if you keep reading in bars."

That's when I told her about Harvey's visit, how watching him got me thinking about what's real and what isn't and how can you tell the difference. "We all have blind spots in our field of vision and our brain fills them in. Does that mean part of what we're always looking at isn't there, doesn't exist?"

She told me her name was Kate.

"And how about when you stare at something and it disappears? Why is that?"

She said she'd just moved to South Florida. She's a stockbroker for a big discount chain and they're opening an office in Hallandale. She said, "So what are you going to do with this information?"

"Write a story about a woman with macular degeneration. Her husband dies, but she hallucinates him every day. He helps her prepare lunch, they listen to the radio, she tells him about their children."

Kate forced a smile. I wasn't sure what that was about. I told her that maybe my widow's children want her to go to like Johns Hopkins for experimental treatment, but she's worried if she gets her sight back, she'll lose her husband again. She couldn't face that.

Kate was quiet. I said, "How about I buy us a drink?" She ordered Tullamore Dew. Sounded good to me. I told her how with macular degeneration all you have is your peripheral vision. "But the most interesting things we see are always off to the side, don't you think?"

She said, "Did you make up Harvey Fahlstrom?"

"Harvey's real."

She raised her glass. "To Tim," she said. We toasted.

"Who's Tim?"

"The man who drank Tullamore Dew."

"Tell me about him."

"I met him twelve weeks ago in Houston. When you open a new branch, the company sends you to Houston for ten weeks of training. There were seventeen of us. Tim and I became friends. Close friends. And then he died."

"I'm sorry."

"He was supposed to move in with me today."

I took a drink. Was she playing a game with me?

"I talked to him on Friday. He was so happy. Then yesterday I got a call from his friend Phil. Phil said, 'Tim's dead.'"

I MET THIS nonfiction writer one time at a conference in Vermont. She told me that her child had recently died. We were sitting alone by a stone fireplace. I was sipping cognac. She cried. I gave her my handkerchief, expressed my condolences. I felt terrible. She apologized, told me she had thought she was over the death enough to talk about it. I asked would she like a sip of my drink. She told me she was Mormon.

She said, Joshua was five. He had a white dot in the center of his left eye. Turned out to be a tumor behind the retina. It spread—the cancer did. She described the gruesome progress of the disease—the radiation, transfusions, the chemo. She spent a year watching her child waste away. I tried to imagine her pain. She said on the last night at the hospital, she was actually relieved when Joshua died. She felt released, she said, from the prison of his illness. She felt guilty about her relief, a guilt she will carry the rest of her life.

She stared into the fire. She whimpered, keened. She wiped her eyes. I said something meant to express kinship, to offer solace, something sincere but inadequate. She blew her nose, told me she was lying. I said, "About what?" She said, "My son is a twenty-two-year-old med student." She lit up a cigarette. She laughed, looked at me. I said, "Are you psychotic?" Ten minutes later she was dancing in the barn at the writers' party. I watched her jitterbug with the famous handsome poet. I told my friend Stuart what she'd done. He said, "Sounds like maybe you were a little gullible." I said, "Stuart, I read fiction, my job is to be gullible. I believe anything anyone tells me except for people who write memoirs."

The next evening in the lecture hall, the woman who was not a bereaved Mormon mother after all read an essay about a hike into wilderness mountains. She told us all how she got naked under the stars and bathed in a river while a bear watched her from the bank. People were moved, many to tears. They stood to applaud. Young writers wished they could be as noble, as undiminished, as intuitive, as honest as she. "Bullshit," I told Stuart. "Every word." He said, "Sometimes we're better than ourselves when we write."

KATE SAID, "We were lovers. I've never felt anything so intense in my life. And I don't expect I will again. We spent every second of ten weeks within twenty feet of each other. We were like magnets. I know I sound silly."

I told her she didn't at all. Told her I'd just reread *Romeo and Juliet*, and this time I cried for me, not for them, because I realized that kind of consuming love would never happen to me again.

Kate said, "Tim was married. Two boys, four and six. I was a home wrecker, a disgrace to sisterhood, but I couldn't stop.

Two weeks ago our training ended. He went home to his wife in Fort Myers. I moved here. We made our plans on the telephone. Friday he told his wife and his kids he was leaving them. I guess things got out of hand. Penny—the wife—got hysterical. The boys were crying. Relatives arrived. People screamed. When he called later, Tim said he didn't want to go into the sordid details just then. He was going to sleep on the boat. He'd call me in the morning. We'd be together soon. He told me he loved me. That's the last thing he said to me. Maybe to anyone."

Kate drank her whiskey. I ordered two more. I thought how terrible for the wife and the kids that he had to tell them and then die. But if he hadn't told them, he wouldn't have been on the boat. What about the boat?

Kate said, "It was Penny's boat actually. Her daddy owns a marina on the Caloosahatchee. Tim loved the boat, the peace and solitude of the river."

"What happened? Did he crash or something?"

"They found him asleep. I mean dead. Dead in his sleep—which I guess you can't be, really. Seems there was a leak or something in the heater, gas leak or whatever."

"Jesus."

"The funeral was this morning. I couldn't go, of course. It's tearing me apart. All that life we had planned, gone. Our ten weeks will be the dearest of my life."

I asked her did anyone suspect the father-in-law of sabotage. He had access to the boats and all. I thought if I were to write this story, what would I do? Change Kate to, let's say, Paulina, make her a sales rep for a pharmaceutical company. With a Ph.D. in organic chemistry. Where did that come from? Give the boyfriend another job, another home. Could the boat be a camper? Then again, why change anything? What's the chances anyone involved would ever read their story?

Kate looked at her watch. "I'd better be going."

I gave her my phone number, my address, said we were neighbors. "Call," I said, "and we'll have a drink." She thanked me for the hospitality, for the story, for listening. I said, "My pleasure. Nice to meet you. Really. Nice to chat. And I'm sorry. I am. About Tim." I stared after her until she was gone. She has not called.

What Are We? What Are We to Do?

Iris snuggles next to Tom on the leather couch, rests her head on his shoulder. She folds her chenille robe over her knees. TV's on. *Seinfeld* rerun—the one where Jerry steals bread from an old lady. Tom knows that what he's doing is crazy, inconceivable. He's about to leave his wife and his two young daughters. Here he's been Mr. Trustworthy all these years, Mr. Domesticity, Mr. Model Husband, and now this. He thinks, Wait till this news hits the neighborhood grapevine. Well, he'll be gone by then. Love makes being crazy acceptable. That's what Paulina told him. Paulina. His love for her is a hunger. Paulina—the sound of her name is all the food he needs. He remembers something he must have read somewhere: if you have love inside you, and you do not bring it forth, that love will destroy you. If you bring forth that love, it will save you. Something like that. He never used to think like this—about love and other qualitites, not until he met

Paulina. The first time they talked, they talked about truth, goodness, and love, and he was surprised that he had had anything to say. Didn't even know what he knew.

He looks at the photographs on his den wall. He and Iris on the beach in Barbados. He and Iris aboard the *Calusa Queen*. That's the day the twins were conceived. He can't just leave, vanish, walk out like some guy in a country-and-western song. Well, maybe he could, but he won't. This is part of the new self he's inventing. Be honest and forthright. Suffer the consequences of your actions. Harbor no venom. He owes Iris this much. Owes her much more. He'll make the clean break; then everyone can get on with their lives. His shoulder hurts; he needs to move his arm.

Iris asks does he want popcorn? "No." "You sure?" "Sure." Iris looks at him, screws up her mouth, squints. "You okay?" she says. "Yes." Commercial's over; she turns her head. Tom is uncomfortable with the irony he's privy to—that one minute, this minute, Iris is blissfully ignorant of his duplicity, the next, she'll be desolated by it. Tom wishes he hadn't fallen in love— at least at this moment he wishes that. But he had. Entirely. He sees Paulina now in front of his eyes, and he smiles. Her beauty is such that his vision is enhanced. He's never seen so clearly. He looks at his watch. If he tells Iris now—it's eleven-fifteen—no one will sleep. Better wait till morning. She'll need her strength, and so will he. Iris draws a circle into his palm with her fingernail. He wishes she'd stop.

Later, after Iris has kissed him good night and gone off to bed, Tom turns out the lights, checks the locks on the front and back doors, drinks a glass of warm milk, looks in on the girls. He reminds himself it's not just a wife he's leaving.

He's leaving two children. Well, not *leaving* leaving. He's their dad, always will be. He'll take care of them still. He'll dance with them at their weddings. Things will work out. They always do. It'll be hard for a while. They'll be hurt, angry, sad. This is what he'll do. He'll talk to Iris before the kids wake up. He'll let her vent. He'll calm her—with hope if he has to: *Anything is possible, Iris.* He'll take the kids to Ben & Jerry's, buy them sundaes, tell them how Mommy and Daddy aren't getting along just now, but we love you guys very, very much. Start with that. Answer their questions. *Not far, just a hundred miles down the road. Yes, her name's Paulina. Every weekend, every summer.*

He touches Greta's hair, slips it off her cheek. He kisses her and then Sonja. He cries, but this does not lessen his resolve. What is it about Paulina that's making him put all these lives at risk? Her slim body coiled around his, her fragrance, her teeth on his lip. Her laugh. He'll regret leaving— having to leave—no matter how brilliant life is with Paulina. Better to regret the leaving than lament the life.

TOM CAN'T SLEEP. It's three A.M. He's reading a book on galaxies. He hoped the reading would take his mind off tomorrow. Not tomorrow, today! Jesus. Iris is snoring beside him in their bed. He's got to get some rest. He closes his book and puts out the lamp. The light leaves the room, but he wonders does it continue to shine elsewhere? What is darkness anyway? The absence of light or a mute and invisible force? He closes his eyes and sees the afterimage of the lamp, a green and violet tulip. And then he sees a long table set with fabric foods: silk and cotton pizzas; satin cookies; calico pies with latticed, rayon crusts; frilly layer cakes, iced with lace and gingham. And he sees his mother-in-law Berjermy. She's arranging the food just so. That's what she does—she makes what she calls "culinary sculptures." When Tom was still the boyfriend, when he first saw a red velvet cake with yellow taffeta roses on Berjermy's kitchen counter, he went along with the joke and said, Birthday cake for a diabetic? Only it wasn't a joke. Iris pinched his arm. The family is terribly proud of Berjermy. She is their artist. She and her husband Bungo sell her creations at craft fairs and flea markets. But why is he thinking about her?

Tom knows if he gets up now, he'll be tired later. He'll end up sleeping late, and his plan will be ruined. Once again, he goes over what he'll say to Iris and how he'll say it. He pictures them in the kitchen. He can't see Iris's face just now because he's behind her looking at himself. He wonders will he be able to look at her face when he actually tells her. He'll say, You know, very often it's the one who leaves the marriage who has recognized the problem, that the relationship is stagnant, that the husband and wife—you and me, us—have settled into a numb and drowsy life. We live like cattle. She'll say something. He'll say, It would be a shame, a tragedy to waste our lives like this, and you know it. You said yourself we never do anything anymore. What he won't say is how it takes courage to be the one. He'll tell Iris he doesn't know why it happened. His infidelity was not planned. *Why* is not important. The fact is, it did happen, and it cannot be undone. Tom opens his eyes. He and Iris disappear. Maybe he should get up, have a drink.

He's been unhappy for years and didn't know it. He's never felt happiness until now. He had assumed that what other people called happiness was this not-unpleasant tranquillity he often experienced. He was complacent and constant—balanced, unperturbed, unrealized. His life wasn't difficult as much as it was meager and circumscribed. And that's not what he wants for his life. He loves Iris, will never stop loving her. But it's love without passion. It's temperate love, benign and dutiful. With Paulina, however—

Iris turns in her sleep, moans, clacks her tongue. When Tom thinks of their marriage now, it's like looking down a barrel of gas at a doomed star. When he thinks of his life with Paulina, it is a bright ring of starbirth at the core of a galaxy. It's the fiery cradle of possibility, the vortex of hope. He looks at Iris, at the mole on her neck. He feels like a spy in his own house. Iris—sweet, comfortable, obliging Iris. It's true, he doesn't admire her. He feels his treachery like a blast of adrenaline. He feels his heart strain against its skin. He gets out of bed.

IRIS CAN HARDLY breathe. She's choking on her saliva. Her eyes burn and her face is slick with tears and mucus. She feels brittle, nauseated, volatile. She rocks in her seat to steady the quaking and seething within. She twists a tissue in her hands. She means to lift her head to look at Tom, but she can't. She cries and cries. He needs space? What could that possibly mean? Words—instruments of his betrayal—are useless to her now. Her sobs come in bursts at the expiration of each obstructed breath.

Choke, gasp, sob. Choke, gasp, sob. Like some sputtering machine. It's driving Tom nuts. She's been at it now for two hours. The poor girls were so alarmed they went out and hid—probably in their treehouse. Jesus. Where is her sense of reason? They've been through it all. What else can he tell her? No, he won't change his mind. Yes, this *is* the first time. Some men would have kept you in the dark for years. At least I had the decency— He stops himself.

Iris says, "Our life was like a fairy tale. What have you done to it? How could you?"

Tom shakes his head. He considers saying that fairy tales are all about *Once Upon a Time*. This is the here and now. But he doesn't bother.

She says, "How can ten years of marriage be undone in ten weeks?"

Even if he wanted to answer, even if he had an answer, she wouldn't hear it over her weeping.

She says, "What have I done to deserve this?"

He says, "It's nothing you've done. Don't blame yourself."

She says, "I'm blaming you, you bastard."

And out of nowhere a sentiment that he's probably read somewhere occurs to Tom. "You know, Iris, when you blame someone, you give up the power to change," and he understands, even as he speaks, that this bromide sounds false, inane, condescending, brutal—not at all the way it must have sounded when it impressed itself into his memory.

Iris raises her fists above her head and slams them to the table, flipping her cup, splitting the saucer. Her scream is an assault. Tom leans away, blocks his ears. A scream so profound, so chilling, so eloquent that he knows at once how annihilated she is and knows as well that now he can never come back to her after what he has done. His presence in the house would be a daily hammer to her heart. He has opened a wound that will not heal. Iris has cut her hand, and it's bleeding into the puddle of spilled tea.

Tom is humiliated by Iris's suffering and is so angered he wants to shout at her, tell her she has no ambition, no enthusiasms, no energy, no imagination. How's that for why I need to leave? You're sucking me into this dull and lifeless existence. But it's Iris who shouts at him. "I'll do whatever you want. I love you, Tom. Don't kill me like this!"

NOT EVEN A KNOCK. The door opens and in walks Berjermy and Bungo wanting to know what the hell's going on. Bungo says, "Greta and Sonja showed up at our house in pieces. Your children run away from home, and you two don't even know it." Tom stands, looks past Bungo. He says, "Are they all right? You got them with you?"

Bungo puts out his hand. "Sit," he says. "You sit right there. It's you they're running from." He says, "What's going on here?" And Iris tells him what: "Tom's leaving me for his whore." Berjermy hugs her tight, swaddles her with love. "Now, now," she says. "There, there."

Bungo lays his pipe wrench on the counter. He must have come right from work, Tom thinks. Got his coveralls on. Berjermy's in her housedress. Bungo takes a towel from the rack, dampens it at the sink, and kneels beside his daughter's chair. He cleans her wound. He looks at Tom and shakes his head. Tom wonders what has given him the strength, if that's what it's called, to go through with this—with what must look like the assassination of a good woman. If he had ever needed proof of his ferocious love for Paulina, this steadfastness must be it. His love for her is like a prayer, an adoration. He imagines Paulina across his kitchen, only she's in her kitchen, and she's reading his letter and thinking about what a terrible torment he must be enduring. She thinks that his enormous sacrifice will make their love as strong as death.

Tom will begin a new life with Paulina, will fashion a better, more compassionate self. In this house, he's just Iris's husband, the twins' daddy, the provider (and, of course, now the philanderer). He's trapped. In this life he's done all he can do. Ahead lie security, retirement, senility. What he thinks is he's a better person with Paulina, that being in love makes you a better person, visible evidence notwithstanding.

And then he remembers his dream from this morning. (He must have fallen asleep on the La-Z-Boy.) Dreams of bad weather, of driving in foreign cars on slick roads, of a reticence to play sports, of Rolf Whitehead. And he thinks there was an eight-legged sheep, some kind of cloning mishap. He shouldn't be thinking about this, but sometimes your brain takes you away just to save itself some pain. Rolf Whitehead was a man in the training session with him and Paulina up in Orlando. In the dream, Rolf said, "O, love, where are you leading me now?" And he didn't move his lips when he said it.

Tom says maybe it would be better if Berjermy and Bungo leave. "Iris and I need to be alone." Iris says yes she'll be okay. She wants time to talk some sense into him. "I won't let this happen." Bungo says he'll be back to check in. He looks at

Tom. "You psychotic or something?" he says. Tom says no, he isn't. Bungo stands, squeezes Iris's shoulder. It's like she's seven, and he's picking her up at school, walking her home past the spiteful girls on the corner. "Let's go," he tells his wife. He picks up his wrench, slaps it against his palm. He says, "You hurt my little girl, you best not set your ass back in Lee County. Capisce?"

Tom imagines Bungo coming at him with the wrench, realizes he wouldn't mind so much being the victim for a while. A little violence might even accelerate his departure.

THIS TIME BUNGO knocks before he comes in. Tom tells him that Iris is sleeping. That's how she deals with stress. She hopes to wake up on the other side of trouble. Bungo says, "When you canceled the wedding that first time, she slept for three days." Bungo looks in on his daughter. He sees that Tom has packed a suitcase and an overnight bag. Bungo sits at the edge of the bed, leans over and kisses his daughter's ear. Iris wakes, stares up at him, looks around at where she is, and remembers. She says, "I don't know what I'll do, Daddy." He tells her to sleep. "The kids are watching cartoons with your momma. I'll stay," he says. "You sleep. Everything will be all right, sugar. I promise."

Bungo wipes coffee off the seat and sits. He tells Tom he could have at least cleaned up the goddam mess. "You know, Tom," he says, "guys all over the world have been having affairs since the beginning of time. But most of us are smart enough to keep quiet about it. Most of us are mature enough to understand the difference between a roll in the hay and a

family, between ten minutes and a life." This is not something Tom can talk to Bungo about. How can he tell his father-
in-law that he doesn't want a mistress, can't even understand
that kind of hypocrisy? He wants possession and access. If he
thought Bungo would understand, he'd tell him, you have to
love the person you're having sex with. Passion is not a fleeting thing. Intimacy is not casual.

Bungo says, "Look, I know how hard it is to keep a marriage together these days. The pressures. Family values down
the crapper. Whole world's loco if you ask me." Bungo blots
spilled coffee with the bloody towel. "You're awfully quiet,"
he says.

Tom says, "I've been through the wringer."

"Have you?"

"Bungo, I'm sorry about all this."

"Are you?" Bungo tosses the towel into the sink. He says,
"How is she going to face her friends? Her own self? How's
she going to know who she is anymore? How's she going to
take care of herself or the kids? You think about that? How
does a person become another person that she didn't want to
become?"

"Iris is stronger than you think."

"What are you going to do with yourself?"

Tom shrugs.

"I mean tonight. You can't stay here."

"I want to see the girls."

"Not tonight. They're too upset. In the morning you come
see them. Sleep on the boat tonight. Think about what you're
doing to your precious ones. Tomorrow maybe you'll see
more clearly."

"Thanks, Bungo. I am pretty exhausted."

"Like I care. Go, before I change my mind."

TOM FIGURES he'll cruise upriver to a favorite cove in the wildlife refuge. You go upriver here and it's like you're not in Florida anymore, at least not in the twenty-first century. This could be the Amazon or the Congo. He carries his bags into the cabin, sits on the bunk. He calls the girls on the cell phone. He gets Bungo on the answering machine, telling him that his call's important, blah, blah, blah. Tom waits for the beep, says, "If you're there, pick up. It's Tom. It's Daddy. Hello. Want to say hi to the kids. Okay, then. Greta, Sonja, Daddy loves you a bushel and a peck. See you tomorrow. Kiss, kiss."

He opens the suitcase and takes out the framed photos of his daughters, puts them on a shelf over the bunk. And then he calls Paulina and gets a busy signal. Who could she be talking to? He feels like she's being inconsiderate, and he's angry until he realizes he's being foolish. It's like he can feel every nerve in his body. He gets up and stretches. He hits *Redial*. She picks up. He tells Paulina that, yes, it's been rough, but he doesn't want to get into all the sordid details just now. "Poor baby," she says. "I wish I could be there for you."

"You are," he says.

"It must be terrible for Iris, though."

"For all of us," he says, and he wonders if Paulina's concern isn't presumptuous. "I'll call you tomorrow. Early. I love you, too," he says.

. . .

ROGER BANNISTER and Clark Gable. Tom's on the bunk, staring at the cabin wall, playing this game where he thinks of famous people whose names are parts of houses. John Locke. Jane Curtin. By concentrating on the absurd, the mundane— are they identical?—he can drift off to sleep, usually before he gets to James W. Hall and Farah Fawcett. But tonight, he has been unable to erase this unordinary day. And besides, he's chilly. Tom hears the grunt of a female alligator calling her young, the slap of a mullet breaking water. He gets up, slides the cabin door shut. He puts on a pair of socks, gets the bottle of Irish whiskey out of a galley cabinet. He pours a shot, sits on the settee by the table.

Tom feels like he's not quite safe, hasn't quite escaped. Iris will be there in the morning. All of them will. He'll need to be resolute. He wishes he would not have to tell Iris yet again that he is leaving her, but knows he will. Maybe he could just stay on the river, slosh off into the swamp. He laughs. His nose is cold. He pours another shot, gets up to check the thermometer. He clicks the heater on, picks up the wrench, and puts it in the tool trunk. He sits again with his drink. No, he doesn't want to be a drug rep for the rest of his life. What a ridiculous obsession—money.

Tom thinks maybe he'll go back to school, at least part-time. Study anthropology like he did before he switched to business. He remembers himself in class listening to a lecture on cargo cults and beginning to understand how and why man creates his gods. He can hear Professor Grandone say *Vailala Madness*, but he can't recall what it means exactly.

In those days—could it be fifteen years already?—what he knew was not so important as what he did not. The world was a miracle, and *wonder* was a verb, not a noun. He knows that this joy he remembers is somehow connected to Paulina. Was it an unconscious yearning for astonishment and hope that led him to find her, or someone like her? Or had Paulina carried him back to his innocent and curious self?

AND DOES it matter?

One and done, he thinks, and pours himself a final shot. He thinks about his girls, but in the future when they're happy and in love themselves. They'll understand Daddy then. Greta will say, "Don't be silly, Daddy, of course you didn't hurt us. We love you. If the marriage didn't break up, something worse might have happened." Sonja will say, "It's so much worse for kids to grow up with anger and tension in the house, to witness their parents wallowing in regret." And she'll give her dad a big hug.

Tom stares at the driftwood planter on the table. He sees a face in the grain, and then he doesn't. A face he recognized. He looks again, squints, and it reappears. It's Mr. Marco, who owned the little market where Tom bought his Snickers and his Mr. Pibb. Dead ringer—mole on the cheek and everything. Tom remembers getting high one time on wacky weed and seeing Bob Hope on a spinach leaf. He saved the leaf to show Lonnie, his girlfriend, but it wilted in his pocket, and Bob was gone. Tom realizes that he's sleepy at last. He sees himself making out with Lonnie in the front seat of his idling station wagon. He wonders where on earth Lonnie is. He swallows what's left of the whiskey, walks to the bunk. He feels like he's moving in slow motion. He lies down.

He's a bit nauseated, but who wouldn't be after all the stress he's been through? His eyes won't stay closed. They see Paulina across the cabin, and for a moment Tom thinks she's really there, that she's learned how to transport herself through time and space. He almost talks to her. He decides he's had one drink too many. Decides, too, that that's where the future is—on the port side of the cabin. He takes a deep breath and feels his brain expand to fill his skull—not unpleasant at all. Maybe he should stay awake and enjoy it. No, he has to be alert in the morning. Anyway, you never solve problems with worry. Some problems you can do nothing about. Once you are helpless and admit it, you are free. You let go. He let go.

And suddenly his dad is beside him in a chair with a book of fairy tales in his hand, a finger tucked into the page where he'll read. Tom knows this really isn't his father. His father died when he was twelve. Drowned. His father begins: *Once upon a time there dwelt near a large wood a woodcutter.* Tom smiles. His favorite story. He thinks he hears a phone chirp. In his mind, he answers the phone, but no one's there, and the chirping continues. He counts the chirps. Finally they stop. His father says, *How can you bring your heart to leave my children all alone in the wood?* Tom tells his dad he wants a sister. "I'm lonely without one," he says. "Mom says one kid's enough, but it's not." His father says, *I will eat a piece of the roof and you can eat the window.* Tom says, "Where did you go when you went away?" His father says, *I was with you whenever you needed me.* He takes Tom's chin in his hand and says,

"Remember this, a father will do anything to protect his children." Tom sees that Paulina is no longer across the room, understands that he is here in the past, the starboard side of the cabin. He closes his eyes, listens, and imagines a fiercely burning fire, pearls and precious stones, a wide expanse of water, a heartbroken father welcoming his children home. *Then all their sorrows were ended, and they lived together in great happiness.*

YOU'RE AT MACY'S,
KILLING TIME,
WHEN IT HITS YOU

THERE ARE MOMENTS IN YOUR LIFE WHEN YOU think you can change absolutely everything—your disposition for starters, your past, your values, your weight, your I. Q. score, your obsessions, your friends, your unflattering habits, your future, your heredity—by making that one small, but consequential change in the kitchen. You realize, for example, that this bread machine you're staring at could be the first step on your path to a life worth living.

You'll make your own bread every day. You've always wanted to give it a try. You'll begin with boughten mixes, just until you get the hang of it. You imagine the aroma of yeast and baking bread, and your childhood flashes before your eyes and so does that trip you took to Paris a decade ago—has it been that long?—when you swore to yourself you'd never drink American wines again.

Once you get the feel of the machine, you'll create your own recipes. You'll experiment with crust and crumb and grain. You make a list in your head of the breads you'll bake: oatmeal, Portuguese sweet bread, anadama (like your grandmother made), pumpernickel, potato, challah, raisin, Swedish rye, olive, sourdough (you'll make your own starter, the *mother*, and you'll feed her, nurture her for years). Eventually, you'll give up the machine for your oven. It's only been a year, and already you're feeling healthier, wiser, more independent, more *connected*—that's a word you find yourself using a lot. You no longer watch television or color your hair. You're reading those eighteenth-century British novels you never got around to. The world bristles with possibility. You're up at six, kneading, proofing, listening to Mozart.

One evening you notice an ad for a farm in the country. On a whim—you've learned to trust your intuition—you call the real estate agent. The owners, she says, are flexible, willing to talk. You move to the farm, grow your own wheat, barley, and oats, organically. You don't do this yourself exactly; you hire a man from town. This quiet man who's lost his wife. His name's Raymond. You envy his sadness and respect his solitude. You teach baking to a few students to help meet the mortgage payments, finance the new oven. These students admire you so. They are like your children. You tell them life, like baking, demands meticulous attention to detail.

A local entrepreneur urges you to open a small bakery. Health is hot, he says. He calls you a culinary folk artist. He mentions franchise possibilities. Banks want to loan you money for the project. With money you could go back to Paris. You picture yourself at a café on the rue des Écoles, black summer dress, blue espadrilles, a breeze luffing your hair, veiling your face. You take a walk down to the brook behind the house, sit under a willow, watch the trout splash in the shallow pool, rising to the mayflies. You hear the *see you, see yeeer!* of the meadowlark. You tell the entrepreneur,

Thanks, but no thanks. This is what you were meant to do. You have, you realize, kept a covenant with your childhood. You are whole.

And you buy that bread machine, the one with the recipe memory, the easy-clean pan, the detachable kneading rod, the removable crumb tray.

for Fran Parker

THE NUMBER OF STAIRS IN A FLIGHT, BOOKS on a shelf, cars in a lot, peas on a plate, words on a page, scenes in a movie, people in a crowd, petals on a flower, bones in a face. Curtis is the kind of guy who counts things. Numbers are knowledge. Knowledge is power. Power is wearing the pants, being in the saddle, laying down the law, having it your way, holding all the cards, having the world under your thumb.

After he murdered his fiancée's girlfriend at the self-storage unit two blocks from campus, after he'd shattered her teeth with a wine bottle. After he'd sodomized and strangled her (124 seconds), Curtis sat the naked body in the passenger seat of his Chevette, secured it with the lap and shoulder belts, and drove back to school. He switched on the radio to KIX 98. Al Green. "I don't know why I love you like I do." He lowered the volume so he could talk without shouting. He felt he needed to explain himself, tell her why he'd done what he'd done. Hadn't he warned her? Thirty-seven phone calls, sixteen letters, the "chance" meeting at the Rathskeller. *What did you think, I was kidding?* He had his future to think about, he said, his marriage to Laquiesha, captain of the basketball team, Oprah wannabe. And no trashy white girl was going to ruin his life.

When he stops at the red light by the bayou bridge, he thinks about this lesbian's lips on Laquiesha's lips, and he can't help it—he whips a backhand at her mouth, cuts his knuckles on her jagged teeth. *Bitch!* He pulls up to the Education Building and hauls the battered corpse to the Dumpster, lifts the body over his head and drops it in. He pumps his arm. *Two points!* He changes out of his torn shirt and bloody slacks and returns to the basketball game at the Pantherdome. Laquiesha scores twenty-three. Lady Panthers win!

In the morning, a custodian, three months shy of retirement, discovers the body. *Sweet Mother of Jesus!* Her blue eyes are opened, blood has dried around her mouth and nose, sugar ants carry crumbs up her leg. The police detective, who will die of cancer before the case is closed, a cancer he doesn't know he has, makes a note about the gold bracelet on the victim's left wrist, lists its charms: clown with moving legs, basketball, diploma, ladybug, angel, four-leaf clover, Mickey Mouse, frog on a lily pad. And then what happens is this:

1. Curtis drives his car to his cousin Walter's house in Winnsboro, asks Walter could he wash it, clean it, detail it.
2. Friends of the deceased tell the detective about the existence of a threatening letter that Curtis wrote to her.
3. The letter and a diary cannot be found.
4. Curtis is arrested, booked, indicted.
5. Laquiesha claims to love him, says that she was a "sister" to the deceased, the disturbed Miss Doe, and that Curtis was like a big brother to Miss Doe,

always calling her to see how she was doing, sending her encouraging notes, watching out for her at
parties.

6. Laquiesha's mom says she was with Curtis all
night, from dinner at Frankie and Janie's (crawfish and oysters) right through to the final whistle
at the game—he never left his seat.

7. Curtis's wealthy and connected parents hire a
costly and brilliant attorney from Shreveport to
defend him.

8. The brilliant and charming attorney uses a pre-
liminary hearing to ridicule shoddy police proce-
dures, to uncover contaminated evidence, and to
root out discrepancies in what he calls the prosecution's flimsy case.

9. The charming, gifted, and handsome attorney is
struck by lightning and killed. (Truth is stranger
than fiction.)

10. Curtis's wealthy and connected parents hire
another famous trial lawyer from New Orleans.

11. The district attorney, running for reelection in a
racially divided parish, appoints an untested prosecutor, a young black woman, to the case.

12. On the stand, Curtis is not asked how he managed
to change his clothes while in the stands. Or why
he would.

13. The local African-American community protests
the trial, calling it a witch hunt, a rush to judg-
ment. Persecution not prosecution!

14. At a news conference, the basketball coach denies

allegations of homosexuality on the team. When asked about the scandal that involved her former assistant's recruiting players with sex and gifts, the coach says, The Lady Panthers are not on trial here.

15. Curtis is not asked how he cut his knuckles or how his fingerprints might have gotten on the wine bottle, Exhibit 7.

16. Witnesses, who have signed depositions that they saw Curtis outside the Pantherdome while the game was in progress, are not called to testify.

17. The Lady Panther players, all witnesses to Curtis's constant intimidation of Miss Doe, of his many public threats, are not called to testify.

18. Campus police, who saw Laquiesha taking several items from Miss Doe's Toyota after the murder, are not called to testify.

19. Curtis's juvenile record of violence toward girl-friends is inadmissable evidence.

20. Professor A., who had once given Curtis a C+ and was subsequently stalked by Curtis, testifies on Curtis's behalf.

21. Professor B., who had an affair with Curtis while he was her student, testifies on his behalf.

22. Miss Doe, we learn, was molested as a child by her older brother, or so she said. She also claimed that she was gang-raped after a high school football game. She was a regular visitor to the school shrink. She had quit the basketball team in mid-season. She had flunked English Comp 101. Miss Doe, we learn, was a confused child.

23. Curtis is acquitted.

24. Curtis and Laquiesha, and Laquiesha's mother and sisters, and Curtis's parents, and the famous and masterful attorney and his winsome and earnest intern celebrate Curtis's vindication with a victory party at the River Oaks Country Club.

25. The masterful and triumphant attorney tells his earnest and perky intern that they just got a guilty man off. She seems surprised, stunned. She sits up, lights a cigarette, asks him, If that's the case, how are we supposed to live with ourselves? He tells her, We defend the Constitution; our client is the Constitution.

26. Curtis's parents buy him a Porsche.

27. Curtis and Laquiesha move to Memphis. (He works as a security guard at Graceland, but you wouldn't believe that.)

28. Curtis buys a remote control Corvette which he plays with every evening after work in the parking lot of the Paradise Pointe Apartments.

29. Laquiesha complains to Curtis about their finances, about her dated wardrobe, about his seeming indifference to their plight. He reminds her she has twenty-two pairs of shoes, fifty-four dresses, seven hats, and eighteen warm-up suits. She tells him about Raymond Dorling from work.

30. Curtis batters and strangles Laquiesha, dumps her body in a slough by the St. Francis River near Forrest City, Arkansas, Al Green's hometown.

31. Curtis's parents drive to Memphis and rent a U-

Haul. They clean out Curtis's apartment, including all of Laquiesha's belongings, including the
bloodstained bedspread. They tell the nosy manager that Laquiesha will pay the rent.

32. Curtis's parents hire yet another eloquent and
bombastic attorney. They sell the Porsche.

33. When the body is discovered, Memphis and
Arkansas police argue over jurisdiction. Memphis
loses and takes the case. They are not interested in
anything that happened in Louisiana. They have
so tainted the evidence that they have no leg to
stand on. They listen to the bombastic and per-
suasive attorney, and Curtis walks.

Actually, he drives to Hollywood, Florida. As fine a place as
any. He rents Room 12 in a residential motel on Dixie
Highway, the Dixiewood, lands a job testing blood at National
Health Labs. He's trying to meet the right people, to make
friends, to start over. He eats lunch with his colleagues in the
canteen; he shoots the breeze with the clerks at the 7-Eleven
on Federal; evenings he goes to clubs to unwind.

For someone who loves to count, Curtis can't keep a
beat. He's an awkward, self-conscious dancer. He keeps
stepping on feet, bumping into people. He knows how com-
ical and graceless he must look, and he asks the young lady
he's just met if she would mind sitting this one out. She
says, Maybe we should before you kill someone. She says
she needs another Long Island Iced Tea. Yes, she knows it's
her fourth.

They sit in a corner booth. Curtis, who's calling himself

Austin, tells Lourdes that he's a doctor, an oncologist. She says, You mean you carry a beeper and rush to the hospital for emergencies? He doesn't know if she's joking. He says, Cancer. She says, Scorpio. No, no, he says, I treat cancer. He tells her he's just finished his residency at Sloan-Kettering. Curtis is reminded that this is all he's ever wanted to be, a doctor, a healer, a helper, a respected man in his community. Find the tumor and cast it out of the body. Where once was death now there's life. And how will his dream come true now? The Tudor house in the country, the Italian suits, the German cars? Lourdes says, Why don't we get out of here. I'll drive, he says. She gives him her keys. Seven of them. He steadies her on the walk to her car, opens the door.

He drives by his motel. An overweight bottle-blonde in a halter top is sitting on the hood of a rusted Mercury drinking a beer. She waves to him. Lourdes says she feels like shit. She cracks the window, takes three deep breaths. Curtis says, Let this be a lesson to you, young lady. You need to act more prudently. A pretty girl like you could find herself in a bucket of trouble. She says, Okay, Daddy. So Curtis figures he should tell her what she's done tonight, for example. He says, I've killed two women. She says, Not with your looks you haven't. He says, I'm serious. She tells him her address and closes her eyes.

Curtis gets her into her apartment and lays her down on the couch. He slips her shoes off her feet, covers her with an afghan. He gets himself a glass of milk and a bag of ginger snaps from the kitchen. He sits in the rocking chair and stares at Lourdes. She snores. He dunks a cookie in the milk and eats it. Lourdes collects unicorns. There's a purple and pink unicorn print above the couch, glass figurines on the end table, a ceramic herd on the TV. He wonders what that's all about.

Sitting there, feeling at home somehow, enjoying this domestic scene, Curtis suddenly feels misunderstood. Folks think if you've killed a couple of people, that you'll just keep on killing, that you're some kind of natural-born menace, some monster, that you're out of control. Curtis knows that he is in complete control, and knows that he's capable of great acts of kindness, in fact. Like tonight, carrying Lourdes home. There are lots of scumbags who would have taken advantage—the predators and psychos.

He looks at Lourdes. He doesn't want to touch her, kiss her, disturb her, doesn't want to hurt her. He wants to explain to her about rage, how it can't be manufactured. How it's not something you summon at will. And, of course, how it cannot be faked. Rage is a kind of furious sincerity. That's what so many people don't understand. Your sociopath will kill for pleasure, but a normal person needs that rage in order to kill. Murder shouldn't be enjoyable, and it shouldn't be taken lightly. It's an aberration, not a habit. Yes, I've thought a lot about this, Lourdes.

He eats another ginger snap, brushes crumbs from his hands, sips his milk. He says, Think of it like this. I'm a pistol, and I'm pointed right at your face. Rage is my hammer and disrespect is my trigger. Now, you'd have to be a fool to pull that trigger knowing where the gun is aimed, wouldn't you? Yes, you would indeed. And yet some people do just that, Lourdes. Boggles the mind.

Curtis misses Laquiesha so much. They were *this* close to marriage, to success, to happiness. He shakes his head at his enormous loss. He cries, wipes his eyes with his shirtsleeve, apologizes to Lourdes for the waterworks. He says, I hope you never have to suffer the loss of your soul mate. He remembers one afternoon when he and Laquiesha sat at the table in her momma's kitchen, drinking iced tea while Momma fried chicken, and all three of them were joking and laughing to beat the band. He hopes Momma isn't blaming herself for what happened. She only lied that first time to save her daughter's reputation. A mother has a duty to protect her child. That's her job. He thinks how it's hard to steel yourself for irony. He laughs at his pun. Curtis decides that next paycheck he's sending Momma a dozen roses.

He empties the contents of Lourdes's pocketbook onto the coffee table: a pack of Marlboros, two sugar packets, four tea bags, three zinc lozenges, tubes of toothpaste, lipstick (red velvet), and Super Glue, a Swiss Army knife, Chap Stick, Monistat, Midol, seven Band-Aids, and a red wallet with a cartoon of Wonder Woman on the front. Lourdes has twenty-one credit cards. She really *is* going to get herself in trouble. She has six photographs, each of her with a different friend. She has $67 in cash. Curtis settles accounts. He figures $25 for the drinks and $10 for his taxi home. His scintillating conversation, his escort service—all free. He uses the bathroom, cleans up his mess. He wipes drool from Lourdes's chin. He decides to keep the $10 and walk home. He shuts the apartment door quietly, checks to be certain it's locked. He sings as he walks down Sheridan Street. "I'm full of fire, full of fire."

Lourdes is alive and asleep. Curtis doesn't need thanks. He doesn't expect it. First of all, do no harm.

And:

- The cautious DA loses his reelection bid, returns to his law firm, argues with his partners, and withdraws a half million dollars from the firm's account that he feels belongs to him. At his trial he claims to have mistakenly burned the cash along with sacks of deer corn out in the backyard. He sticks to his story. He suffers a nervous breakdown. Following an eighteen-month prison sentence, he's elected mayor.
- The humiliated and pregnant prosecutor resigns her position. The father of her child, a court bailiff, refuses to leave his wife and family. The former attorney and her baby move to Nacogdoches, Texas.
- Laquiesha's momma eventually collects $25,000 on her daughter's life insurance policy. She's able to pay off the mortgage on her bungalow.
- Laquiesha is buried without a headstone.
- The basketball coach resigns, moves to Perryville, where she raises border collies and works on her book about the killings.
- A month after the headaches started, a week before he enters the hospital, two weeks before he dies, the detective responds to a domestic disturbance call on Fink's Hide-a-way Road. Tyson Nightingale has busted out all the windows and broken all the mirrors in his house. The detective manages to calm

him down, bandage his bleeding fists. They sit at
the kitchen table.

The detective says, Tyson, what the hell have you
done?

Tyson says, They tooken me up in their ship.

Who did?

The aliens did.

Why would they do that?

They make doubles of you. They take you and
twist you till you're backasswards and inside out,
upside down, crisscrossed.

Am I talking to that double now?

Doubles live in glass.

The detective says sure he'd like a drink, why
not, and Tyson takes down a bottle of bourbon from
the cabinet. They sit quietly until the detective says,
You know and I know you weren't abducted, Tyson.
There ain't no aliens. There ain't no angels. Ain't no
ghosts. There's just us. Tyson cries. The detective
tells him it's okay. He says, Tell me what's really
going on.

EPITHALAMION

"Lovers don't finally meet somewhere.
They're in each other all along."

— R U M I

BRANDI'S GETTING MARRIED ON FRIDAY AT TWO-
thirty at Centerville City Hall to a Bulgarian gentleman with
whom she spoke for the first time on Monday night over the
phone. She met Radomil ("Call me Rado; all my friends do")
on Tuesday morning at the Tick Tock Diner. She arrived before
he did. The sign on the diner's screen door said, NO OUTSIDE
FOOD. Rado's name means "happy favor." He's been searching
for a wife in America and was beginning to lose hope. His
visa expires Thursday week. Without a green card, it's back to
Plovdiv. Rado has a gold loop pierced through his left eyebrow, a gold stud in each ear, and a tattoo of a serpent on his
right bicep. Brandi ordered biscuits and gravy; Rado, eggs and
hash. Coffee for both. At the counter, a fat man in a yellow
Purdue University T-shirt and baggy blue pants ordered sweet
potato pancakes. The man wore a cloth hat with a leather lace
tied under his chin, and he'd decided to fold the brim up on
the right and down on the left. Rado squirted mustard on his
sunny-side eggs. He ate his toast with a knife and fork. Brandi
sipped her coffee and watched him chew and chew. She won-

dered if Rado was circumcised. Mr. Purdue asked for a doggie bag. Rado, it seems, was a tireless masticator. His lips glistened with yolk.

Brandi knows that she has a twin in a spiral galaxy 10 to the 10^{28} meters from Centerville. She's read all about it for astronomy class. In infinite space even the most unlikely events *must* take place somewhere. There's an exact copy of her, who is not her, but who also lives on a blue planet called Earth in a solar system with eight other planets. The life of Brandi's double has been identical to Brandi's in every respect until now. Now the doppelgänger Brandi, in her parallel universe, puts down her fork, wipes her face with a napkin, says to her Rado, Thanks, but no thanks, and walks out of the diner. The sign on the diner's screen door is worn and faded and says, NO OUTS.

For her not-inconsiderable troubles, Brandi will earn $2,000, money she could use toward her tuition. She's an English major at the local branch of the state university. She'll get the first $500 on Friday. Well, more likely $300 because this morning, Wednesday, she made Rado buy her a $200 diamond solitaire ring at Zale's. We're going to do this right, she told him. She'll get the next $1,000 at the three-month meeting with the INS. ("We're trying so hard to have a baby, aren't we, sweetie?") She'll get the remaining $500 on their second wedding anniversary when the divorce proceedings will get under way. On Thursday Rado will move in with Brandi for one week. Right now Rado rents a shabby third-floor studio apartment over by the Defiance County Farmers' Museum. The walls of his crib, as he calls it, are decorated— well, that's not quite the appropriate word—are embellished with magazine photos of lavishly bosomed women in scanty swimsuits. After the week, Rado will move in with some pals from work.

Brandi thanked the waitress for the refill. She told Rado, You can understand, can't you, how this is a significant disappointment?

You'd be helping me out, Brandi.

A wedding is supposed to be one of the highlights of a woman's life.

Helping yourself out.

It's not supposed to be a good deed, a casual business proposition.

It's not the wedding that matters, Brandi. It's the marriage.

And what kind of marriage will this be?

One without deception. Better than most.

Marriage should be the start of a new life.

We have a saying in my country: Marriage teaches you how to live alone.

In her Intro to Lit class, Brandi couldn't keep her attention on Professor Rivard's lecture about Henry James Joyce Kilmer or whoever it was. She'd get the notes from Gretchen the brainiac after class. Brandi wrote her new name on the cover of her literature notebook. *Brandi Kostov. Brandi Blythe Kostov. Mrs. Brandi Blythe Kostov. Mrs. Radomil Kostov.* She liked the music of it. When Brandi got the notes from Gretchen, she asked Gretchen if she would be her witness at the wedding. Friday. Yes, this Friday. Yes, I'm serious. And could you bring a camera?

Brandi lives practically alone in her stepfather's house. Her real father, Bob Forbes, is an independent insurance agent in town and can't catch word of the upcoming nuptials, or he'll try to stop them. Bob Forbes is connected. The step-dad, Sonny O'Loughlin, spends most of his time over at his girlfriend Rosemary's house, or else the pair of them are parked at the bar at the Ron-de-voo. But every afternoon Sonny comes by the house to take a shower. Sonny told Brandi he wasn't so sure that marrying the Bulgarian was such a brilliant idea. Of course, Sonny once married Brandi's mom, Georgette, who is certifiable, and who goes through men like candy, so he's not exactly the best judge of suitable marriage material. Granted, I've made my mistakes, he said, but what do we really know about Bulgaria, Brandi?

There are four beds in Brandi's (Sonny's) house: Brandi's queen, Sonny's waterbed, and the bunk beds in the guest room. The bunk beds and the room once belonged to Brandi's brothers Roy and Ray, before they got involved with crank and motorcycles, before they drifted away to God knows where. Rado sleeps days. He works the graveyard shift at the Wal-Mart out on Old New Concord Road. He cleans floors. The work is subcontracted, so Rado is not actually part of the Wal-Mart family. He's part of the Flawless Floor Care family. He makes more money cleaning floors in Centerville than he could make at any job in Plovdiv or Sofia. He owns an Ericsson cell phone, Dolce & Gabbana sunglasses, a Rolex watch, and a Hugo Boss suit. He wears Air Jordans and Prada shoes. He smokes Marlboros, drinks Rémy Martin. He dreams of opening his own beauty salon: Radomil Chic. In Bulgaria, he designed accounting and business management software. He speaks three languages. Brandi thinks Rado is hot. He has thick, dark, shoulder-length hair that shimmers with highlights in the sun. Brandi adores blue eyes, but she'll settle for brown eyes in her first husband. That's how hot Rado is.

When they went shopping for the wedding ring, Rado wore a yellow tank top, snug black slacks, and a black leather jacket. Brandi wore her hair down and also wore a black leather jacket. As they came out of Zale's, they each turned into the wind, let the spring breeze luff the hair from their faces, and they each put on their sunglasses like they were synchronized dancers, like they were moving in slow motion. Fred and Ginger. Kismet.

Rado called Brandi on Wednesday afternoon while he was jogging in Miller's Glen Park. We have a little problem, he said. Brandi's friend Kelly's mother was demanding at least a share of the $500 finder's fee. Rado explained that his friend Klaus, not Kelly's mother, had introduced him to Brandi. Brandi called Kelly's mom, who told her that she had given Brandi's phone number to Klaus and was only asking for her just reward. Brandi asked Mrs. Druin to please try to understand. This is my future we're talking about. Your quarrel is with Klaus. Mrs. Druin didn't like this one bit, but she did back off her demand. And yes, she would speak with that son of a bitch Klaus. And no, she would not contact the INS.

Brandi hopes to consummate the marriage. She also hopes that Rado won't hurt her. When they filed for the marriage license, Brandi asked the clerk what the $10 Domestic Violence Fee was all about and was told that it's sort of a prepayment to help defray the cost of the police officers who might be called out to intervene should domestic affairs turn nasty and brutish as they so often do. Rado explained to

Brandi how their marriage, unfortunately, makes consumma-
tion impractical. Or rather, the eventual, inevitable divorce
does. But after the divorce, when they're both single again,
what's to stop them from dating, from falling in love, from
raising a family, from living happily ever after?

On Tuesday night Brandi dreamed about Texaco. Texaco
was a former boyfriend—if you can count one disagreeable
date as a boyfriend—who had subsequently stalked her for six
months. He called her 312 times in a single day. He tossed
stones at her window. He mailed her dozens of lurid post-
cards, sent her photographs of his uncircumcised penis. He
followed her home from work. He stood outside restaurants
while she ate. In the dream, Texaco is played by the actor who
played the priest-killer in the movie she saw on cable the
other night. Texaco's wearing the left brim of his hat down so
that you can't see his eye, and he's telling her that she had better do just as she's told when Brandi notices the pierced brow.
Now that she knows his secret Bulgarian identity, Texaco will
have to kill her, but before he gets the chance to, Ryan comes
to the rescue.

Ryan has blue eyes. He's Brandi's boss, the night manager
at You Wanna Pizza Me. Brandi has had a mad crush on Ryan
ever since she met him. Ryan seems not to have noticed. Ryan
is not what most girls would think of as handsome, but he is
a dreamboat in Brandi's eyes. She calls him "Sweetass" when
he's not around. Ryan lives twenty minutes out of town in
New Concord. He lives alone now that his undeserving wife
has left him. On Sunday night, Brandi told Ryan, whose name
means "young royalty," that he should just stay at her house
instead of driving home so late in the pouring rain, in the fog.

He didn't stay, didn't say, Thanks, but no thanks, didn't compliment her generosity, didn't offer an excuse, didn't feel the need to. Ryan's divorce becomes official on Friday. Is that a sign or what?

All the while at work, this eighteen-year-old tramp, Elise the Piece, Brandi calls her, has had her mitts all over poor Ryan. Elise knows how Brandi feels about Ryan, but she's always pawing at the poor guy regardless, kneading his shoulders, touching his arm. When Brandi called Elise a whore right to her freckled face, Elise slapped her across the cheek.

Brandi called Ryan at work on Wednesday evening. Just to talk. I've got a rush here, Brandi. Call me later. Brandi went to the party for the visiting writer at Professor Fell's house. The beer and bourbon were flowing, and then Phil, the senior theater major, took out his guitar, and when everyone got to singing, Brandi took her turn and led them in "Blue Eyes Crying in the Rain." She was weeping herself by the end of the song and so was Professor Fell.

Brandi stopped in to see Ryan on her way home. She helped him fold delivery boxes. She told him she was getting married on Friday and would be in to work after the ceremony—well, it's not really ceremonious, is it? After the performance. The do-to. After the fuss and after a quick bite at Sabrina's Toast of the Town. Ryan said, You're what? and Brandi's heart leaped. I'm getting married. Ryan's jaw dropped. It was as if his face were set in cement. Brandi had hoped that when she told Ryan about the wedding, he would at long last profess his undying love for her, and if he did, she would call off the wedding with Rado. But he did not. No, Ryan said, he could not envision anything going on between them outside of You Wanna Pizza Me. Brandi said, Of course, I'll deliver pizzas on Friday, Ryan. Nothing's changed.

Brandi has been wondering how things will turn out for her other self on the distant planet Earth—the self who walked away from Rado—but she knows she'll never find out. Even if she traveled forever at the speed of light, Brandi could not reach Brandi because the space between them is expanding faster than the speed of light. It seems unfair to have to remain a mystery to yourself. Better not to know that you also live in another galaxy than to know but be unable to talk to yourself. And yet the knowledge is strangely comforting as well, knowing that all of this—the pizza job, the empty beds, the graveyard shifts, the visiting writers, the reluctant darling, the Bulgarian suitor—that this is not all there is.

ELECTRIC LIMITS OF OUR
WIDEST SENSES

I LEFT DENTALAND, SWUNG BY THE HOUSE TO pick up Spot, and drove on out to Pembroke Lakes Animal Hospital where he wasn't known. My fingers tingled—evidently I still had nitrous oxide in my brain. I stopped for a green light on Federal Highway, heard tires squeal behind me, horns squawk. I had been thinking about the note my girlfriend e-mailed me: *Johnny, we don't have much time left.* What did she mean by that? We have all our time left.

Spot loves sitting in the pickup, but hates when it moves. He starts whining, drooling, turning circles on the seat. I told him to keep his paws off the dashboard. I said, I'll buckle the seatbelt on you if you don't quit it. He stared at me. I said, I mean it, Spot. Do you want me to pull over right here? He sat nicely, gave me a muffled but defiant woof, and looked out the window.

At Sheridan and Dixie I noticed a hand-lettered sign staked into a patch of grass: NO TRUSTPASSING. I read it to Spot. He ignored me. Earlier when I was getting my lateral incisor filled, while I was in my delirium, I heard my telephone ring, and I thought, Well, that's it then, my day is ruined. I waited for the answering machine to pick up, for the caller to leave a message. The voice said, *If you need your house painted, call*

Ducky Langlois at—and he gave me a number to call. Here's the thing. Ducky was a childhood friend of mine. I haven't seen him since he moved away from the housing project in fifth grade. I hadn't even thought about him in ten years, I bet. His eyes were tiny, blue, and crossed. I wanted to call the number he left and ask him, How did you track me down, Ducky? And how did you know about the water stains on the stucco? But before I could dial, I heard the dental assistant ask me if I could sit up.

Spot and I stopped at a crosswalk on Taft and watched a line of schoolchildren parade by. Spot's tail thumped the seat. He's crazy about kids. I thought how Ducky's the same age in my head as these kids here on the street. Why did he show up in my dream after thirty-five years? What sort of man did he grow up to be? Did he grow up to be a man? I remembered Ducky and me sitting on our front steps with his cousin Rodney Demarco. This was in Massachusetts in the sixties. Ducky's in a T-shirt and dungarees with red stretch suspenders. Rodney wears thick glasses and two hearing aids, the beige wires disappearing under his shirt collar. He has a crewcut and a tube of butch wax in his shirt pocket. I can't see myself, but I'm there. I'm like a camera. We're waiting for the store bus. I have to buy my mother a pack of Pall Malls. She smokes Pall Malls, which she calls Pell Mells, because of the quotation on the pack: "Wherever Particular People Congregate." Some day we'll be fancy, she says. You just wait. Ducky and Rodney are trading baseball cards. Ducky wants three Yankees for one Yaz.

Spot stuck his head out the window and barked hello to the kids. I lifted my eyebrows, smiled, waved to the crossing guard. She ignored me, or rather she looked right at me and wilfully did not respond. I thought for the umpteenth time that I was tired of living in a place where every sociable gesture is suspect. I should move to the country, to some small town where people are civil and benevolent. I should make this crossing guard regret her rudeness. That's a part of me I hate—the vengeful part.

When we walk with the leash, Spot holds it in his teeth. This makes him think he's walking me. He led me across the parking lot and into the Animal Hospital. The waiting room had a painting on the wall of dogs playing golf—little plaid knickers, tweed caps, and all. A bulldog's making a side bet with a poodle and the collie's addressing the ball with his niblick. I don't actually know if it's a niblick, but I like the word. Could be a cleek or a mashie. I sat in the corner. Spot lay down and began to chew the metal leg of the chair. I scolded him. I gave him his pig's ear. He held the ear upright on the floor between his paws and gnawed at the notched peak. The elderly woman beside me had a caged lovebird in her lap. She introduced herself as the Happy Rooker. She told me she lived in Davie with several hundred birds—canaries, budgies, macaws, parrots, cockatiels, pigeons, and a kookaburra named Dundee. Only the big guys got to stay in the house. The rest of them slept in the barn. She opened her wallet and showed me a photo of Razzle and Dazzle, her peahen and peacock. They had the run of the place, she told me. The Happy Rooker leaned toward me and whispered that Dr. Lincoln was in there now with an emergency—a spray-painted cat. She tsked. Who could do such a thing? She said what's even more obscene was people who sold newborn kitties for python food. They call the kittens *pinkies*, she told me. Imagine.

The Happy Rooker asked me why I looked so morose. Was it going badly with the *d-o-g*? she said. Spot looked up. I said, He's here for a heartworm check. I told her how I'd gotten a call from my old friend Ducky. I said it like it really happened. And it had, of course, only not physically. I said I'd been stuck in my childhood ever since the call. She said, Is it a happy place, your childhood? I told her I'd thought it was then, but it didn't feel like it now. You miss your young self, she said. Don't you?

The other patient was a Labrador with a tumor on his neck the size of a muskmelon. I had trouble looking at it and not looking at it. They'd waited a long time to get the growth treated. The dog's owner, though, told me that Shep wasn't here for the tumor at all. He held up the dog's front paw. The dog whimpered. Spot cocked his head. The paw was wrapped in duct tape. The owner said, Got bit by a raccoon, and it won't heal up proper.

The receptionist leaned over the counter and said, Dorothy, you're next. That's me, the Happy Rooker said. Before she stood, Dorothy nudged her bird off the nesting box and slid open the door. Inside was a single peach-headed chick. Splay-legged baby, Dorothy said. A cripple. I wished her and the birds good luck. She touched my wrist, smiled, told me I was kind.

My girlfriend says I'm susceptible, like a person who's always coming down with colds or a person who is easily swayed by orators. But I'm susceptible, she says, to sensory stimulation. What she's talking about is how when I see something I immediately connect it to some memory or other, some bit of stored imagery. What she doesn't understand is that I don't do this so much as my brain does it, and

I have nothing to say about it. Like when I saw the crossing guard—before I got angry with her—I recalled the crossing guard at our grade school. She had a downy, bleached mustache and wore mirrored sunglasses. In winter she tied a wool scarf over her garrison hat and smeared Vaseline on her face. Or like the day I went to Bath & Body Works to buy Annick— my girlfriend, I might as well tell you her name—this particular Country Apple body lotion she likes, and a clerk invites me to rub an antibacterial cream into my hands—Alpine Summit, especially made for guys, she tells me. She says, I like to rub it in my hands during the day—smells like men. And for a week after that I noticed women everywhere rubbing lotion into their hands and smiling, and I thought, Has this been going on all my life?

And the very idea of smells gets me thinking about vanilla and frying garlic and gasoline, and when I think of gasoline, I'm back there at Mulcahy's gas station, and my old man's inside playing pitch with Billy Marley and Whitey Martin, whose brain is wired by the CIA, and with Addie Nadeau, who will die shortly at thirty-six while mowing his lawn. I'm outside sitting up against the building, talking to Maurice Walsh, trying to convince him that the Kinks were a better band than the Beatles. My father smelled like bay rum. Annick smells like garden soil.

Annick wants to know why do I do that, why do I think every little thing is significant. I tell her it's a provocative world out there, honey bunny. She also tells me that not every person has an ongoing conversation with himself, not every life is narrated by a voice in the head. But I don't think I believe her.

Dr. Lincoln asked me about Spot's diet. I said he was omnivorous and adventurous. Reason I ask, he said, is he's got a sliver of yellow plastic between his back teeth here. I can get it out, but maybe we ought to clean his teeth while you're here. I said, Next visit we'll do that. Spot bit Dr. Lincoln's stethoscope, yanked it, dove off the examining table. Not very disciplined, Dr. Lincoln said. Have you considered obedience school? I made a joke. I said, For me or the dog? He didn't laugh. He told me to get Spot back up on the table.

I dragged Spot out from under the table, asked him not to embarrass me any further. On the table, Spot rolled on his back, a submissive gesture, he wanted us to think. He slapped the doctor's arm away. Dr. Lincoln gave me a long-suffering look. He said, You're one of those people who buys a pet because you need love. I couldn't speak. It had never occurred to me that there could be any other reason.

Dr. Lincoln said, Animals need structure and discipline. They need limits. Dogs especially. They need to be told when to sit, eat, play, and defecate. Spot grabbed the cuff of Dr. Lincoln's lab coat and growled. Dr. Lincoln slapped him on the muzzle. He turned to me, said, This dog's out of control. I came clean. I said, Spot's always been a bit hyperactive. Irish setters are like that. He chews things, anything, everything. He eats my pens, my glasses, flashlights. He runs loose in the neighborhood, comes home whenever he feels like it. Dr. Lincoln shook his head. He said, So put a fence up in your yard. I said, I have. Doesn't work. He jumps it. Then get an electric fence, he said.

I said, That's cruel.

He said, Dogs can't be left to roam.

I said, Some dogs are rambunctious, free-spirited.

He said, There's a leash law in Broward County.

They like to explore, I said. It's good for them. They're like people—they need to get away, push themselves, even if others don't approve.

Excuse me, he said, but society functions because we each have our place and we know it. What you're talking about is anarchy.

I said, Look, some folks fit properly in the mainstream, some don't. And some dogs do, some don't. Not everyone has to be normal.

Dr. Lincoln scratched Spot's ears. I could see that Spot the Recalcitrant was grateful, transported, unhinged. Traitor. Dr. Lincoln said, We all end up normal no matter what we do. Age is the great normalizer. We all wither the same. Even if you want to be wild at eighty, you can't. You want to hitchhike across France, but you'd always be worried where the next bathroom is. And suppose you need your medication?

I said, Why are we talking about this?

Electric fences, he said. They turn young dogs into old ones rather quickly. Dogs learn to love their yards, their tiny worlds. They forget about the greener pastures. They come to their senses, settle.

I ran into the Lab's owner in the parking lot. How's old Shep? I said. He said, Need to put him down. Got the cancer. I looked at Shep in the back seat of the car. He licked the dressing on his wound. The owner said, Don't need to pay no one to do the job. I'll put him down myself. I owe him that much. When I was, I don't know, about five I think, four or five, my aunt Robinella took me to a Disney movie at the Loew's Poli. Bought me Junior Mints and a root beer. We sat in the first row of the balcony. I thought of the ceiling as the floor and the chandeliers as crystal trees growing from pots. The lights went out. *Old Yeller.* A boy and his dog. An hour into the movie I wanted a golden Lab of my own, and I was figuring out how I could convince my dad it was a good idea even though pets weren't allowed at the project, when I looked up and Tommy Kirk's holding a rifle. He's crying. He's aiming at Yeller. This can't be happening. Uncle Walt's duplicity: You love this dog, don't you, Johnny? Well, now you sit right there and watch while I kill him. And don't you even think of turning away. How cynical and manipulative can a person be? I can still hear Fess Parker telling his boy that "Now and then for no good reason a man can figure out, life will just haul off and knock him flat." I was five, barely standing. I wouldn't drive within fifty miles of Disney World.

At the park, I let Spot run on the baseball field. I sat in the dugout and watched him lean into his turns, tongue flapping, ears folded back, making wider and wider circles. I thought about my day, how all those people from my life had come together without regard for time or logic. When I thought of myself now and myself then, I saw no cause-and-effect at work in my life. No plot. Plots are for stories, accidents for life. Chance seemed more significant than choice. A disturbing notion.

When I was young, I had planned to leave the country, work my way around the world. Take five years. Maybe come back. Maybe not. I had researched, planned, mapped, corresponded. I had my first job all set up on a farm in Wales. In Carmarthen. But one day I stood in the license renewal line at the Massachusetts Department of Motor Vehicles reading

Dylan Thomas. Why did I decide to go on that day? At that hour? Why did I stand in Line 7? Anyway, a red-haired girl in the adjacent line asked me for the time, and I told her, and she said, I've had eighteen straight whiskies; I think that's the record, and I said, Excuse me? and she tapped my book and said, Thomas's last words, and one thing led to another, and a year later we were married, and twenty-four years later I'm single again and living fifteen hundred miles from her, and I never got to Wales.

I say single, but I have Annick, my sweetheart, and she has me. We're in love; we're just not married. I have my house, she has hers. We're intimate companions. Best friends. We're in league, Annick says. I've never been happier. If I could stop time, I would, and every day would be today, and every day would end with Annick and me talking, touching, listening to Puccini or Jimmie Dale Gilmore, snuggled in bed with Spot snoring on the floor beside us.

As a kid I could not imagine being married. Being married I could not imagine being divorced. Alive, I cannot imagine being dead. Being dead I cannot imagine. Who I was has nothing to do with who I am, what I did then, with what I do now. Where's the sense in all that?

I called to Spot. I whistled. He stopped, dropped, rolled on his back, squirmed like a fish. One day Ducky and I were down at Great Brook catching tadpoles, when two big kids walked up and told us to beat it; this was their brook. Ducky said no it wasn't. The tall boy called Ducky a cockeyed faggot and shoved him into the water. When Ducky stood, the fat boy grabbed him from behind and the tall boy tried to stuff a tadpole into Ducky's mouth. Ducky wriggled and kicked. The boys laughed. I pitched a rock and hit the tall boy flush on the temple. He screamed, dropped the tadpole, and grabbed his bleeding head. He fell to his knees in the brook. The fat boy said he'd kill me, but I could see he was rattled. Ducky broke free, and we ran all the way home. We caught our breath on the front steps. I figured I'd be punished if my parents ever found out I'd hit someone with a rock. Ducky told me I should have minded my own beeswax. He was going to offer the beating up to God just like he did at home. He said, You do that you hardly feel a thing. I said, That's fucked up, Ducky. He said he'd get to heaven before me. I said, What's your hurry? I yelled to Spot, told him we were going to Annick's, which he likes because she saves him steak bones, which he dislikes because he can't sleep on the bed.

That night Annick and I sat up in her den drinking Irish whiskey and talking. I asked her about her *we don't have much time left* e-mail. She said, Change is not a choice, Johnny. That's all I was saying. I said, So what should we do about it? Be aware of it, she said. She leaned her head into my shoulder. I told her, Whatever time we have, we'll have it with each other. But I wondered if you can really *have* time or is time what we're made of. It just makes me sad, she said. Spot growled at his biscuit ball. I poured us another drink. We held hands. Jimmie Dale figured he was gonna go downtown. His love, his love had gone away. Annick said, I just wish we had more time, you know. I told her I'd settle for what time we had, just so long as we didn't have to come to our senses.

ARLIS & IVY

WHEN MY SISTER ELVIE DIED, I MOVED THE Amana freezer in from the porch and set it in a corner of the kitchen where it belonged. And when I did, the face of Jesus disappeared right off it. I taped up a handy shopping reminder from Saterfiel's Sack N Save on the freezer door—you just put a peg beside bread or milk or Little Debbies or whatever you need. Elvie and I had been together all sixty-six years of my life, all of it in this, our daddy's house. When people die, you begin to notice the space they had taken up with their bodies and voices, with their scent, with the air they displaced with their motion. I'm not proud of what I done, but I could not tolerate solitude, and so I went to the True Vine Powerhouse Church of the Saved but Struggling, not to find Jesus—He has a way of finding me—but to find a widow with the same itch. We married, Ivy and me. I did not impose myself on Ivy in a husbandly way. I started out shy. I ain't much to look on. But I seen worse. Neither of us was very comfortable at first, but we were curious enough and sad enough to get on with it. Ivy felt out of place here, and I told her she ought to make the place hers and she did—moved the freezer out to the porch, and didn't Jesus come back. Looked like he'd aged a bit, but not so much as me. He seemed happy to be back, Ivy said. I got to tell the world. I said, I wish you wouldn't. She said, Arlis, it's a miracle. I said there's miracles everywhere we look, in the bark of trees, in the linoleum, in the bees at their hive. It's a miracle how you run your hand up my arm.

THE DEAD OF NIGHT

HE'S TIRED AS A TOMBSTONE. CLOVIS COY CAN barely keep his eyes opened, and yet here he is driving his pickup on an empty two-lane desert highway in the dead of night. Should've stopped back in Loco Hills, found a room, slept the sleep of angels, woke up bright-eyed, and driven on in the morning. He's listening to Los Lonely Boys and singing along to stay awake. *How far is heaven?* He drinks the last of the cold coffee from a plastic cup, rolls down his window, and breathes deeply. He remembers asking his dad that question when he was four, and Dad saying, Heaven's just down the road a piece, son. Clovis almost doesn't see whatever-the-hell-it-is in the middle of the road, but he swerves to the shoulder and misses it. He brakes and looks into his rearview mirror. Whatever it is, it hasn't moved. He backs up. Unless he's hallucinating, there's a plaid loveseat straddling the yellow line. Clovis gets out of the cab, looks around. He shuts his eyes and opens them. He sits on the loveseat. He's not dreaming.

Clovis hoists the loveseat into the bed of the pickup, shuts the tailgate. He hears an owl hoot and then what must be a jackrabbit skittering through the sage. He starts up the truck, turns on the radio. He pulls out onto the highway. The man on the radio says, "We've got Christine on line three. Hello, Christine, you're speaking with the Dream Doctor."

Christine says, "In my dream, my mother's dying." Clovis tries to picture Christine. She's sitting on a couch in a darkened living room, feet curled under her. She says, "Mother's in a canopied bed, and I'm like standing by the door, and I want to ask her if she's a lesbian before it's too late. I don't want her taking any secrets with her to the grave. So I try to speak, but all that comes out of my mouth is baby talk. Goo goo, ga-ga, like that."

The Dream Doctor says, "Are you a lesbian, Christine? Is this dream really about your secret?"

Christine is quiet. Clovis figures she just swallowed a bit of that red wine she's been nursing. She says, "Well, I think I might have been one, you know, but then I dated this gay boy, Shaun, and he kind of like brought out my feminine side."

Clovis punches up another station and finds ranchero music. He sits up straight. He thinks about how much he'd like to be having a dream right now. When he sees a rest area, thank God, Clovis pulls in and parks. He leans his head against the window, shuts his eyes, but he's been driving for thirteen hours, and he dreams he's driving still, can feel the tremor of the road, hear the hum of the tires, only now he becomes aware of flashing lights, and he thinks he might have been speeding. He opens his eyes and remembers that he's parked. He looks out the side mirror and sees a state trooper checking the loveseat with his flashlight. Then the trooper shines the light at the mirror and blinds Clovis. The trooper steps to the cab, one hand on the butt of his service revolver. Clovis says, "Just trying to get some sleep, Officer."

"Well, you can't sleep here."

"It's a rest area."

"It's not a bedroom."

"I'm dead tired."

"Get moving."

Clovis stops at a convenience store for coffee, asks the cashier how much he owes. The cashier, who's cleaning his fingernails with a key, doesn't look up from the magazine he's reading. Clovis says, "How much for a large coffee?" And then he notices that the cashier's wearing a button that says LOOK AT ME: I READ LIPS. So Clovis steps closer and bends his head to catch the cashier's gaze. He holds up the coffee, rubs his fingers together. He mouths the words in an exaggerated fashion. "How much do I owe you?"

"You don't have to shout!"

At a gas station outside Antelope, Clovis fills the tank, goes in to pay. He can barely lift his boots off the pavement. He feels like if he collapsed on the floor by the display of snack food, he wouldn't be able to stand. The clerk looks through binoculars at the gas tank and tells Clovis, "Twenty-two, twenty-one."

Clovis pays. "Would you mind if I slept in your lot for a couple of hours?"

"There's a motel eleven miles up the road. On the right."

"Lot wouldn't be safe?"

"American-owned."

"I can do that."

The clerk hands Clovis his change. "You look like you're circling the drain, cowboy."

Outside the gas station, Clovis watches a car drive very slowly on the shoulder. The driver of the car, pasty face and slicked-back silver hair, watches Clovis as he drives. Green rubbish sacks are piled on the hood and trunk of the car.

Clovis pulls into the Alamo Motel parking lot. He's so grateful he made it, he wants to cry. He kills the engine, steps out, puts on his cowboy hat, stretches. No one's at the office desk. Clovis hears the mumble of a TV from the back room. A handwritten sign on the wall reads, NOT RESPONSIBLE FOR LOST OBJECTS. The clock isn't working. Another sign says, ONCE A ROOM HAS BEEN OCCUPIED, THERE WILL BE NO REFUND! Clovis clears his throat, taps the reception bell. "Hello!"

The desk clerk comes out from behind a beaded curtain eating a drippy burrito. His hair is tousled. He hands Clovis a registration form. Clovis tells him the pen doesn't work. The clerk tells him to bear down. Leave an impression. He tells Clovis it'll be thirty dollars, plus tax.

Clovis slides the form across the desk. "Could you use a loveseat, by the way?"

"Cash."

"I found it on the highway. It's yours free."

The clerk points to the sign. "Not responsible."

Clovis takes out his wallet. "Where am I?"

"La Promesa."

"Thirty."

"Plus tax. Two-fifty. Plus a two-dollar key deposit, a five-dollar phone deposit, and a ten-dollar cat deposit."

"Thanks, but I don't need a cat."

"Yes, you do, hombre."

"I'm allergic."

"You got a snake with you?"

"What for?"

"We have mice." The clerk leads Clovis to the back room. There's a young girl, can't be more than fifteen, lying on the sofa, sucking her thumb. She doesn't take her eyes off the TV where a Mexican cowboy warbles a love song. *Este amor apasionado . . .*

Next to the shabby recliner are twelve plastic kennels, each with a cat, a bowl, a litter box, and a scratching pad inside. The cats' names are written on the kennels in black marker: Tom, Belial, Diablo, Salvador Dali Llama, and so on. The clerk sucks his teeth, sings along with the cowboy. *Yo so perder, yo so perder.* He says, "Pick one, señor."

Clovis chooses Molly. The clerk tells him he's made an excellent choice and hands the kennel to Clovis. "You don't have to let her out. The mice can smell her."

All the rooms are dark and quiet except Room 10. There's some kind of ruckus going on. Clovis stops by the door, hears a man say, "Esperanza, when you're up to your chin in shit, the only thing to do is sing."

Clovis opens the door to Room 11 and stands in the doorway, looks around, listens. He puts the kennel down, steps into the room, snaps on the light. Cockroaches scoot along the paneled walls. He kicks the bed, the desk. He opens the bathroom door and steps back. He puts the kennel on the bed, sees that the red message button on the phone is flashing. He picks up the phone, punches a button, and listens to a man say, "Words cannot describe the pain, Rhonda. Words only come when the pain is over. When everything is over. *Comprende?* Everything."

Clovis turns on the TV. The screen's snowy, the sound staticky. He tries a few channels, turns it off. There's a linen post-card on the TV of a desert sunrise: ocotillo and sage, and in the distance a yellow sun peeks over purple mountains, brightening the indigo sky to silvery blue. He turns the card over and reads. "Life is a journey, my ass. We're never going anywhere. We'll never get out of here. Rhonda." Clovis lies on top of the bed, covers his eyes with his hat. Esperanza screams from next door. Molly cries, and Clovis lets her out of the kennel. She purrs and rubs her side along his leg. Clovis takes the Bible out of the bedside table. If he reads, maybe he'll fall asleep. "These also shall be unclean unto you among the creeping things that creep upon the earth, the weasel, and the mouse . . ." Molly's ears perk up. Clovis hears scratching along the baseboards. The bed in Room 10 creaks. Clovis reads about the eating of swine's flesh in the garden until he hears what sounds like scuffling from 10. Esperanza cries. What-could-be-a-body slams against the wall. Molly leaps from the bed. Clovis goes next door and knocks. Inside, the man says, "Shut up or I'll really give you something to cry about."

Esperanza says, "No, please, Joey."

Clovis knocks again. The crying stops. Joey opens the door a crack. The security chain is in place. Clovis says, "Is every-thing okay, miss?"

Joey says she's fine.

"I didn't ask you." Clovis looks past him to Esperanza. "Are you all right?"

"She's my wife."

"That makes it okay to hit her?"

"Get the fuck out of here before I tear you a new asshole."

Esperanza says she's all right. Clovis asks her if she'd like him to call the cops. She says, "You don't understand English? I said I was okay."

"You heard the lady." Joey shuts the door.

Back in the room Clovis tells Molly, "No cats in the Bible, honey, no rest for the weary." He pulls back the bedcovers and sees the rats, two of them. He grabs his hat, his boots, and Molly, and backs out the door. He hauls the loveseat off the truck, puts it on the walk in front of his room, and lies down. Molly climbs on his chest, kneads his shirt. He stares up at the starry sky.

"What do you see?"

He's startled by Esperanza. She's wrapped herself in a blanket.

"Everything."

She looks to the sky. "I can never see not one of those consolations they all talk about. Just a mess of glitter to me."

Clovis yawns. "Can't sleep."

"Then you can't dream."

"One time in my life all I did was sleep."

"All I did was dream."

Clovis scoots over, holds Molly in his lap. Esperanza sits. She smells like she's been in storage. "What's with you and Joey?"

"He has me dancing before the music starts." She closes her eyes, wets her lips with her tongue, and smiles. "You ever have a woman do that for you?"

"I haven't."

"Put that on your list of things to do." She closes her eyes. Clovis watches her. In a minute, she's snoring. Clovis gets up, pulls the blanket to her shoulders.

Molly's asleep on the dashboard. Clovis closes the truck

door as quietly as he can. He crosses the parking lot to the doughnut shop. When he steps near a souped-up muscle car, he sets off an alarm. A siren wails and a voice says, "Step away from the car. Now!" A guy in sunglasses steps out of the shop, clicks his remote, and the alarm stops. Clovis says, "This your car?" The guy ignores the question, opens the car door, cranks the engine, revs the motor. The windows are tinted black. Purple and pink neon lights glow around the base of the car. It's like a spaceship.

Clovis sits at the U-shaped counter, his back to the door. At the end of the counter to his right, a slim man shakes and shakes a carton of orange juice. To his left a few seats away, a man who may be drunk mutters to himself. The waitress, middle-aged and attractive, a pencil in her blond hair, says hi, and, "Can I get ya'?"

"Coffee, please."

The state trooper from the rest area strolls in, walks behind the counter, takes the coffeepot from the waitress, and pours his own. He stares at Clovis while he does. He walks to a booth, puts his hat on the table, and sits. The waitress returns with the coffee.

She says, "You look beat, my friend."

"Haven't slept in thirty-seven hours."

"You ought to try it."

"I did." He points with his chin at the trooper. "Smoky wouldn't let me."

"Espinoza? If he was rain, he wouldn't fall on your field."

A boy walks in and heads for the cigarette machine. He sports a spiky raspberry Mohawk. He's wearing bondage pants, combat boots, and a Rancid T-shirt. Espinoza stirs his coffee and smirks. He says to the boy, "My, my, my, rebellious youth. Son, you are a stereotype."

"And you're a cop in a doughnut shop." The boy smiles and walks out. The slim man is still shaking his juice. The waitress asks Clovis where he's heading.

"Home. Haven't been back in nineteen years."

"Why now?"

"Nowhere else to go."

"They say there's no use running if you're on the wrong road."

"I've set out to go home plenty of times, but never made it."

"The house will be smaller than you remember."

The trooper stands and puts on his Stetson, drops a coin on the table, and walks out the door. The waitress grabs a damp rag and walks to the table. The slim man slaps a pack of cigarettes into the palm of his hand. The drunk wipes his nose with a napkin. His eyes are red and swollen. He tells Clovis his dog died, and Clovis says he's sorry. The drunk takes a photo from his wallet and shows it to Clovis.

"How did it happen?"

The man studies the picture. "He drug the garbage from the kitchen to the living room. I said no. He tore open the Hefty bag, snapped at me." He shows Clovis where the dog's teeth broke the skin. "I tied him to the charcoal grill out back, shot him twice in the back of the head."

"That's not funny."

"Am I laughing? Second was a mercy shot."

"You killed your dog?"

"We had developed an adversarial relationship." He cries and lays his head on the counter.

The waitress says, "Take it outside, Ricky."

"I lost my best friend, Rosalee. For chrissakes, have some sympathy."

Clovis says, "That's fucked up, Ricky. Pardon my French, Rosalee." He likes the sound of her name, the way it flows off the tongue, the soft vowels and easy consonants. "So, Rosalee, what do you do in—where are we?"

"Alejado. And you're looking at it."

"Got a family?"

"Not anymore."

She goes to answer the phone. Clovis watches her, admires her figure. Too lovely and sweet to be alone. He imagines her in a small house, flowers on the porch.

She comes around the counter and sits beside Clovis. He says, "So what keeps you here, Rosalee?"

"Where would I go?"

"Your roots are here?"

She shakes her head. "I love the desert."

"So do I. Why do we?"

"Love walking out there, back into the hills, and hearing nothing but my heartbeat."

Clovis yawns. "It's time for me to head west."

"I can give you something to keep you awake."

"I'd rather sleep."

"Free no charge."

"Thanks. I can make it another two hours."

"You must live up around Los Cielos."

"I do."

"God's country."

"I'll take a cup of milk if you have it." Clovis takes two bills from his pocket. The slim man stands beside him, still slapping the cigarette pack against the heel of his hand. He says, "Y-you're h-heading w-west?"

"Need a lift?"

"Y-yes."

"No smoking."

Rosalee puts a cup of milk on the counter. "Maybe you'll be back this way."

Clovis puts the cup on the floor and Molly laps up the milk. He pours water from a plastic jug onto a bandanna and washes his face. The slim man paces in front of the truck. "What's your name, partner?"

"T-Terry."

"I don't suppose you drive?" Terry laughs or barks, Clovis can't tell which. "I didn't think so."

Terry sits in the passenger seat, plucks his eyebrows with one hand and bites the fingernails of the other. He rocks in his seat.

Clovis says, "You're a bundle of nerves. Been jittery all your life?"

Terry nods.

"The stutter, too?"

Terry nods and bites his fist.

"Do they know what causes the stutter?"

"Hate." Terry pats Molly, who's brushing up against his leg.

"If you stopped hating whoever it is, maybe the stuttering would stop."

Terry points to the side of the road. "D-drop m-me h-here."

"Where do you live?"

"B-by t-the d-doughnut s-shop."

"I don't get it."

"I d-don't s-sleep. N—need to w-walk."

"Why don't you sleep?"

"M-might n-not w-wake up."

"Sounds pretty good to me right now." Clovis pulls to the shoulder and stops. Terry opens the door. Clovis says, "Stay off the highway, friend. You'll get yourself killed."

A while later Clovis veers off the road, feels the truck bounce along the shoulder and scrape against a barbed-wire fence. He stops the truck, gets out, and does some deep breathing. He gets back in. Molly sleeps in the passenger seat. He leans his head against the window, puts his hat over his eyes. Just then an eighteen-wheeler roars by, blasting its air horn. The whole pickup shakes. Clovis realizes he can't stay here. He pulls onto the highway. His eyes nearly close, and then they do for one, two, three seconds, and then his head drops and he snaps awake. He sits up straight, realizes how lucky he was, touches the cat. He tells her how he just fell asleep and dreamed that he was driving. His eyes were closed but he could see. Whew! He decides he'll sing to the snoozing cat. "Are you sleeping, are you sleeping, Molly-O, Molly-O? Morning bells are ringing, ding dang dong." And as he sings, his voice grows breathier, his words become slurred, and the car drifts over the center line. Clovis doesn't hear a horn blast rising in pitch, doesn't feel or hear a crush and thud of metal. He just drives on into the boundless dark.

The door's unlocked, and Clovis walks in. Rosalee was right. His head almost touches the ceiling, and it's so bright inside, like the house has its own sun. He calls to his mother and father, yells hello. He walks down the hall. "I really didn't think I was going to make it. Almost drove off the road. Hit a guardrail or something." He sees a note on the fridge. "Clovis, I'll be back after the funeral. Can't wait to see you. Love, Mom." How did they know he was coming? He goes to his old bedroom. A poster of Hendrix over the bed. He'd forgotten about that. He picks up a model plane, a B-25 Mitchell Bomber, and remembers the stormy afternoon he built it. He lies on his bed and closes his eyes and falls into sleep. He dreams he's driving and swerves to avoid someone or something on the road and loses control of the truck.

On the highway, Trooper Ezpinoza guides the occasional car around the accident scene. A pickup truck is on its roof. Clovis is trapped inside. A paramedic is on his stomach, half inside the cab. He tends to the victim. "You're going to be all right. Soon as the Jaws of Life arrive, we'll have you out of here in a jiffy."

Clovis says, "I just want to sleep. Please!"

"We need you to stay awake, sir."

Espinoza hunkers down. "How we doing?"

"Got the Heimlich valve inserted, the paramedic says. "Breathing's okay, but the pressure's dropping."

Clovis says to Espinoza, "You wouldn't let me sleep."

"We can't let you sleep," Espinoza says. "We need you to work with us."

Clovis recognizes the paramedic as the man with the rubbish on his car. "How did you know where I lived?"

"Can you tell me your name?" the paramedic says. He takes Clovis's blood pressure. "Keep those eyes open, amigo."

"I haven't slept . . ."

Clovis is fast asleep in his bedroom when he hears his

mom calling him from the kitchen. "Come on, now, Clovis, rise and shine. You'd sleep your life away if I let you." Clovis pulls the pillow over his head. "Breakfast is on the table. School bus is here in twenty minutes."

The paramedic reaches in and adjusts the oxygen cannula in Clovis's nose, checks the pulse. "Come on, now. Stay with me. Wake up." Clovis opens his eyes. "There you go. Do you understand what happened to you, sir?"

"Not responsible."

"Who's this Rhonda you talk about?"

Espinoza says, "They'll be here in ten."

The paramedic shakes his head. "Talk to me, sir."

"When the pain goes away."

Clovis opens his eyes and sees his ten-year-old self sitting at the end of the bed. The boy says, "Who are you?"

"Who you'll be."

"What do you do?"

"I get by."

"I don't want to get by. I want to be somebody."

"You see, this is why I didn't want to come home."

"Not a failure."

"I kn-knew I'd have to p-put w-with y-your sh-shit." Clovis holds back tears, takes a deep breath. "When you get to be my age, you'll understand that you don't judge a man's worth by the job he holds, but by the dreams he dreams."

"That's not what my dad says."

"Or by the people he loves. Or by what he sees. Or something."

The boy runs through the beaded curtain and out of the room. "Mom, Mom!"

Clovis grips the paramedic's hand. "Mom! Just five more minutes." His grip slackens. The paramedic checks his pulse and pressure. He shuts Clovis's eyes, removes the blood pressure cuff. He stands and walks toward the ambulance. Molly skitters off into the sage. The day dawns in the desert. A yellow sun peaks over purple mountains and the indigo sky brightens to silvery blue.

TALK TALK TALK

THAT EVENING AFTER SUPPER, AFTER HE HAD pruned the wisteria, walked the dog, set the recycling bins by the sidewalk, Rance Usrey went into the den and turned off the TV. He told Emma they needed to talk. She folded her paperback novel, looked at her watch, said, "My show goes on at nine."

Rance leaned over and kissed his wife on her forehead. "It's about work." He opened the liquor cabinet, took out the sherry and the two cordial glasses.

Emma said, "You've been drinking an awful lot lately."

Rance told it just how he'd rehearsed it, how he wanted, *needed* really, to change his life, how he'd been numbed by the routine of law practice and jaded by the legal system, disgusted by it, really.

Emma rolled her eyes.

He said, "Honey, don't get exasperated." He poured the sherry, handed her a glass. "Hear me out." He cleared his throat. "In America we're not interested in justice. We're not after truth; we're after victory." He was, he told her, in danger of becoming as cynical as his partners Jack Bruyninckx and Kirby Ogg. He sipped his sherry, stared across the room at the leggy and dusty philodendron.

"Is this about O.J. again?"

"Jurors are told they mustn't allow their feelings to interfere with their decision, as if that were possible or desirable. The law is life lived without emotion. That's what this is about. It's life without nuance or ambiguity. It's preposterous, false, and suffocating. I don't want to be a part of it anymore." He looked at his hands when he said, "I'm going to quit the firm."

"Are you insane, Rance?"

"I'll give them time to find someone, of course. I'll finish up the work on the Loudermilk case."

Emma walked across the room to the cluttered desk and picked up a pile of bills. She let them drop. She said, "And who's going to pay these?"

Rance hadn't rehearsed this part because he was hoping that his decision would be embraced by Emma, and that this would lead to a discussion of their mutual dissatisfaction, of their desire to live simpler, more meaningful, more creative lives. He didn't want to have to say that maybe we could *both* work. He didn't want to say, We could dip into our savings, cash in a 401(k) if we need to. He didn't want to say, Maybe we don't need two cars, two phone lines, pagers, cell phones, satellite TV. Maybe we don't need to go out to eat five nights a week. Emma said, "And are we always going to live in this squalid house?"

THAT WAS two years ago. They had been married for fifteen. Three years earlier, they had brought Dave, their Maltese, home from Planet Pet, and understood—this was what

Emma believed—that they had already decided not to have children, but could not say so to each other, had decided that their life now was everything it would ever be. Dave was the emblem of their quiescence. The room that Emma thought of as the nursery had long ago become Rance's office. On Dave's first night in his new home, Emma held him in her lap long after Rance had gone to bed. Dave trembled, whimpered. She rocked him, sang to him, patted him, told him he was a good puppy, yes, he was! She put Dave into her canvas book bag, slipped the bag over her shoulder, and walked around the dark and empty house. She jiggled Dave, reassured him, rubbed his back through the canvas until he settled into sleep. The truth was she couldn't see a child fitting into her life of charities, volunteer board meetings, and housekeeping. She was so busy she hardly had time to plan her week, never mind her life, but then when she thought about her suddenly well-defined future, she felt desolate and emboldened.

IN THE THIRD year of their marriage, Emma miscarried in her second month. She wept for days, apologized to Rance for her failure, for her tears, for everything, and then she cried some more. She had allowed herself, you see, to imagine the baby she knew would be a girl, to imagine this baby, Annie Rose, asleep in the new crib—she shouldn't have bought the crib—little wisps of black hair, scarlet cheeks, her tiny, dimpled hand working itself into a fist. Rance was just then waist-deep in a nasty trial that you may have read about. The firm's client, a former district court judge from a venerable Bastrop family, stood accused of the sexual assault and murder of two thirteen-year-old girls. He drugged the girls, raped them, wound them in shrink-wrap, and buried them alive. After the last-minute plea bargain and the sentencing, Rance took Emma on a Caribbean cruise, and her spirits did seem to lighten. They agreed to try again for a child when she felt strong enough.

RANCE PROPOSED to Emma six months after meeting her and two weeks after passing the Louisiana Bar. He took her to New Orleans for the weekend. They stayed at the Monteleone, dined at Commander's Palace. After the bananas Foster, Rance presented Emma with an emerald cut diamond engagement ring. She could barely catch her breath. She was so elated that evening, so buoyant, so believing, that she looked ahead to her entire life, and there at the end of that life she saw her and Rance, hand in hand, walking down an oak-lined lane to their home, or was it to their reward?

RANCE NEVER did leave his law practice; Emma wouldn't hear of it. But he did get involved with the Morehouse Parish Community Theater. He played Arlis in *The Freezer Jesus* and Tom in *The Glass Menagerie*. Rance loved acting, loved the way you could lose yourself in someone else. He took a creative writing class at the college. He wrote poems and stories about the lawful and the lawless, and on every other Saturday night he drove to Monroe to read his work at the Beer 'n Bards open mike at Strawberry Fields. Emma took these opportunities to rendezvous with Douglas Bleeker, a married father of four, at the Bide-a-While Tourist Court in Perryville.

Rance knew all about the State Farm agent. You're in good hands with Douglas Bleeker. When Rance confronted Emma about it—*I found his business card on your dresser and a size-seventeen shirt in the Subaru*—she denied it; quote on homeowner insurance, she said, mixup at the cleaners, but he knew. And he had known about Lenny Stranieri, the wedding photographer, *their* wedding photographer. For the first dozen years of their marriage, Emma had worried that Rance was having an affair with one woman or another, with his secretary, with a public defender, or that he would leave her for someone younger, classier, blonder. He could never settle her unwarranted anxiety. She called him at work, met him for lunch, organized their evenings, held his hand at cocktail parties.

BY THE TIME Dave was paper-trained, Emma had taken up with Lenny Stranieri, who told her he never forgot a beautiful bride. Lenny tended bar at the Tom Cat Lounge on Wednesday nights. He was handsome enough, but nothing special. A couple of afternoons a week they met at the Downtowner Inn on Third, and that went on for like five and a half months. When she told Lenny how unsavory she felt, how dishonest, he told her that if you don't have a secret, you're just not living. When the lamentable affair achieved its tawdry conclusion—he stopped returning her calls, found excuses not to meet, claimed to be away at photo seminars—Emma was overwhelmed with guilt and disgrace. And, surprisingly, with loss. She had not expected to miss Lenny, miss the dangerous afternoons, the drab motel room, that tearful clown portrait over the lumpy bed. She knew that Rance had grown suspicious, and she was glad it was finished and glad, too, that she'd done it. The exciting little secret exalted her, she thought, above the decent women at the County Market, the uncomplicated women at the River Oaks Country Club.

RANCE HOPED that a romantic weekend together might rekindle her passion for him. So for her birthday, Rance surprised Emma with a Lovers' Getaway Weekend package at the Arlington up in Hot Springs. A lavish suite, continental breakfast, mineral baths, and massage for two. (Douglas Bleeker bought her a black lace zip-front bustier.) On the way out of town, they dropped Dave off at the Bark Avenue kennel.

On Friday night Rance took Emma to a new French place on Central Avenue, the Restaurant Renady. Emma said she didn't *get* French food, so Rance ordered. They had crème de cresson, poulet à la grain roti, ravioli à la Nicoise. They split a bottle of Chateau Croizet Bages, which Emma thought tasted like bananas, and said so. The little restaurant had four tables and was run by a French family. The father cooked, the mother and daughter—Rance guessed she was about ten—waited tables. The mother and father joked in French. There was a pencil-drawn portrait of a cat framed on the wall beside

Rance and Emma's table. The cat was smiling. Rance felt cheery and assured.

He said, "What should we do with the rest of our lives?"

"Oh, please!"

"I'm serious."

The little girl stopped at their table with a dish of chocolates. Emma smiled, shook her head. Rance took one. *Merci.* The girl curtsied and returned to the kitchen.

"Why don't we move to New Mexico or somewhere? Adobe house, desert sunsets."

"Why would I want to leave my home?"

Rance bit into his chocolate. Praline caramel. "How about you want to go because you're curious?"

"I'm not going to move at this point in my life. I've got an infrastructure. Dentist, doctor, stylist, mechanic. I'm not going through that all over again." Emma excused herself and went to the ladies' room. Rance realized that a new beginning didn't require a new geography. All it needed was for the two of them to reinvent themselves—and not as some imaginary, ideal couple, but as who they were when they married. Take some amnesia to manage that.

Emma used the pay phone, called Douglas Bleeker's cell, got his voice mail. She called his home, hung up before anyone could answer, but did not take her hand off the handset. She closed her eyes and put her forehead against the wall. Her birthday! Her goddamn birthday! She ached all over, felt weary and leaden, like if she relaxed, she'd collapse to the floor. Forty-one! She remembered her first birthday party, her yellow sundress, her silver party hat with the blue number 4, how they all played pin the tail on the donkey and musical chairs, and she remembered Charlie Engdahl's snug white curls and the chocolate icing on his nose and cheeks. She remembered how she hugged him so he wouldn't leave with his momma, and how he got frightened and cried. Emma straightened herself, took a fortifying breath, and returned to the table.

Rance told Emma that when he was, oh, nine or so, he was on a bus going home, maybe from the movies, and a woman pulled the bell cord and stood by the back door. When the bus squealed to a stop, she smiled at the bus driver and said, "Thank you and good night." The driver didn't look up or acknowledge her in any way. She stepped off the bus and walked by Rance's window, her eyes cast ahead at the driver. Rance heard the clicking of the turn signal, saw that the woman was hurt. Rance saw her now, the pocketbook slung over her left shoulder, the cradled shopping bag, the dark eyes and ivory skin, the paisley kerchief. That was the first time he understood that silence was a bludgeon, that life doesn't get any sweeter when you grow up.

Emma was thinking about Gwen Bleeker, who was just then in the hospital getting a mastectomy. She could die from the cancer. Rance ordered *deux cafés crème, s'il vous plait.* Of course, Gwen's illness made it impossible for Douglas to leave her. Emma wouldn't respect him if he did. If the worst happened, God forbid, and Gwen were to die, Emma hoped Douglas wouldn't expect her to raise his four kids. She wouldn't put herself in that position. Gwen's going to pull through this crisis. She'll be fine. She's strong. The kids'll have their momma.

Rance watched the little girl carry a tureen of soup back to the kitchen. He didn't want this family to change, didn't want the daughter—Chloe, her mother called her—to grow up, to go off to a university, meet some boy, and move to St. Louis or Knoxville, didn't want Papa to get prostate cancer or Mama to luxuriate in flirtations with other men. He didn't want this restaurant to close, not tonight, not ever. We could just sit here, he thought. He looked at Emma. We could never move.

She said, "Well?"

Rance suggested they stop in for a cocktail at the Ohio Club, and Emma figured anything was better than going back to the room. They sat upstairs at a back table. The music hadn't started yet. Rance said, "Do you think they were lovers?"

Emma said, "Who are you talking about?"

"The woman and the bus driver."

"I wouldn't know." Emma took out her compact, brushed her face with satin blush.

Rance ordered two Cosmopolitans. He toasted Emma's birthday. "Here's to forty-one more!"

"No, thank you."

"Not having fun?"

"I'm bored, Rance."

"With Hot Springs?"

"With us."

"Do something about it."

"I have."

Rance sipped his drink. "You have indeed."

"Douglas Bleeker."

"Why?"

Emma shrugged. "You're always trying to make sense of the world, Rance. Me, I know it doesn't make any sense."

"You need a reason to do what you do."

"No. Sometimes you just *do*."

"I was hoping you would give him up."

"Hope is what keeps us from living our lives."

Mr. Nevermind, a jazz trio, took the stage to a smattering of applause.

Emma said, "You accept your circumstances and get on with it."

"You know you're hurting me."

"You don't act hurt."

"Do you enjoy being the other woman?"

"Not when I think about it. I'm not a monster, Rance."

Mr. Nevermind played bebop mostly, but didn't seem to be having fun. Didn't even look at one another. No excitement, no delight. Rance wondered, Was this what they had in mind as kids when they practiced their scales, took their lessons, listened to their heroes on the radio, this adequate going-through-the-motions so a few people can nod their heads to the beat, snap their fingers, tap their toes? Emma grabbed her purse and stood.

"Where are you going?"

"Back to the hotel."

"Sit down, Emma."

"You talk talk talk, but you don't say anything."

"Please."

"No."

"Just for a minute, and—"

"And no. I said no. I won't. No!" With that, Emma turned and walked out of the bar.

· · ·

A YEAR EARLIER, at a parish Bar Association gala at River Oaks, Rance had found Emma out in the parking lot in the arms of a personal injury attorney. The gentleman mumbled an apology and excused himself. Rance grabbed Emma's arm and slapped her. When she laughed, he slapped her again. Then he cried and begged her forgiveness. Her arm was bruised, her eye was swollen. She said, You'll have to forgive yourself; I'm going in for a drink.

EMMA BRUSHED her wet hair and stared out the window to the bathhouses below. She took off her robe and pulled back the bedcovers. She slid under the covers, put out the light, and stared at the ceiling. She didn't need love, necessarily. What was love anyway but possession? She turned the glowing alarm clock around, shut her eyes, pounded her pillow. She knew what she wanted. Respect and attention. She wanted to laugh. Douglas Bleeker made her laugh. She wanted passion in her life, and she'd take it where she found it. Passion doesn't lie. What she also knew: She didn't want to be alone. She heard the key in the door, the snick of the latch. She buried herself under the covers and pretended to sleep.

Rance unlaced his shoes and kicked them off. He sat in the chair by the window and stared at the bed. "Do you want to talk?" He unbuttoned his shirt. "Emma?" He slipped his watch off his wrist and put it on the coffee table. "I know you're awake."

Emma stirred, pulled the covers off her face. "Why pretend that we have anything to say to each other?"

"I won't live like this." He listened as Emma sobbed, sniffled. He said, "What do you want, Emma?"

"I want to sleep. I want to leave here first thing in the morning. I want to go home."

GWEN BLEEKER survives her surgery, endures the subsequent radiation therapy, and makes a remarkable and heroic recovery. A grateful Douglas Bleeker leaves her, files for divorce, and moves in with Lois Lamb, a third-grade teacher at Grace Episcopal School. Emma is puzzled by this, but not entirely disappointed. As Douglas Bleeker explains it to her, she is still his little side dish. And that's okay with Emma until the night she sees Douglas Bleeker and his lambie pie at Crawfish City. Emma is stunned. That son of a bitch has never taken her to a restaurant, not once, not in all their years together.

EMMA AND RANCE buy a new house, a Greek Revival with a full-facade porch on Riverside. Dave dies of distemper, poor guy. Rance buys a golden retriever puppy he calls Strider. He buys a red pickup. Emma and Rance love their new home. Emma plants an elaborate flower and herb garden. She's out there all the time in her braided straw hat, knee pads, and clogs. When she's not working in the garden, she's sitting on the patio admiring it. She puts Bach on the stereo, iced tea in a thermos, and watches the bees and hummingbirds work at the flowers. She learns the Latin names of all the plants. She enters her tea roses in flower shows. Winters, she reads through seed catalogues. She feels happy, feels close to Rance, and wonders about all her youthful foolishness and indiscretion. She doesn't recognize herself in the sullen, resentful woman she remembers. She's scandalized when she hears about the Baptist minister's affair with the choir director. Emma is diagnosed with skin cancer. Melanoma. She's dying. It's not fair.

RANCE IS AT her hospital bedside every day. For a while he walks her to the window so she can wave down at Strider, who pokes his head out of the pickup window. He reads while she sleeps, which is most of the time in those last days. He reads about an African in Greenland. The water glass on the bedside table has a paper hat. He folds her clothes, packs them in a plastic grocery sack. He puts her brooch, her wedding ring, her pearl earrings, and her watch in his jacket pocket. When she wakes, he holds her hand, holds the straw to her lips so she can sip. He drops the sack of clothes in the Salvation Army donation box. He pats Strider and wonders what he'll do when Emma dies. He sees himself out West. Boots, Stetson, plaid shirt, and Wranglers. Dawn. He's sipping coffee on his porch, staring off to the black mountains on the horizon. He puts the house up for sale, gives his notice at the firm. He's fifty-six; his whole life is ahead of him.

AFTER THE PRIVATE service at the Pine Grove Cemetery, Rance picks up Strider at home. They drive to Lake

Providence and back. They stop for a stretch in Mer Rouge, and Strider chases a cotton rat through a soybean field. Rance is amazed when he considers his marriage, the nearly three decades of it, and how it all seems to have happened in seconds. Just like that. Over and done. A blur.

JUST BEFORE she dies, Emma signals Rance to lean closer; she has something she wants to tell him. He puts his ear to her lips. She swallows, squints, shuts her eyes. But she can't remember what she was going to tell him. She whispers, "Never mind." Her last words carry Rance back to that night in Hot Springs years ago, to the unimpressive jazz trio, to the dismal and aborted weekend at the Arlington. He remembers watching her sleep that night. He would have bet the marriage was over. But he didn't leave. You don't walk out on responsibility. You take heart. You trust in time. And then he remembers the Saturday night that he and Emma walked into Crawfish City, and he has to laugh. Emma saw Douglas Bleeker sitting there, dining with a young woman, and she walked right up to their table and clapped her hands three times, like she was wiping them clean, brushing the grime of Douglas Bleeker from her life, and said, It's all over, Douglas Bleeker. That's it. End of story.

CONGRATULATIONS, YOU MAY ALREADY BE

RICHARD'S LISTENING TO WTAG, TALK RADIO, AND a caller from Grafton Hill wants to know why he should have to pay for parking at the Galleria. He has a point, Richard thinks. Why should you have to pay to spend money? Richard's writing a letter to Ed McMahon with the directions to his house. It's not so easy to find. *And when you get here, go around to the back (the landlady hates for anyone to use the front), go past the bulkhead, and come on up to the third floor. Don't mind the mess in the hall.* This just in case he does win the Publisher's Clearinghouse Sweepstakes. He probably won't, but it would be wicked sick to win, and then they can't find you, and the money goes to some runner-up from New York. *I'll have a drink ready for you. Scotch, I'll bet. Am I right? You probably won't come yourself, though—that's just for the commercials. Maybe you could pass the map (not to scale) on to one of your functionaries.* Richard puts the letter in an envelope, puts his coffee cup in the sink, the jar of Folgers Instant in the cupboard. He leaves the radio on for the cat.

Richard's got his gloves and his tools in a ten-gallon plastic bucket, and he catches the bus to Hope (somebody's idea of a joke) Cemetery. He scrubs his mother's headstone. He washes and dries the plastic flowers, returns them to their galvanized vase. He trims the grass against the headstone. He sits beside his mother, opens his lunch bag, eats his sandwich (olive loaf) and an apple, and thinks about what he'd do if he won the million. He heard on the radio about a guy in Canada who won the lotto, bought a muscle car, rented a cabin in the woods, threw a party for his pals till the money ran out. That's not what he'd do. Right in the bank, live off the interest, live like a king. He wouldn't let incredible wealth go to his head.

At Denny's, Richard eats with his ball cap on and a cigarette burning in the ashtray. He studies the guy at Table 16, guy with a gray brush cut, pants hiked up to the middle of his round belly, hearing aid, gray and white checkered shirt. The guy's got a black leather wallet attached to a chrome chain attached to a belt loop on his pants. Wallet like that would be nice, Richard thinks.

He goes back to his paper, reads about a woman in the jungle who is the last person alive who speaks her language. She says she dreams in this language, but can't tell her dreams to anyone. Richard thinks there's something wrong with our own language when the same word, *dream*, means what you see in your sleep and what you hope to do in the future. Denise, his waitress, pours him another coffee, leaves him the check. Macaroni and cheese + coffee + apple pie + tax + tip = $9.75. The article says that each language contains words that uniquely capture ideas, and when the words are lost, so are the ideas.

That night Richard dreams about a man with no left arm. They are in the jungle, and the man is jolly enough and asks Richard to tie his shoe for him. In the morning, Richard calls his sister Paula in Maine. She tells him about the surgery she's had for the cancer and how her arm is now paralyzed from the operation. Which arm? Richard says. When he hangs up, Richard asks himself if there's a word for this: for a person whose dreams may be real, but whose hopes may not.

JOHNNY TOO BAD

Barbie

I'M NOT PROUD OF THIS, BUT I'LL TELL YOU ANY-
way. My dog Spot has a Barbie doll that he carries with him
everywhere he goes. She used to be Malibu Barbie, but then
Spot ate her splashy little lounging outfit, and now she's
generic, brunette Barbie, or as my girlfriend Annick says,
she's Housing Project Barbie. Spot stole the doll from Layla
Fernandez-Villas who is five and lives two doors down. Layla's
mom Gloria (Call me Glow!) hammered on my door, told me
what had happened, said her daughter, her baby, was in her
bedroom right now weeping hysterically. I told Glow to take a
deep breath, offered her some iced tea. Sweet or un? She said
something to me in Spanish, something about my *cabeza*. I
stayed calm. I explained that while Spot was admittedly rambunctious (how could I deny the *chorizo frito* episode?), and
while, yes, he *was* decidedly mischievous, though I preferred
the word *frolicsome*, and certainly he could be naughty on occasion, and granted, he *is* impervious to discipline, I'll give you
that, Glow, still he's an honorable dog, and he would never—

I heard the clicking of Spot's toenails on the terrazzo and
turned to see Barbie dangling by her legs from Spot's jaws.

She was naked to the waist, her buttery body slimed with drool, her belly punctured, her arms flung above her head. Her hair was perfect. I ordered Spot to come. He backed away, wagged his tail. I snapped my fingers. I said, Drop the doll! He shook her. Glow said she didn't want the goddam doll any-more—what good is it? I said, Please, let's not make this any harder than it already is. Spot dropped Barbie on her head, dared me to reach for her. He snorted. I said, My goodness, Glow, is that the Greenbergs' cat on our coach? Spot looked at me, at recumbent Barbie, back at me. He growled. When I reached for Barbie, Spot snatched her up and bounded toward the kitchen. He stopped when I refused to chase him. He woofed. Had I forgotten the rules to Keep Away? Spot hun-kered down on his forelegs, Barbie between his paws, his butt in the air. He lifted his brow. Glow told me her husband Omar would not be happy about this. Omar sells discount cosmet-ics and knockoff perfumes out of his silver Ford Aerostar. He claims to be the man responsible for this new look where women paint their lips a conventional red and then outline them with a violet or brown. So we know he's a dangerous man. Naturally, I bought Layla a new doll—Los Alamos Barbie. She wears a spiffy, starched—and discreetly reveal-ing—lab coat, high-heeled hiking boots, and she glows in the dark.

Bigfoot Jr.

Yesterday afternoon, Spot and I walked to Publix, our super-market. Usually, I'll buy Spot a scoop of butter pecan at Ice Cream Cohen's next door, but today he wouldn't release his beloved Barbie, so I tied his leash to the bike rack and went inside. The place was mobbed. I stood in the express checkout lane with a twenty-pound sack of dog food. There was some confusion at the register. The customer, a great-bellied fellow in a white T-shirt and black Speedo, spoke only French, the cashier only Spanish. Apparently the trilingual manager was being summoned. I put down the sack and plucked a copy of the *Weekly World News* off the rack. A woman with a hirsute toddler on her lap posed for a rather artless photo. The headline over the picture read *I Had Bigfoot's Son!* I wasn't sure we needed the exclamation point. Krystal Drinkwater had confessed to the astonishing copulation, but did not reveal the how or the why, did not mention where Dad was at these days, whether they kept in touch, shared custody and support. I wondered, too, if Krystal had simply used Bigfoot for reproductive purposes, or had she been in love with the big palooka all along? And what do her neighbors think? (I imagined a trailer court at the edge of the woods, gravel yards littered with rusted hibachis, baby strollers, automobile tires, and Big Wheels. In the window of a yellow and white Skyline, an aluminum Christmas tree.) And is the child, Kirk, being ridiculed by his playmates at preschool, pitied by the teachers? Is breeding outside the species something that Bigfeet regularly engage in or was Krystal's inamorato a sexual pioneer? I wanted to learn about the ecstasy, the trepidation, the dream. I wanted to be in that delivery room. And, of course, I wondered what had made Krystal so—desperate, was it?—so reckless that she would make this preposterous claim to her family, her friends, the world. Because, really, there is no Bigfoot, is there?

And then I heard folks behind me in line talking about the approaching hurricane and how Publix was already out of bottled water. I turned. Hurricane? I said. *Fritzy,* the Asian woman told me. I saw my incredulous face in her sunglasses. Hurricane Fritzy? I said. Was she joking? She wore a coral-colored, low-cut T-shirt with HOTTIE in blue letters embroidered across her breasts. She wasn't joking. How had I been so preoccupied that I'd missed the news of an approaching hurricane? I excused myself and went in search of batteries. Once again, I'd waited too long to order storm shutters.

Victim Soul

I made grits and cornbread, sat in front of the TV. The folks at the Weather Channel said it was still too early to determine the storm's landfall, but we should all stay alert and tuned in. You could see how sober and calm the meteorologists were trying to be, and how really jaunty, cheery, and hopeful they felt. No doubt Jim Cantori was home packing his Gore-Tex windbreaker and his personal anemometer. I knew that Channel 7 (*I, Witless News,* Annick calls it) wouldn't think it too early to call for a direct hit on South Florida. I knew they'd already be reveling in the potential devastation. I switched channels, but the local news was over. The *Jeopardy* theme music played, and Spot came zooming into the room, dropped perforated Barbie, and howled. I put the TV on mute. Spot looked at me and whined. How many times does he have to tell me he hates that song? He collapsed on the floor, his muzzle against Barbie's back. I apologized. When I saw Alex Trebek, I put the sound on. Defending champion Betsy wanted *Geography* for $200,

Alex. Alex said, It's the largest freshwater lake in the world. Betsy buzzed in. She said, What is Lake Superior? And Alex said she was correct, but she was not. Am I going to have to dash off another letter to these people? The truth is (or the fact is) that Lake Baikal in Siberia contains twenty percent of the world's fresh water, more than all of the supposedly Great Lakes combined. I hate misinformation.

I surfed through the channels and found an *Unsolved Mysteries* segment about a miraculous girl from Worcester, Massachusetts, and naturally I watched because Worcester's where I grew up (in a manner of speaking). Turns out that the girl, Little Rose, drowned in her family pool ten years ago, but did not die. Not quite. She's in what the doctors call a state of akinetic mutism. She seems to be awake—her eyes are opened and mobile—but she is fixed and unresponsive. People call her a victim soul, say that she's crucified on her bed, that she takes on the suffering of others. She's developed the stigmata. Oil drips from the walls of her room, oozes from the holy pictures at her bedside. A statue of the Virgin on Rose's dresser weeps. The oil and the tears are collected on cotton balls, packed in Ziploc bags, and given to visitors, who use them to swab their tumors, their ulcerated skin, their arthritic joints, and so on. Little Rose's mom says that her daughter was visited by a woman with ovarian cancer, and the woman was healed. When Rose manifested symptoms of the cancer, X-rays of her ovaries were taken and showed not a tumor at all, but an angel.

During the commercial, Spot the Vigilant heard me shift in my chair, or he sensed my larcenous intentions, and he bolted awake, took Barbie to his sheepskin-lined bed across the room—a very expensive bed that he's never used except for storage—and dropped Barbie inside next to his squeaky tarantula, his plush duck, his soccer ball, and his wooden shoe. Then he lay in front of the bed and stared at me. I said, She's not good enough for you, Spot. He blinked and yawned.

The Little Rose story resumed with a shot of a football stadium where a Mass was to be celebrated in her honor on this the anniversary of her drowning. Paramedics wheeled her into the end zone on a gurney. She wore a white gown and a gold tiara. Her abundant black hair tumbled off the mattress and trailed to the ground. I was afraid it would tangle in the spokes. People in the stands wept and prayed. They raised their arms to the Lord, shut their eyes, swayed their bodies.

When I was a boy I worked at this very stadium selling soda at Holy Cross games (only we called soda *tonic*, so I sold tonic, and we called a water fountain a *bubbler*, and pronounced it *bubba-la*; we called lunch *dinner*; dinner *supper*; sprinkles *jimmies*; a submarine sandwich a *grinder*; a hard roll a *bulkie*; a porch a *piazza*; a cellar a *basement*; a rubber band an *elastic*; and a milkshake a *frappe*. We called a luncheonette a *spa*). And then I saw myself at ten, no gloves, maroon woolen jacket, holes in my P.F. Flyers, torn dungarees, nose dripping, Navy watch cap pulled to my eyes and over my ears, lugging a tray of drinks up the stairs in Section 14, where I knew my old man and his buddies would need cups of ginger ale for their flasks of Canadian Mist. I could smell November in the air, and I knew when the game ended I'd have two dollars, and I could stop on the way home at Tony's Spa for an English muffin and a hot chocolate, and if the schoolyard lights were still on, Bobby Farrell and I would shoot some hoops. I heard a cheer, and I looked up to see if Tommy

Hennessey had scored a touchdown, and I saw Little Rose being carried to the altar at the fifty-yard line. I wanted to be cured of my aging. I said, Little Rose, take away my years. I waited. I switched off the TV. This was one miracle she could not perform. And apparently there was another: she could not heal herself. Which made me think. What would all of these people do if she were no longer the victim soul, just another fifteen-year-old girl in love with pop singers and sassing her mother? And what about Mom? Does she want her little girl back or does she want her little saint?

What I know and what most viewers of *Unsolved Mysteries* do not, is that Worcester is mad for the miraculous. When I was at St. Stephen's Grammar School, Dicky Murray's sister Mary and her friend Patty Shea were praying at the side altar in our empty church when they saw the statue of the Blessed Mother move. Patty hyperventilated and passed out. Mary Murray wept and pledged her life then and there to Jesus. She would become a nun. When word of the miracle got out, the church was mobbed every day with pilgrims come to give praise, come to witness the dynamic evidence of God's love and compassion. And many were not disappointed. The plaster Virgin might wiggle a finger one day, cast a glance the next, flare a nostril, flex a toe. Her movement was subtle, not grandiose, that being her way.

Dicky told me that at night when he was in bed he could hear his sister through the walls speaking with Jesus. She wrote down their conversations in her diary. Dicky knew where she hid the key. Mary claimed that she could taste the love of the Sacred Heart, could smell sin on people's clothing. Jesus called her His Maple Sugar Valentine. Mary told the nuns at school that Jesus had asked her to suffer for their sins. This did not go over well. Eventually, Mary was pressured by the monsignor to recant, to admit that fasting for Communion had left her and Patty dizzy and befuddled, that perhaps the flickering lights of votive candles on the altar, the dancing shadows, had tricked them into thinking the statue had moved.

Not long after the Ecstasy of Mary Murray, a Father Leo D'Onofrio was assigned to St. John's parish down the hill, and he set about healing the infirm. His hands, it seemed, made whole. Busloads of crippled and otherwise ailing supplicants arrived from around the country on the first Sunday of every month. Father D'Onofrio made the lame to walk, the deaf to hear, the dumb to speak, the blind to see. He shrank tumors, cleared arteries, purified blood. People abandoned crutches, prostheses, and wheelchairs in the aisles of the church. We took my uncle Armand for the cure. Uncle Armand got shell-shocked in World War II. When Father D'Onofrio laid his hands on Uncle Armand's head, my uncle spit in his face and never did regain a healthy mind.

I wonder what it is that makes people in Worcester so hungry for preternatural religious experience or what makes the city so hospitable to the wondrous. The TV beeped twice and a weather alert scrolled across the bottom of the screen. Hurricane Fritzy was now a strong Category 3 storm and was located about 270 miles east of the Lesser Antilles. Fritzy was heading due west at thirty-one miles per hour. Less that two days away, looked like.

I heard Spot snore, wheeze, snuffle. I turned off the TV. His forelegs twitched. Probably dreaming about chasing a stretch limo up Sheridan Street. I stood. He opened an eye, looked my way. Don't even think about it, Johnny.

The Bathtub

Spot is so terrified by thunderstorms that I tell myself we ought to move to the desert, and maybe we will someday. (And then I think: dry and flaky skin; nosebleeds; flat, flyaway hair.) As soon as Spot hears the first grumble of thunder he starts panting, whining, pacing the house. I take a bottle of cognac, a plastic cup, and a pile of magazines to the bathroom. As the storm intensifies, Spot starts digging at the tile or the rug with his front paws, trying to furiously scoop out a protective bunker. I figured out that the safest place for us in a storm was the bathtub, where Spot could dig all night without hurting himself or our house. I sit at the faucet end of the tub and drink and hug Spot when he tires and takes a fretful break on my lap. I pat him. I sing lullabies. I read him stories from *DoubleTake*. I tell him, It's okay; Daddy's here. So you see why I was worried about a hurricane. I wasn't sure I was up for thirty-six hours in the tub.

One Saturday morning last July I woke up, and Annick was staring at me. I said, What? She said, Are we too old to be spontaneous? I said we weren't. She said, Let's do something unexpected. Usually when we're together on Saturday, we sit on the couch and read our books until afternoon, when we plan a menu, shop, cook, eat. I said, Like what? We drove to Key West. We left Spot in the garage with food, water, leather bones, and an open door to the backyard so he could do his business. Spot wasn't allowed in the house alone because he'd eaten most of a Mission end table I'd bought at Restoration Hardware. Annick and I planned to have a late lunch at Blue Heaven, listen to junkanoo music over a couple of drinks. On the drive home, we'd stop to see the key deer. Be back before dark. We hadn't counted on the weather. We ran into a line of violent thunderstorms at Mile Marker 56, and we took a motel room on Grassy Key.

In the morning I dropped Annick off at her house and went home to rescue Spot. You could tell from the downed branches and the flooded streets that the storm had hit hard. I opened the kitchen door, and Spot charged me. He was so deliriously happy to see me that he zoomed across the living room, ran over and across the couch, the comfy chair, the coffee table. He made that circle three times and then he was back licking my face. Spot had chewed and dug his way from the garage, through the drywall and the plywood, and had come out in the cabinet under the sink.

What My Sweetheart Annick and I Are Not Doing Tonight

We're not in her kitchen preparing spaghetti puttanesca, sipping martinis, making naughty jokes about noodles and sauce. And we're not sitting on the deck of the *S.S. Euphoria* sailing to the Bahamas, holding hands, staring up at Cassiopeia, chatting about our aspirations. We're not at the movies, partly because I refuse to go anymore. I find them all dishonest, disheartening, and disappointing. Body parts and body counts. So Annick goes alone or she goes with her friend Ellen. She thinks I'm ridiculous about this, thinks if I love her I ought to be able to sit for ninety minutes by her side. But we'd only end up arguing. I'm insufferable, and I know it. It's all because I loved movies when they told stories about decent people in enormous trouble, when acting was a special effect.

When we first dated Annick told me she liked *Forrest Gump*, and I felt the life force drain from my body. I thought, If she tells me she's a Republican I'll scream, and then I'll take my leave. When I'd mention Truffaut, she'd roll her eyes. I'd say Cassavetes or Spielberg: principle or spectacle; sentiment or sentimentality. She'd say, Cassavetes?

We're not at the movies and we're not in my bed, not in her bed, not in bed at the Riverside Hotel in Fort Lauderdale, which is what I had planned for this, our fifth anniversary as a dating couple. Dinner at the Himmarshee Grille, cruise up the New River on a water taxi, nightcap at Mark's on Las Olas. These days Annick considers herself my ex-sweetheart.

Screening

I left Spot with Barbie, went to the kitchen, and telephoned Annick. I got her machine. *Hello, you've reached Annick. Today's words are cosset, oast, and judder. Leave your name, your number, and your word for today, and I'll get back to you as soon as I can. Maybe.*

I said, Annick, it's me. Come on, pick up. I know you're there. Annick? One, two, three. Okay, then. Call me. My word is *vaticination*. 'Bye. No sooner had I spoken my word than I wanted to take it back. And that's the terrible thing about speech—once it's articulated you can't revise. I hung up. A crumby Latinate word that will never enlarge anyone's world. A pretentious synonym for *prediction*. If I had thought a moment longer I could have said *rick* or *larrikin* or something interesting. With speech there's no time to see what you say until it's too late.

Ennis

Back in college, my friend Ennis Murphy fell in love with a girl from the Midwest. He married her in 1972 and divorced her in 1974. A year later he married again (both wives had the same first name and the same blond hair) and had two kids, one of whom, the boy, got into some criminal trouble when he was fourteen. So Ennis and Viola search around for a proper boarding school for their son. Get him away from the crowd he's running with was their thinking. Ennis's wife's friend, a visual artist, suggested a school in Mitchell, South Dakota, that has a terrific reputation for turning wayward boys around. Saved her nephew Peter's life. Was into sniffing spray paint and now he's a clinical psychologist. This was in 1994, and Ennis could not have told you if his first wife was even alive.

So Ennis and his son flew to South Dakota, and Ennis spent a week at the Corn Palace Motel while his boy settled into his dorm and his routine. One morning over coffee at the Lueken Bakery, Ennis noticed an article in the paper about his ex-mother-in-law. He couldn't believe it at first, but there was her photograph, and Marlene didn't look much older than she had twenty or so years ago. She had won first prize at Dakotafest for her honey-spiced cornbread. And she lived in Epiphany. Ennis checked his road atlas, saw how close that was, smiled, called information, and got Marlene's address.

When she answered the door, Ennis said, Marlene, you may not remember me, but I was your son-in-law. Marlene stepped back, opened the screen door, said, Ennis Murphy, you're like some ghost, and she hugged him, and ushered him into her kitchen. He sat at the table while Marlene brewed coffee, warmed some cornbread. She told Ennis how her husband Tubba had died of emphysema six years ago. Never did quit smoking. That's when she sold the place up in Huron and moved out here, away from the hustle and bustle. She said her daughter lived in Mitchell now, taught literature at Dakota Wesleyan. Ennis had never known his ex-wife to be interested in literature. I'd call her right now, Marlene said, but she's in Rapid City at a conference. Ennis said, Well, you tell her hi for me. Marlene said, We know all about you, Ennis. We follow your career. We're so proud of you. (I should tell you I've changed Ennis's name. He's a moderately famous musician whom you might recognize.)

A year later, Ennis returned to Mitchell to perform at his son's school. He sent his ex two tickets to the show. She came alone. They got together later for drinks. She was a Willa Cather scholar, it turned out. Head of her department. Ennis told me, It didn't take us long to realize that our divorce wasn't working. After that weekend, he went home to his unsuspecting wife of twenty years, his devoted wife, and told her he was leaving her for his other wife. She said, This is some sick joke, right? It isn't funny, Ennis.

Ennis told me it was his great happiness over his resurrected love that gave him the strength to do what must have seemed so cruel to an observer. He told his wife he hadn't planned for this to happen. She said, Weren't we happy? He said, It was fate. She said, You can't do this to me. He said he was sorry, truly sorry that it had to happen, but it had happened, hadn't it? You'll be better off, he said. She hit him in the face so hard that she broke her elbow. Ennis drove her to the emergency ward. He was questioned by the triage nurse and then by two sheriff's deputies. His wife was hysterical. He waited for her in the lobby. His left cheek was bruised, his eye swollen shut. He called South Dakota with the news.

Ennis remarried his first wife on what would have been their twenty-fourth wedding anniversary. Their first marriage, I remember, took place in a field of wildflowers at an Audubon sanctuary in Barre, Massachusetts. We were all barefoot and garlanded, and high as kites. The second marriage was performed in a Lutheran church in Mitchell, and Ennis's son, an A-student, was his best man. His daughter refused to attend the ceremony.

I made the mistake of telling Annick this story as we lounged on the couch the same night that Spot stole Barbie. So now she thought I wanted to reunite with my ex-wife. I said, That's crazy. She said, You made that story up. I was hurt. I said, If I'd made it up, you'd have believed it. She was crying now. She put down her wine glass. She asked me how I could have told her such a desolate story. I said I thought it was a story of enduring love and grand passion. Annick shook her head. She said my past was the one place she could never be. And then she stood, told me she was leaving, and walked to the door. Spot followed her, wagging his garrulous tail. She patted his head, scratched behind his ears, under his chin, called him *Spot the Loony* in her baby voice, and let him lick her face. She told him to stay. After she shut the door, Spot sniffed at the threshold, whimpered. He woofed at me.

At first I was angry with Annick. I mean, you think you're building a cozy and resilient relationship with a person, and then she proves you wrong. It's not at all intimate like you had imagined, but merely amicable. It's not irrepressible, but rather fragile, unsubstantial. But then I considered my motivation. Why *had* I told her about Ennis and the two Violas? Had I meant it, unconsciously or not, as an unsettling cautionary tale? Was my story a smile and a shrug? A nasty little assertion of my independence? A gratuitous nod to the treachery and caprice of Time? And then I was angry at my vicious self. I realized that I had committed an unpremeditated, but intentional, nonetheless, act of cruelty. I've caught myself playing this game before, the game of undermining my emotional prosperity. Something irrational inside, something ungovernable and unknowable, some fear or impulse has convinced me that the road of happiness leads to the house of sorrow.

Canine Theater

I cleared my dishes, rinsed them, poured myself a drink, and went out to sit on the deck. I put my feet up on the rail, leaned back in my chair. Spot sat at attention and stared at me. He wanted to know where I'd hidden Barbie and, more importantly, why would I do such a thing. I said, Maybe she found out I was suing her for alienation of affection and decided to skip town. He put his paw on my leg. I said, I don't think obsession is healthy for a dog. He yipped. He rested his head on my arm, looked up at me with his Pagliacci eyes. He's good.

Barbie was in the exercise room, which is not where I work out, but where I store all the training equipment I've foolishly bought over the years, the free weights, the Soloflex, the stationary bike, the Abdomenizer, the StairMaster, the treadmill, the NordicTrack. You might ask why have I kept these reminders of my failure and my unfitness around. Well, I paid for them, and I can't bear to give them away. The financial loss would only compound my distress. I've also got a closet full of shoes that I haven't worn in years. I've got red clogs, green espadrilles, white bucks, dirty bucks, oxblood brogans, black wingtips, blue huraches, cordovan penny loafers, chestnut Earth shoes, purple creepers, saddle shoes, beaded moccasins, Beatle boots, cowboy boots, chukka boots, engineer boots, fringed suede knee boots. I've even got a pair of particolored bowling shoes that I wore home from Gasoline Alleys Candlepin Lanes when they gave my sneakers away to someone else. If I ever put in a garden, I'll wear the bowling shoes to till the soil because who cares if they get wrecked.

I wanted to take Spot's mind and heart off Barbie, so I figured we'd play Canine Theater. Spot's quite a fine performer. I like to think he brings clarity and dignity to every role he plays. Of course, he doesn't like the Scottish play. When Annick, as Lady Macbeth, rubs her hands and declaims, Spot runs for the door and whines to be let out.

I stood. I looked at Spot. I said, "Biff, what are you doing with your life, goddamit? You've got unlimited potential."

Spot cocked his head.

"Don't look at me like that, Biff. Your brother Hap, he's doing gangbusters. But you, Biff, you're the smart one. You've got the winning personality."

Spot woofed.

"Out West? There's nothing out West for a man with ambition."

He growled.

"You're wrong, Biff. New York's the place for the Lomans. Willy and his sons."

Spot barked.

I picked up the Nerf football from the deck. I said, "Go long, Biff." I threw it as far as I could. Spot just sat there. I gave in. I got Barbie.

pannick@hailmail

I checked my e-mail: Speed Up Your Net Connection in Minutes GUARANTEED!!! Investor Alert! A Canadian Package That Matches Your Request. Archie MacPhee's On-Line Catalogue. And this from Annick:

> Johnny, I'm trying to give my future a shape. I don't want it
> being just more of the present. All my days are so alike now
> that they slip seamlessly into the past, and the past may be
> a fine place to visit, but I don't want to live there. Sometimes
> you make me so tired. It seems to me like I'm walking, you're
> standing still. You're stuck in your blue period. I'm going out
> to buy new paints. Time to get on with it. The opposite of

change is death. Say hi to Spot. Have you heard about
Fritzy? Annick

I went back to the deck.

Ways of Seeing

Some things you look at, and some things you stare at. You
look at a photograph, but you stare at a flame. You *look* with
intent and with intensity, but you *stare* without purpose or
motive. When you look, you distinguish. When you stare, you
witness. To look is to examine. To stare is to accept. Looking
leads to comprehension, staring to reflection. *Look*, and you
are fixed in time and space. *Stare*, and time dissolves, the
world around you drops away. Me, I love the imposition of
looking, but I prefer the susceptibility of staring. And that's
why I love the night. Darkness obliterates distraction. I sit on
my deck and stare at the stars. I see Perseus, Lacerta, and
Cygnus adrift in the Milky Way. And I see beyond the stars to
infinity, and in staring out I see within, see the faint shimmer
of who I briefly am. Emerson said that if you want to feel
alone, look at the stars. And I do. I feel alone, but also a part
of something incomprehensibly vast and sublime. And I feel
small, but not insignificant because I can wonder at it all,
because I can think about the stars, and the stars cannot think
about me, because I can tremble at the mystery.

The wind rattled through the queen palm. I smelled curry
coming from the Pannus' house. I heard the squawk of a
night heron. I saw the Northern Cross, and the Cross made

me think of Ray. Rayleigh Baravykas, my girlfriend just before I met my wife. Ray and I were in our sleeping bag in the dunes in Provincetown, and Ray pointed out the Cross and Andromeda and the dim galaxy beyond it, and we stayed awake to watch the Perseid meteor shower—a night of shooting stars. And then a thunderstorm.

The next morning we sat together at the laundromat, and a woman with a baby on her lap stared at us and smiled. She said, "You two look so beautiful together." But we're not together. Maybe we didn't believe in our beauty. I wondered how Ray was doing, and wondered how you could go from finishing each other's sentences to not talking for twenty years. There was a time I wouldn't let Ray out of my sight, and now I'm not even sure what she looks like.

I heard rustling in the heliconias. Probably a possum. Spot heard it and woofed. He's afraid of possums. I said, It's only Pogo. He growled unconvincingly. I guess my theme for the night was loss, or it was loneliness, because then I thought about two ex-friends who had the same first name (no motif intended). I've known the first Tony since second grade. He's my oldest pal. We used to sit in the schoolyard and talk about movies. Later we read Thoreau and Muir together, listened to obscure acoustic music. We planned trips out West, to Coeur d'Alene, to the Sawtooth, to Glacier. I'd buy maps, plan the routes, research the parks and campgrounds, and Tony would go with someone else. One morning he wouldn't be home and his mom would say he's off with Gary Smart (or Brian Houde or Henry Welch) to the mountains. I'd get to see the slides when they got back. Each time I was afraid to ask for an explanation.

One Friday night he called from his college dorm to tell

me his girlfriend had left him, and how devastated he was, how suicidal. That Sunday morning I hitchhiked the fifty miles in subzero weather to see him, and when I arrived, his roommate told me that Tony was at a motel with the woman in question, and then he went back to sleep. *Miles* was the roommate's name. Miles to sleep. Miles to go before I sleep. Funny, I hadn't even known I knew his name. Miles, who later moved to Australia. Why do I remember that?

Tony was an only child. He had one aunt and no cousins. His aunt and parents died. Tony has known me longer than he has known anyone. I tell myself it's his childhood he's running from. But I think it's me. I call every six months, on Christmas and his birthday, and leave a message on his machine.

The second Tony and I did travel together—to Europe and across America. For years we were inseparable. And then he stopped talking to me. He told friends that I was stuck in the past, that I hadn't grown up. He may have been right, of course. He told them I had an indiscriminate sense of humor. Maybe it *is* better to put the past aside, but I never can. Tony moved back to his mother's house after she died. I wondered did he sleep in his old bedroom or move into Mom and Dad's. There's some cruelty in that thought, I know. I miss the Tonys. We could be having fun right now.

What if Ray and I had never split up? I tried to picture us now. (Yes, it's futile to think *what if?* about your life, but I've been doing it since I was a kid. What if Mom and Dad die in a car crash on the way home? How would I handle all that trouble? Could I go live with Aunt Bea in California? What if I had sprung my grandfather from the nursing home? (Would have needed a miracle here. In fact, I went to the nursing home, said, Pepere, you want to get out of here, never come back? He said, I know I'm supposed to know you. Could you tell me who you are?) I could only see Ray and me in a cold place. Ray in a bulky wheat-colored sweater. We're on a farm in coastal Maine. Goats. Wild raspberries. And then I remembered her grandfather's farm and what happened there. Ray's uncle Edwin shot his father in the head and then shot himself, but not before he doused the parlor with gasoline and dropped a match.

I went back to the kitchen, made some coffee, sat at the table, and wrote a poem about Ray:

Still Life with Ray

Ray tells me what Sister Cecilia told her and the other
girls back in sixth grade, that St. Lucy plucked out her
eyes and sent them to her tiresome and lascivious
suitor, the Consul Paschasius, to save herself from
shame. Yikes! It's 1969 and Ray and I are on the
beach in Provincetown waiting for the sun to set over
the bay. We have wine and chocolate and Portuguese
bread. I wonder did Lucy have the eyes wrapped in
silk and did she pay the boy who delivered them. I
make a joke about how Lucy was from the school of
aggressive chastity. I'm in love with Ray. Ray's mother
has just died. Ray says eyes don't see, the mind does.
I touch my forehead to her temple, and when she
speaks I feel her words in the bones of my head. She

says we never see only one thing at a time. Ray is a painter. She says if you look at anything for a long time, it melts and shatters. I wonder if she's talking about her memory of her mom or about the beach grass, sea rocket, and bayberry in front of us. When the sun sets Ray stands and looks behind us to the eastern sky. I look at the fuchsia sun, the purple sea. I look at Ray, her blond hair aflame. She tells me to look at the purple band low in the sky. I put my chin on her shoulder and look ahead to where she's pointing, and finally I see it. We watch the band rise in the sky and then dissolve into the darkness. Ray says we just watched the earth's shadow cast on the sky. I hold her face in my hands. Ray averts her eyes.

I typed it. By now it was the middle of the night, and I still couldn't sleep. My uncle Armand told me how the world was destroyed every night and put back together again by God before morning. I looked through photo albums and found what I knew I would—a black and white photo I had taken of Ray and her grandfather on one of our Sunday visits to the farm. Ray is sipping soup from a spoon and looking over at me with her turquoise eyes, and old Joe is holding his ball cap by its visor and scratching his head. The tip of his index finger is missing. He's wearing a torn corduroy coat over his coveralls over his sweatshirt. Beyond Joe on a shelf over a dry sink sits a tub of Jewel lard, a pitted enamel washbasin, a chalkware collie, a hurricane lamp, and a box of Ohio Blue Tip matches.

I took a drink with me out to the deck. Something else Uncle Armand told me: you can tell the real voices from the crazy voices because the crazy voices are just outside your ear. We look out to the end of the universe racing away from us. We can only look back, it seems. The future is invisible. How shall we know it?

Glow & O

When you tell people that you write fiction, they tend to respond in one of three ways. There are those who will stop talking to you because they assume you are going to write about them, you're going to appropriate their precious lives for your squalid little stories. My family's like this. Years ago I was made to promise that I would never again reveal the kind of familial impropriety that had gotten my uncle Didi blackballed at the Singletary Rod & Gun Club, that I would not embarrass my parents or aunts or in any way muddy the family name. Otherwise I could spend my holidays in solitude. And I have kept my word although I do have a dozen or so stories filed away awaiting the deaths of certain cousins and in-laws.

Then there are the folks who think that writers write only about themselves, and so they assume that writers lead adventurous, troubled, and reckless lives. These people are eager to listen to your madcap tales of turmoil and self-destruction. You tell them you don't smoke, don't drink (you lie) or carry on with the wives of friends. You explain that you no longer shoot heroin and you don't roam the predawn streets with packs of other writers. You tell them you sit in a room and work. These people are hurt that you don't trust them with your indiscretions. The hurt festers into anger and resentment.

The third response comes from those who think that fiction writers make everything up. These are sweet, kind, and naive people who want to make your job easier, and so they tell you stories from their own lives. Like my friend Ennis and his two Violas. Or like the seventy-five-year-old woman I met in Winter Haven who told me she'd carried on a forty-year love affair with a married physician, a radiologist, a man with a wife and four children. Moved here from Los Angeles to be near him. They went on a cruise to Paradise Island, and he died in their bed in his sleep. She had to call the wife from her cabin with the tragic news, arrange for the transport of the body back to Winter Haven. She could not attend the funeral. He was the love of her life.

Gloria and Omar fit into this last category. When Gloria first stopped by to welcome me to the neighborhood she was very pregnant and smelled like vanilla. As we sat in my kitchen and talked, she ate the empanadas she had brought me. She told me that her husband—the Big O—was away on business, meeting with the Latin American Cosmetics King in Caracas. She told me how she knew that O loved her: since she told him how much she loved his lavender shirt, he'd worn it every day. She told me she took lessons: voice, dance, acting. It was O's ambition that she get her own program on Telemundo. I told her I wrote stories. She told me her voice teacher's cousin knew Gloria Estafan's housekeeper. I said, So, you have an in. She raised her brow, pointed at me like I was on to something. She asked me what my stories were about. I told her love and death. She wiped crumbs from her mouth, leaned back in her chair. She said, You can write my story.

When she was sixteen, Glow was madly in love with Billy

Cassidy. They'd been going steady for a month when Billy's mom died quite unexpectedly. At the wake, Glow sat between Billy and his sobbing father and accepted the condolences of strangers. Billy chewed gum. His jaw cracked. He held Glow's hand for what must have been comfort, but felt to her like restraint, detention. Glow wished she could say a prayer at the casket, express her regrets, whisper to Billy that she'd be there for him, and leave with their other friends.

In the following weeks, Glow spent her afternoons and evenings at the Cassidy house, cooking, cleaning, watching television. Billy had become more affectionate, but less amorous, more tender, but less demonstrative, more reliant, grateful, needy, and therefore less deserving of her passion. She wanted love, not domesticity, wanted to be an obsession, not a substitute. She told Billy she was sorry about his terrible loss, and then she returned the silver crucifix ring he'd given her. She told me she missed him, always had. He teaches high school in Miramar. And then she told me the hidden meaning to her story: "Death is stronger than love, Johnny."

When I first met Omar he was wearing a silky red and gold soccer uniform, shin guards, and wraparound sunglasses. He handed me a beer, and we leaned against his van. He told me his team, the Jaguars, had just defeated the Lions of Judah at Boggs Field. He scratched Spot's muzzle, spoke to him in Spanish. Spot sat, gave Omar his paw. I noticed the cases of lipstick in the van and asked Omar how he liked his job. He said a man's job was to love a woman. Whether the woman loved him back was unimportant. The woman's job was to be loved. He asked me did I have a woman. I said I did. He asked me to describe her complexion, eye and hair color.

I said, Cream, coffee, copper. He put down his bottle, cut open a case of lipstick with a key, pulled out a gold tube, and handed it to me. "Cinnamon Spice. For your woman."

"Thank you."

"My wife tells me you write stories."

"Yes."

Omar smiled, looked toward his house, leaned into me, and told me his secret. He had another family in Venezuela. A wife, Graciela, and three sons, Pablo, four; Carlos, three; Celestino, one and a half. "*Omar* is my American name."

"You wouldn't lie to me?"

"What would be the point?"

"You have two identities? Two passports?"

He smiled. "I love them all."

What Else Could It Be?

I squished my earplugs in as far as they'd go, adjusted my padded eyeshade, taped my Breathe Right nasal strip on my nose. I thought how this was a secret I kept from Annick. She'd never seen me armed for sleep. When we stay together, I sleep unfortified. I would be too embarrassed. Anyway, I like my dreams and want to enjoy them without interruption. But I'm a fretful and uneasy sleeper. Wind in the oleander wakes me, the refrigerator's hum, the dawn's light, passing cars, my own snoring. I puffed my pillow, smoothed the sheet, stretched my legs, relaxed them. For an insomniac, going to bed is like going to therapy. All the cargo you've weighted down with forgetfulness and disregard, and then dropped into the deep, comes popping back to the surface. Like my dad.

He had left a message on my machine, and I hadn't returned his call. He told me about the hurricane and about a woman named Fritzy that he knew during the war—before Mom. My dad was an inventor before he lost his sight. He didn't so much make new things as he found new uses for existing things. He made fishing lures out of bottle openers and tea-spoons, made coat hooks out of plastic duck decoys. He once made a shaving mirror for the shower out of a harmonica holder and a woman's compact. And that's how he appeared to me as I tried to sleep—naked in the shower with the holder around his neck and the opened compact case snapped into the spring tension clamp. His face was lathered. He held a shaving brush in one hand and a razor in the other. He was far-sighted in those days, so he wore his reading glasses, which had fogged. He cracked me up sometimes. One day he ran out of shaving cream, so he shaved with Reddi-wip. He would point at an object and ask me what it was. I'd answer, and then he'd tell me what else it was. Like I'd say *ladder*, and he'd say *towel rack*. Or I'd say *ashtray*, and he'd say *soap dish*. *Wooden shoe—planter; flat iron—door handle.*

The reason I hadn't called my father back, the reason he was keeping me awake, had to do with the tape he wanted me to make. He wanted me to read my last book into a recorder so he could listen to it. I told Dad that Spot was in the book, that he belonged to the central character, a writer, not so unlike myself. I told him the writer's father had vision prob-lems, so naturally he assumed the father is him. I did not tell him that the writer and his father have a problematic rela-tionship. I did not want my father hurt by his misperception. Even if I told him now that he's not the character, he'll think

I'm lying. Spot's Spot, after all. The writer's a pathetic little scribbler who left his loving wife, after all.

I took off my eyeshade. Maybe if I opened my eyes, I wouldn't see my wife. But there she was holding a peeled orange to her mouth, holding it with both hands, biting into it and crying. I pulled out the earplugs. Once again, thoughts had murdered sleep. I know that I made the novel up. I also know there are resemblances to my life. I know why the writer left his wife, but I don't know why I left mine. I like to pretend that writing is a plunge into reality, that it forces me to deal with what I'm ashamed of, with what I regret, with what I don't understand, with what I don't want to know about myself, but it can also be avoidance. Flight. It's easier to make someone up, after all, and give him the trouble and deal with his turmoil, than it is to deal with your own. And I knew if I didn't do something soon, I'd be writing about the writer who lost his girlfriend.

I sat on the edge of the bed. I keep a memo pad and pen on the night table. I wrote this down: *A father is always a son; a son's not always a father.* I'd figure it out in the morning. If I hoped to get any sleep, I needed to get out of bed.

The Dead of Night

I've been despondent in my life. I've felt ponderous and numb, desperate and disabled, brittle and disposable, lost in a gloom so profound I wanted at once to hold on to anything and let go of everything. But I've come to understand that hope, our brief candle, is my only light in the darkness, and so I keep it with me.

I sat in the living room, feet up on the ottoman, staring toward the window. Spot snored on the couch. I realized you can't look at space, but only at objects in space. Without something to be seen, you are blind. I also realized I was avoiding what hurt. It was so quiet I could hear everything, the CFX freight rumbling alongside Dixie Highway, blasting its whistle at every intersection. And when that faded, I heard a semi whining along the Interstate. I pictured the driver wearing a T-shirt, smoking a cigarette. He knows he has seven hours to Savannah and then one more load to carry up to Augusta before he gets home to Myrna and the boys, gets a few days of rest and a chance to work on the dragster. He's thinking, because he always does, that he shouldn't have gotten into the long-haul business in the first place. Never at home. But how could he give it up now? That's what the car's about and why he needs to get it humming: the new life, the dreamed-of life, the real life he's not yet living, the life of a drag racer. He'll enter out at Silver Dollar this spring and then maybe Rockingham. He doesn't want to think about all this. He'll just get sad. He puts on the radio. Every station's in Spanish. Where the hell am I? He plugs in a Willie Nelson tape, and every song calls him home.

The night is both our blessing and our curse. It's a sanctuary from turmoil, a respite from the routine and clutter of our lives. Our days seduce us with activity. Our nights confront us with stillness. The night may seem false in its solitude, but it's the lie that speaks the truth. At night, we're reminded of this hurried interlude between oblivions. And that's why we choose to sleep, to dream. Dreams are the madness that keep us sane.

I saw Spot's legs twitch and realized my eyes had adjusted to the scant light that had been here all the while. I wasn't despondent. I was afraid. I thought about what I was missing. When I first met my sweetheart—this was at a bookstore café—she told me her name was Annick, but she danced under the name Blaze. *Blaze* was the setup. After our espressos, she shook my hand, said how nice it was to meet, to chat and all. She needed to find a book. I discreetly followed her, hoping she didn't head for SELF-HELP or NEW AGE. She went to ART & ARCHITECTURE, and this gave me the courage to approach and ask her if I might call her. She gave me her card. I read it. I said, Very funny, Miss Pascal. You don't dance at all, do you? She told me she was a freelance set designer and worked mostly with local theaters. I said, Are you related? She said, He is my great-great-great-great-great-great grandfather. Later she told me her joke had been a test. If I hadn't recognized the name, she wouldn't have answered the phone.

Annick says that the only way to know the future is to imagine it. I'm not sure I want to know it, but I try. I see Annick and me in twenty years. We're living in Taos. It's a Saturday night in July, and we're driving down to Chimayo for dinner. And then I think, Twenty years—no Spot, so I just get up and go to the kitchen to make coffee. I turn on the TV. There's a live remote from Home Depot. It's half-past four in the morning, and the place is packed. People are buying generators, sandbags, flashlights. The store's already out of plywood.

Walkies

I used to bring Spot to Bark Park up in Fort Lauderdale for his exercise, but he's been banned, *canis non grata*, labeled chronically aggressive, which is a lie, or, at best, a misunderstanding. What Spot did was he got a lot of otherwise docile and obedient dogs riled up, got them in touch with their inner-puppies, so that in their exuberance, they ignored their owners' commands. Apparently, these dogs had never seen anything remotely like Spot's exhilaration and abandon. They watched Spot run like mad around the perimeter of the park, his ears waving, his tongue flapping, his body leaning into the turns like it does. He'd stop to pee on the statue of Dr. Dolittle or to chew some piece of canine agility equipment, and then he'd be off again, dogs following. I saw people calling to their recalcitrant dogs, whistling, gesturing, ordering them to stop chasing after Spot the dervish and get back here this instant! The owners looked at me with narrowed eyes and clenched jaws. I smiled. Spot earned five demerits in his first week.

The final straw came when Spot, who'd been splashing through the drinking fountain, crashed a doggie birthday party at the puppy pavilion, a party to which he'd been explicitly disinvited. He stole a cardboard hat off a beagle and ran off with it. The beagle looked sad, confused. Then Spot bounded back and galloped through the cake. The party's human hostess, a sixty-something platinum blonde, told me I was just the kind of reprobate that gave dog owners a bad name. I told her Spot was just playing. She told me he doesn't play well with others. When I intimated that the party guests were maybe unduly prim, she said no, they were gentle and dutiful. Bootlickers, I said. She said did I understand the first thing about the responsibilities of dog ownership. I said something about the fascist's need to control and dominate. I really wasn't making sense.

So now Spot and I walk around the neighborhood, and I carry a plastic Publix sack so I can collect his poop. We follow a route of Spot's choosing along the mangroves to the canal where he does his business, to the pond where he barks at the Muscovy ducks, and then past the strip mall where I deposit the sack in the bucket behind Asian Nails, and then up Coolidge. (Used to be there were monkeys in the mangroves—escaped from Chimp World in the fifties, but lately the state's been paying poachers to trap them. Haven't seen any in months, which is fine with Spot. They freaked him out. We also have walking catfish here, and marine toads the size of catchers' mitts, and four-foot iguanas, and basilisk lizards that run along on their back legs.) Eventually, we come to Annick's house. So this morning after my sleepless night Spot ran up Annick's porch steps and turned to me. I told him to come on. He sat, looked back over his shoulder to the door. There were treats and hugs inside. I, too, was hoping the door would open, and Annick would be standing there in her cowgirl pajamas, and she'd invite us in for breakfast and rec-onciliation, but it did not. I saw no lights on inside, no activity in the yard.

Back on our block, O was unloading sheets of plywood from a U-Haul truck. Spot sniffed through the hibiscus while I gave O a hand. O asked me did I want to buy some plywood to board up my windows. I told him I wouldn't know what to do with it. He shook his head, told me I ought to be more responsible than that. "Your house will blow away. What will you do then?"

"I'll come stay with you."

O didn't laugh. He opened his cooler, asked me if I wanted a beer.

"Seven-thirty's a bit early."

He opened two bottles of Polar and we sat on the lawn. Layla told Spot he looked adorable. She'd tied a sun bonnet on his head. The two of them sat on the porch steps. His tail wagged a mile a minute. I saw Glow at the screen door talking to someone on a cell phone. She waved to me.

O said that Channel 7 had called for a hurricane landfall somewhere between Haulover Cut and Hillsboro Inlet sometime before dawn tomorrow. I said I ought to paint a bull's-eye on my house. He said we were under a mandatory evacuation order. We've got till dusk, but by three the Turnpike and I-95 will be one-way north and gridlocked. He said he was boarding up, selling what he could of the plywood—Glow's on the phone to the neighbors now—and then taking off. He's got a room booked in Orlando, closest he could find. He told me I should get ready and get out. I said I might have to stay. He said did I have a gun. Did I want to buy one?

Tropical Anesthetic

At home I switched on the TV, and there it was out in the Atlantic, Fritzy's well-defined eye, bearing down on South Florida. I checked hurricanecentral.com and saw the bright yellow cone of probable landfall centered on the Dania Cutoff

Canal. The consensus in the chat room was a powerful Category 4 event in our immediate vicinity with a twenty-foot storm surge, which would put the ocean seventeen feet above the sidewalk. This was not good news. I looked out the window at Spot, studied him. I'd read that animals begin acting strangely before a cyclone hits. Spot was lying in a puddle of sun on the deck. Maybe it was earthquakes I read about. I told myself I wouldn't leave without Annick, and I immediately felt noble, valiant, and self-sacrificing, and I realized as well that Annick would snicker at my idea of heroism, and then I felt embarrassed even though I was alone. You wouldn't think that could happen.

I called motels, and the few that had rooms didn't take pets, no, not even in an emergency. So I just lied to the desk clerk at the Osceola Motel in Valdosta, Georgia, told him I was dogless, even though he hadn't asked. I reserved our room, but we'd have to check in by ten P.M. or they'd rent it out to someone else. I hung up and then thought what if it's one of those motels where you have to enter your room through the lobby? I hate getting caught in lies. I hate sleeping in cars. I closed my eyes and pictured the Osceola. I saw a red sign out by the street with white letters and a flaming white arrow piercing the center of the O, and then a one-story, U-shaped white concrete building with jalousie windows and two red tulip chairs outside each room. I was relieved and chose not to look inside.

I needed to pack what I was going to take, needed to decide what I would save. I walked around the house and realized I had a lot of stuff in my life, most of it you would call junk, evidence of too much time and money spent on eBay: old scrapbooks, movie posters, match covers, baseball cards, advertising art, 78 rpm records, vintage eyeglasses, Viewmaster reels, swizzle sticks. I packed my computer and disks, my notebooks and photo albums. I figured I could get a thousand books in the bed of the truck. I'd just have to hope it didn't rain. Then I thought, Which thousand? Chekhov, naturally. Shakespeare, of course. The Bible. Christ, this could take all day. Which Faulkner do I take? Which Tolstoy? Then I realized that Spot, Annick, and I wouldn't all fit in the cab of the truck. We'd have to take Annick's Tercel.

I put valuables in Tupperware containers in the fridge. I called Annick. Today's words were *pasquinade, herl, dornick*. I told her machine I'd be over in fifteen minutes. She should pack. I said, Our lives are at stake here, Annick. I paused. I said, I'm not leaving without you. Then I thought, I hope she hasn't left already. I told Spot we were going for a ride, and he ran to retrieve Barbie from under the deck. On the way to Annick's I saw that the gas tank was on E. I stopped at the Chevron on Federal and waited in line for twenty-five minutes. They had raised the price by a dime since yesterday. Capitalism is not our finest idea.

I drove to the liquor store. Spot waited in the truck. Prakash and Chandra were boarding up the windows. Don was clearing shelves. He said he kind of figured I'd be along, so he'd saved me a bottle of Hennessy behind the counter. Said they were closing up as soon as they stored the booze in the back. Don's about sixty-five. He has double vision, but he won't go to a doctor because he doesn't have health insurance. He bought an eye patch at Walgreen's, says he's fine. The headaches have stopped.

Annick still wasn't home. I peeked in her garage. Her car

was gone. What if she really *had* evacuated? I enjoy irony as much as the next guy, but to drown while the woman you're trying to save lounges by a pool at the Tallahassee Holiday Inn was more than I could handle. She would not have gone without storing the porch furniture. She's around. I drove home to check messages. Nothing from Annick, but an update from Dad. Seems they'd closed the Fort Lauderdale airport and were flying the planes to safety. I put on the TV. The evacuation of the Keys was over. Whoever wasn't out, wasn't getting out. Card Sound Road and Route 1 south of Homestead were closed. Helicopter shots of I-95 showed six lanes of solid traffic heading north. Meanwhile, in breaking news, two Miami mayoral candidates had each claimed the endorsement of little Elian Gonzales.

I sat on Annick's porch, sweating and fuming, thinking how inconsiderate her absence was. I watched the anoles do push-ups, spread their orange throat fans. The sky was cloudless, the air still and steamy. I looked at my watch. I didn't know why I couldn't leave Annick behind, exactly, I just knew I couldn't, knew without thinking, not even to save myself or to save Spot. I looked at him sleeping on the lawn, collapsed like dirty laundry in the mottled shade of a mango.

I got the house key from under the plaster lawn gnome (Chomsky, Annick called him). I knocked on the door. Waited. I opened the door, stood inside and yelled hello. No note for me on the kitchen table. No dishes in the sink. Nearly noon. We'd need to leave immediately if we hoped to reach Valdosta by ten in this traffic. I opened the garage, stowed the lawn and porch furniture inside. I took down the wind chimes, the bird feeders, the floral wreath, the chili pepper porch lights. I carried Chomsky inside. I changed my shirt. I saw Annick walking up the street. So did Spot. He ran to her. I waited by the truck.

I said, "Where have you been?" and I knew it sounded more hostile than concerned, which wasn't my conscious intention.

"At the beach."

Spot brought armless Barbie to Annick and dropped the doll at her feet. Annick tossed her, and Spot fetched.

I said, "Don't you know we're facing a catastrophe here?"

"Fritzy."

"And you're out strolling on the beach?"

"Thanks for putting everything in the garage."

"We live in a mandatory evacuation zone."

"So why are you still here?"

"I'm not leaving you."

"You don't owe me anything."

She was being disingenuous. "Come on, Annick, you know I love you. Where's your car?"

"In the shop. Henk says I need a transmission."

"Shit. We'll squeeze in the truck."

"Are you trying to insinuate yourself back into my life?"

"I'd like to think I hadn't left it."

We went inside. We turned on the TV while Annick packed her things. Spot dropped Barbie de Milo on the floor and barked at her. He scrunched down, barked some more. He was angry, perhaps because her head was loose. Officials had already made all lanes northbound on the Turnpike and 95, and already the roads were clogged, traffic was stopped. Five million people trying to get out of Dodge. Cars were stalled—

out of fuel and overheated. Fistfights had been reported in several locations, guns fired in Pompano Beach. A ten-car pile-up at Copans Road couldn't be cleared because authorities couldn't get at it.

Annick said she'd rather be at home in a hurricane than parked in a truck on the highway.

AT THIS POINT we had no choice. She told me I could stay. She reminded me that we hadn't made up, hadn't resolved a thing. I said, We'll get married. She said, Don't make fun of me.

"What?"

"You take it all so lightly." She said we'd have to talk about it later. Now we have to get ready. We need to fill up every container we can with water. Need to get out the candles, flashlights, batteries. We need to get to an ATM and take out cash, move the truck away from the trees, check the rain gutters, move everything off the floor that we could, tie cabinet doors shut, and fill the tub with water. I looked at Spot. I said, We can't. Annick smiled. Oh, that's right.

Testimony

Annick and I walked to my place with Spot. We were oppressively cordial, warily chummy. I couldn't stand it. I confessed that I'd been behaving badly, and I apologized. I suppose I thought she would forgive me, would smile, wrap her arm around my waist, lean into my shoulder. She picked up a twig and tossed it ahead for Spot. The thing is I didn't really think

I'd been bad, just honest. And now my graciousness was being rebuffed. How dare she?

Omar's house was boarded up, the rental truck was gone. The neighborhood was eerily quiet. Inside, we filled the tub and sinks with water. I filled a cloth book bag with items from my desk: binoculars, pens, eyeglasses, a portable tape player, headphones, a Howard Finster angel (*One day out of a whole lifetime you will die*), scissors, glue sticks, Eva Cassidy and Louvin Brothers tapes, a stopwatch, and a short-wave radio. We locked up and walked to the beach. The lifeguards had gone. We got lunch at Angelo's before it closed. We watched surfers ride the ten-foot swells as we ate. I said, "Annick, I want to be with you no matter what. And if you want to be married, then I want to be married."

She said, "You just don't get it, do you?"

Strike two.

On the way back to Annick's we spoke to the bridge tender, who told us he was locking the bridge down at three, per orders, and heading out to his girlfriend's house in Davie for a hurricane party. We bought Sterno at Publix, figuring even if the power went out, we'd have fondue. We bought Little Debbie snack cakes at the Dollar Store.

We watched TV reports of the devastation in the Leewards and in the Turks and Caicos. People stranded out on the parking lot that had been the Turnpike were setting up camps beside the highway. A couple of hundred stranded motorists on 95 had broken into Northeast High School and set up their own unauthorized shelter. Stores had been looted in Hallandale Beach and in Lighthouse Point, and nothing catastrophic had even happened yet. Dolph Diaz, the Channel 10 anchor, said he was going home to take care of his family and walked off the set. I asked Annick why we lived here. She said, The climate. At the Krome Detention Center in west Miami-Dade, the detainees, most of them Haitian refuges, fearing for their lives, had busted through the fence and fled into the Everglades. And then we heard the storm was slowing, strengthening. Estimated landfall in fourteen hours.

We turned off the TV and sat out on the deck. It seemed ridiculous that there was nothing we could do but wait. It started to rain. Radio reports indicated that these rain cells had nothing to do with the hurricane, but we didn't believe them. Annick kissed me. I was grateful, restored. I thanked her. We set up the bathroom, which would be our fortification. Candles, the short-wave, a boom box with Puccini CDs, a Coleman lantern, batteries, plastic cups, cognac, Irish whiskey, blankets, water, alarm clock, books, magazines, dog dishes, dog food, dog biscuits, dog nest, dog chewies, what's-left-of-Barbie.

WHEN WE WERE first going out, Annick told me she had been an equestrian in the Big Apple Circus and had dated, had lived with, in fact, the lion tamer, Gunther Something, for three years. So for months I pictured the two of them in their trailer, her in a silky pink, sequined ballerina outfit with a feathery headdress and garish silver eye makeup and him in a one-piece gold and black tank-top deal with gold ballet slippers, the both of them, lithe and graceful, walking quickly on tiptoes around the place, stopping once in a while to pose for the other, to toss back their hair, to acknowledge a glance with upraised arms and a grand smile, to bow deeply, sincerely, with the sweep of an arm. This kept me awake at night. I determined to shape up at a gym. I thought it odd that she never wanted to go horseback riding. Then she told me she'd made it all up. Said really she was a meteorologist—not a weather girl—at KENW-TV in Portales, New Mexico. *Light rain showers will continue this morning across much of southeast New Mexico into the Capitan and northern Sacramento mountains. A few areas of low clouds and fog may reduce visibility. Motorists should use caution.* And I believed that, too, for a while. I even suggested we vacation in her old stomping grounds, told her I had friends in Hobbs we could visit. She laughed, kissed me on the nose, asked me if I'd always been so gullible. I told her I just didn't expect people to lie is all. She said, You lie for a living.

So I can be excused, perhaps, for what happened next. After we set up the bathroom, we sat on the couch. Annick cried. She told me she'd been a mother once. I thought, Oh, she's good! I said, "Bigfoot's boy?" She got up and walked into the kitchen. I waited a minute, pictured her in there waiting for me to take the bait. I heard her blowing her nose, sobbing. I went after her. When I said I was sorry, I half expected her to crack up. Her shoulders trembled instead. I held her, and she told me the story.

She was twenty-seven, not married or engaged, having a difficult pregnancy. Took a leave from teaching. The boyfriend wasn't interested in a child, or in marriage, or in much of anything, really. An optometrist. This was in eastern Pennsylvania, where she grew up. She went into labor a month early. The baby weighed two pounds at birth and lived for two hours.

She named him Jonas after her father who had died when she was fourteen. She told me she still imagined her son alive, still spoke with him. He'd be sixteen.

We lay down on Annick's bed and slept. In my dream I saw a man biting a dog by the nape of the neck, shaking him. I saw men walking upside down on the surface of the water, trees full of perching cats, people with handles on their backs, people floating in air. And I knew if I kept walking I'd see Annick, and I did, and when I reached out to hold her she split into shards of glass and dropped to the ground. Sounded like bells. We woke up with the first crash of thunder and the sound of Spot scratching at the bedroom door.

Miracles

The thunderstorm passed, leaving Spot exhausted. He panted on my lap for a while. Annick sang, "Spot the Magic Setter," his favorite song. I took the mittens off his paws. He hopped out of the tub, drank all the water in his bowl, and collapsed in a heap. The radio report said this line of storms was only a hint of what was to come. Fritzy was nine hours away, wobbling a bit, but still on course for Broward County. Annick and I sat in the tub talking about miracles, which are what Annick figured it would take to get out of this jam. She took a drink of whiskey and passed the cup to me. I told her I didn't believe in miracles. She said walking on water was a miracle. I told her loons walk on water, and Jesus bugs. I knew I was treading on thin ice. Annick's a practicing Catholic, and she's got a shelf full of books in her bedroom about miracles, books she's had me read. She said, "What about the man from Dallas who got a spooky feeling and decided at the last second not to get on that ValuJet flight that crashed into the Everglades?"

I said, "Changing your mind is a decision, not a miracle. Coincidence is not a miracle. Luck is not a miracle. Thinking your dead mother is in the room is not a miracle. A hallucination is not a miracle. An accident is not a miracle. A doctor's misdiagnosis is not a miracle. Finding something you lost ten years ago is good fortune, but not a miracle. Learning from your mistakes is not a miracle. The decision to quit drinking yourself to death is not a miracle. It's a courageous act. Realizing that you've been a ruthless prick all of your life is not a miracle, it's overdue, and you won't change the past or buy your way into heaven by giving your stolen money away, because heaven isn't the White House and God doesn't sell pardons."

"You don't believe in God."

"Figure of speech."

"It's always politics with you, isn't it?"

Annick said she didn't care what I thought, but she believed that God put His hand on that fortunate Texan's shoulder and said, Son, don't get on the plane.

I said, "Then you must believe that that same God sent the other two hundred or whatever people to their fiery deaths without a second thought?"

Spot raised his head when I raised my voice.

Annick said, "It's a miracle that I'm with you." She kissed me, and I realized how wonderful this moment was and how I would be remembering it all my life, the kiss in the tub waiting for the storm, and in that life would be Annick and Spot the

Wonder Dog. Lightning flashed through the house. Thunder exploded and the power failed. "Must have hit a substation," I said, not really knowing what I was talking about. Spot whined, woofed, clambered back into the tub, buried his head in my armpit. I lit the lantern and the candles. We settled in for a long night. I poured cups of whiskey.

The next storm lasted twenty minutes or so. I held Spot while he dug into the curve of the tub. We weren't going to get any sleep. We put on Puccini. Spot howled along to "Maid with the Flaxen Hair."

Pressure Drop

During the night, Miss Fritzy inexplicably braked, wheeled around her eye, and drove south—miraculously, if embarrassingly so, according to the National Hurricane Center. Unfortunately, our miracle was Cuba's catastrophe. There had been no official damage reports from the island as yet, but Havana, apparently, had taken a direct hit. It was nearly nine o'clock. When the last storm ended an hour ago, Spot climbed out of our crowded tub, squeezed himself as far behind the toilet as he could, and fell into a fitful sleep. He was snoring now. According to News Radio 99, South Florida highways remained clogged with parked cars, most of them now in snake-infested water up to their chassis. We had missed the worst, but were not out of danger yet. The hurricane continued to spawn bands of severe storms, some of them potentially tornadic. The governor had declared a state of emergency, called out the National Guard. Public offices would be closed until further notice. All but essential medical and emergency personnel were to stay at home and off the roads.

I stretched my cramped legs, shifted my weight off my numb left side. Annick woke up, smiled, closed her eyes and nuzzled into the pillow on my chest. During a commercial for Griot King Take-Out, I changed stations to a call-in show. A man claiming to be on a cell phone from Havana described the ruins of the presidential residence and said that no one inside could have escaped its collapse. The next caller, who identified himself as a representative of both the county government and the Cuban-American National Foundation, said that as soon as rumors of El Jefe's death were confirmed, there would be an official, government-sponsored gala celebration in the Orange Bowl to which citizens would be respectfully asked not to bring weapons or infants. Another gentleman—*first-time caller from Hialeah; love your show, Rick*—suggested that even if Fidel were alive, this would be an opportune moment for an invasion. I turned off the radio. Annick said that maybe at long last Cuba would be free.

"To install another dictator," I said.

"Don't be cynical, Johnny."

"They loved Batista."

"They don't love Castro."

"The Miami Cubans don't. And that's because he's smarter than they are, and taller than they are, and more Cuban than they are."

"You wouldn't be talking like this on Calle Ocho."

"That's my point."

"So you're saying that some dictators are okay with you?"

"I'm saying I should hate the son of a bitch, but I don't."

Spot whined to go out. Annick sat up. I stood. My knees hurt. My back hurt. I looked at Spot. He woofed.

"All right already, we'll go out."

Spot sniffed the yard in all the usual places. He lifted his leg against the banana tree, turned his back to it, and kicked up some turf with his back legs. I don't know why they even bother. The yard was littered with buttonwood branches, the hibiscus was stripped of its blue and purple flowers. Spot lapped up water from the birdbath. The eastern sky was black, not the serene dark of night, but the ominous green and purple, the bruised black your eye might be if you walked into a baseball bat.

The power was out, would be for days it looked like. Annick and I sat at the kitchen counter eating the Little Debbies and drinking bottled water. Spot chewed on the last of Barbie's midriff. Annick told me about her cousin Destiny, how every six years she commits matrimony with some loser or other. Married at sixteen, twenty-two, twenty-eight, thirty-four, forty, forty-six, and fifty-two. Seven husbands, and in between them a series of even more miserable boyfriends. Dope fiends and drunks, batterers and cheaters. She can't seem to learn. I said, Maybe she's looking in the wrong places. Annick said, You think? I said, No need for sarcasm. She said, You're going to use this, I know you are. I said, Destiny Pascal?

I tossed Spot a piece of a snack cake. "You could look at each marriage as a triumph of hope."

"Just before each marriage ends, she goes in for surgery. She's had her tummy tucked, her ankles thinned, her varicose veins stripped, her eyes lasered, her nose reshaped, and her tear ducts removed."

"Tear ducts?"

"Said her eyes were always watering, and she was sick of it." Annick brushed crumbs from her lap. "What do you think all the surgery's about?"

I sipped some water. I didn't want to say *low self-esteem* or *self-mutilation* or anything else a psychotherapist might say. I shrugged. Tired of weeping! Where's my pen?

Spot heard the thunder before we did. He sat up and whined. He walked to the sliding glass door and barked at the sky. I said, "Okay, sweet pea, I'll take care of you." I wrapped Annick's cashmere tartan scarf around Spot's ears, tied it under his chin. He quieted. I slipped the Gore-Tex mittens over his front paws, tightened the pull cords. We all got back in the tub. Suddenly it felt like we had peaked on a roller coaster and had just begun free fall. The stomach-in-the-throat business. My ears popped. The thunder was now a continuous rumble and Spot was digging like crazy and crying. I held him. The tub trembled. Our liquor bottles clanged against each other. The radio lifted off the floor and slammed into the wall.

Annick said, "Jesus Christ!"

I said, "Tornado."

Spot leaped out of the tub and ran for the closed door. The door sailed into the living room. The little window above us popped like a champagne cork, and the glass and screen vanished. I remembered reading about a man whose brain had been sucked out his ear by a tornado. Then I remembered we were supposed to drag a mattress in here with us to cover ourselves. The walls groaned and quaked. I remembered, too, that you're supposed to open all the windows in the house to prevent a vacuum from developing, and you're supposed to go to the northwest corner of the house. Or the northeast. Too late for us anyway. I grabbed Annick and lay on top of her. I shouldn't have, but I looked up, saw the walls flex, contract, and topple, and I saw Spot, still scarved and mittened, hovering above us, about where the roof had been, and I called to him as if he could have done anything about it, as if he even could have heard me above the earsplitting roar of the storm. Spot floated away from us like a helium balloon. The furniture in the house skated across the floor, tumbled to the lawn, and rolled down the street. The Goretkins' chiminaya flew over our tub and so did a bicycle, a propane tank, a floor lamp, and a television. And then it stopped. We didn't move. We listened to a silence so intense I was sure my ears were blocked. And then a gas grill dropped into what had been the living room and scared the hell out of us. Annick trembled. I held her, kissed her face a dozen times. We cried and then we smiled. I said, "We should find Spot."

Our radio and lantern were gone, but our bottles of liquor were undamaged. I smiled at Annick. I said, "There *is* a God." She picked up a flashlight, tested it. It worked. The kitchen counter was gone, meaning our batteries were, too. The only piece of Annick's furniture in sight was a single kitchen chair. I set it upright. We had an empty sink and a battered stove, minus an oven door. We discovered a providential case of bottled water where the garage used to be. The Lord giveth and the Lord taketh away. Three clown triggerfish flapped their bodies against the Mexican tile floor. I looked at Annick. She nodded. We plugged the sink, poured in two gallons of water, and released the stunned but grateful fish. We watched them float, bodies bowed, at the surface, saw them right themselves, ripple their lacy fins, and dart madly through the tepid water.

We sat on someone else's plaid sofa in the backyard and surveyed the incomprehensible devastation. Annick cried. The sofa wasn't very comfortable. I checked under the cushions and found several dollars' worth of change, a pair of drugstore reading glasses, a TV remote, and a copy of *The Unabridged Journals of Sylvia Plath*. My truck was parked on its side in the next-door neighbor's living room. I hoped that my computer and disks were still in the cab, but I was too afraid to look just yet. I held Annick's hand, and all I could think of was that the worst part of this would be all the standing in all the lines at all the agencies that I'd be doing, all the forms I'd have to fill out, all the calls I'd have to make, all the paperwork and rigamarole involved in getting my life and Annick's life back to normal. And that's when I remembered that triggerfish live in salt water. I decided not to tell Annick. I called to Spot. I whistled. Annick said he'd be okay.

We spent the rest of the morning and the afternoon wandering the neighborhood calling to Spot. We seemed to be the only fools who hadn't evacuated. I found a replacement for my torn shirt in a pile of clothes on Harding Street—a Delta State University T-shirt: The Fighting Okra. We stepped around power lines, fallen banyans, appliances, and household debris. What on earth were we all going to do without homes or possessions? Annick found a portable radio, and we sat on a houseless porch and listened. The tornado had leveled everything east of Federal Highway in Hollywood and Dania Beach. The highways were still parking lots and now the secondary roads in and out were blocked. We told ourselves it wouldn't be looting to take the radio. Annick tapped my leg. Look, she said. Two chimpanzees walked down the street holding hands. When they saw us they stopped and hugged each other. One of them bared its teeth. Then they fled across the golf course toward the water treatment plant.

When we rounded the corner to my street, I half expected to see Spot waiting for us. When he left Annick's house he'd been flying in this direction. I still had a deck and a Soloflex, a washer and dryer, an armoire with a TV in the cabinet, bookcases but no books. We found my tent underneath someone else's Barcalounger. The smart thing to do was to get out of there. Walk to the beach and follow it south until we found a hotel that would take us in. Annick said, We're not leaving Spot. I said, If we haven't found him by tomorrow, we'll have to go.

Annick set up the tent in the front of the house while I walked back to her house for water, liquor, and my computer. I made part of the trip back in an E-Z-Go golf cart I found by the Publix. I got back around dusk. Annick had a campfire going. She'd found sheets and pillows for the tent. At least we'd be safe from mosquitoes and sand flies, from water snakes, roof rats, and God knows what all else. I told her we should just move. She said we couldn't. We still had mortgages. We still owned the property. We'd have to rebuild and then sell and then move. I said if we both sold our houses we could buy a palace in some place more placid and less congested. She said, Montana. I said I didn't want to be cold. We drank cognac, listened to the radio. Castro had been seen on the devastated streets of Havana. In Bangladesh, a hundred thousand people had been killed in monsoon floods. In

Boston, the Red Sox drove for the pennant. In France, union leaders had called for a general strike. We turned off the radio. We heard a helicopter somewhere nearby, and when that faded, the snore of tree frogs, and the exuberant call of a whip-poor-will.

I thought about my pitiful collection of shoes and how years from now some kid kayaking through the mangroves will notice a curious single salt-stained penny loafer wedged into the prop roots, and he'll stop rowing and stare at it, and he'll make up a story about how it came to be there, how one afternoon this junior at South Broward High found out that his girlfriend, his steady girlfriend, his steady, lavaliered girlfriend, was dumping him for a senior who was also the assistant night manager at Pollo Tropical, and how the spurned boy couldn't stand it anymore and started running like mad and eventually found himself sloshing through the swamp, wondering how he got there, and then he lost his shoe in the muck, and the shoe was lifted by the rising tide and floated down the inlet and dropped here, where it may have gone unnoticed forever, except that he, the innocent kayaker, happened along—he could have gone to the beach instead this morning—and happened to be just here when a mangrove crab flashed its white pincer from the cradle of the shoe.

I realized I had been unburdened of the stress and responsibility of proprietorship. I now owned nothing, and I felt reborn. I smiled at Annick. I understood that I was buoyant because I was with her. Privation is not something I could bear alone. In the end, all we have is who we love. My past had vanished, as it were, and now I could be anyone. Annick said, "Did you hear that?"

"What?"

"Jangling."

I shook my head.

"Like sleigh bells."

"Now I do." Coming from down the street. And then we saw a dim light about a foot or so off the ground, bobbing in time with the jingle.

I said, "Goddam."

"What the hell?"

It looked to be a faint halo, an iridescent, scintillating glow. I got the flashlight, shined it at the apparition, and then I saw him, Spot the Sundog bounding toward us with Los Alamos Barbie gripped in his jaw. He ran right past us, the plaid scarf now trailing rakishly behind him, one mitten on, one mitten off. He circled the tent, the campfire. He dropped luminescent Barbie and rolled on his back, squirmed like a fish, exploded to his feet, shook himself like he'd just stepped out of a swimming pool, and dashed into our arms. We petted him, accepted his messy kisses, told him how worried we had been, how happy we were. I threw another Mission end table on the fire. We all crammed into the tent. Spot lay between us, panting, drooling. Then he told us how he'd flown over West Lake and landed in a cushion of fallen Australian pines. He caught his breath, licked our faces, crawled out from between us, and curled into a ball like a roly-poly at our feet. I snuggled into Annick. She kissed my nose. Spot woofed. No more storms, he said. The three of us, we got to get out of here.

AROUND THE WORLD

MY CELL PHONE PLAYS "ODE TO JOY." I ANSWER IT.
It's Peter Martin, the boy from *Around the World,* our grammar school geography textbook, the boy whose place I wanted to take, the boy whose father got permission to take him out of school for a year so the two of them could travel the world while Mr. Martin conducted his international consulting business. Peter's calling from Florence, which he calls *Firenze.* Of course I remember you, I say. Nothing, I tell him, just out walking my dog Spot. He's called to tell me his dad has died, their globetrotting days are over. I offer my condolences. Prostate, he says. Ouch, I say. He tells me the chief export of the Katanga province of the Belgian Congo is copper. I tell him there is no Belgian Congo, no Zaire, no British Honduras, no Ceylon, no Upper Volta, no Rhodesia, no Soviet Union. He says the Yangtze is the longest river in Asia. I tell him I had a cancer scare myself. I say, Why don't you come by for a drink and a chat. Bring your slides. When I tell him where I live, he says, Tomato Capital of the World. Not anymore, I tell him—salt water incursion. The only thing we grow here now is old. I ask does he still have the little briefcase he used to carry, the one just like his dad's. I say, Whatever happened to that little blonde who wore the dirndl, lived in Zermatt? Her dad and yours worked together on the

engineering project. You and she picked alpine flowers together. Spot and I cross Sheridan Street, and he barks at a land crab by the mangrove thicket. Peter says, You mean Analise. And then he's quiet. I give Spot a tug on the leash. Peter says, She married a junkie. Much trouble. I'll tell you all about it when I come by. Do you like bruschetta?

WHO ARE THEY WHO
ARE LIKE CLOUDS?

MARLENE SELF FEELS UNCOUPLED AND OBTUSE, wishes for just a moment that she were dead, and understands that maybe she could be, except for the pain of the knife in her head. Well, then, not dead, but senseless. She'd like to be anesthetized. Marlene has driven from Monroe to Tallulah and back, a hundred and ten miles. She left the kids with Tracy next door, jumped in the Suburban, and drove. Drove because she needed time to think, and the car was the only place she could be alone. But now, back in town, driving west on DeSiard, she can't remember any of the last—she checks her watch—two and a half hours. It could have been five minutes for all she knew. How was she supposed to think with a knife in her brain? And how could she think about the man who buried it there? Marlene turns on the radio to drown out his voice. And what is she supposed to do now? Go home?

This morning, Marlene's husband, Bert, who had told her last month over dinner at Frankie and Janie's that he just needed some time to sort things out, so to speak, needed space, was how he said it, left a message on the answering machine telling her that he's not coming back home after all. Our relationship is no longer tenable, he said. He'd be out of town for the next week, but would call as soon as he got back.

There was silence, and then, Give Danny and Missy my love, and then, These things happen, Marlene, and then, I'm sorry, I truly am, and then a clunk and the dial tone.

Marlene drives to Bert's real estate office on Louisville at 14th. His car isn't there. Neither is the woman's. On the radio, a song she has always liked, but has never known the name of, plays. Willie Nelson sings it. Marlene gets the red light in front of the Bayou Motel. She sees a man and a woman sitting on white plastic patio chairs outside their room, and she knows she's seen them somewhere before, but where? Their little boy pedals his Big Wheel in circles in the parking lot. Maybe at Safeway? At the pharmacy? The boy's about Danny's age. Marlene begins to cry. Why can't she remember? Yes, there was a girl with them, older, like fourteen, fifteen. Yes, it's the girl's face she recalls best. The way she rolled her eyes when the mother talked, the way she openly stared at Marlene. She can almost place them now. The guy in the car behind her leans on his horn. Marlene screams.

The boy looks up at the screaming lady in the big car. Is she angry with him? He sees the lady drive away. The boy's father says, Now there's a gal could use a little loving. The boy's mother looks up from the *TV Guide*, says, Thank you, Dr. Phil. She calls to her boy, Leon, didn't I ask you to stay on the sidewalk? The Bayou Motel is a simple U-shaped yellow-brick affair. Who stays here are truckers mostly, and hookers. Seventeen-fifty a night. The TV works and so does the AC. Truckers park their rigs behind the motel and some of the rigs idle all night. Behind the trucks is a scrubby lot where someone has dumped a stove, someone else a plaid sofa. That's where the woman found the two patio chairs. Beyond the lot is a tank farm.

The man lost his job in the Texas oil patch two months ago. The whole goddam petroleum business has gone to hell. He doesn't know what he's going to do now, but he does know this—he's leaving this shithole town tomorrow. Ain't nothing for him here. Ain't nothing for nobody. Guy at the washeteria said he might could try up in Crosset for a logging job. God's country up there, the man said. The husband opens the cooler by his chair and takes out two cans of Budweiser, hands one to his wife.

The door to their room is open; the TV's on. The girl is on the phone talking to a boy she met in the last town they were in. DeRidder, she thinks, or was it Eunice? She tells the boy how this actor who used to be on a soap, how he's this bad guy in the movie she's staring at, how he's such a total creep, stalking his girlfriend like that. You know the guy, she says, used to be a doctor with an evil twin brother.

Outside, the father sprays lighter fluid on the briquettes in the hibachi. He tells his daughter she's been on the phone long enough. His wife says, Let her yak, Joe. It's the boy's nickel. He says, She ain't never going to see the boy again. Well, his wife says, she don't have to know that, does she? You think it's easy for her, no friends and all? A girl her age. He says, Jesus H. Christ, you think it's easy for any of us? He sits back in his chair. He reads the beer can label—for what, the nine hundredth time?—and that's what he thinks of himself, he's the king of beers.

When the charcoal is ready, the woman takes the luncheon meat out of the cooler, slices it, lays the slices on the grill. She's got the paper plates, the ketchup, the cookies, the lemon drink, set up like a buffet on the dresser inside. Her husband thinks if this were a hundred years ago, he could just find a piece of land and build a cabin, fish for their food, plant a garden. But now somebody or other owns everything. Every goddam inch of this country is someone else's. He tells his daughter to hang up now, it's supper. But the girl ignores him. He looks at his wife. I won't be defied by my own daughter, he says. His wife understands this. He walks into the room. The girl tells him one more minute, Daddy. He takes the phone from her. He tells the boy, This is Kristie's father, whoever you are, and I don't want you bothering with her no more. You got that, trash?

When he hears the dial tone, Theron hangs up. Look who's calling who trash, he thinks. He stares at the phone. For a minute he closes his eyes, stays on his bed, and tries to send Kristie a telepathic message—his brain to her brain. In the message, he tells Kristie to wait till her old man's asleep, take the cash out of his wallet, and get a bus back here to Eunice. And then he imagines waking up in the morning and Kristie's out there in the kitchen with his Mom and they're making breakfast. Yeah, right.

Theron grabs a beer from the fridge. He opens the junk drawer and takes out his daddy's pistol, yells to his mother that he's going out. She puts the TV on mute and turns her head toward the kitchen. Where the hell do you think you're going on a school night? For a walk, he says. She shakes her head like he's out of his mind and turns back to her program. Just go to your room, she says. Theron sees the top of her head, all that stiff hair over the back of her chair. He aims the gun at it, says, Pow. He opens the cabinet over the sink and takes down the box of bullets. He loads one into the pistol.

Theron winds up in City Park across from the Squire's Lounge. Probably his old man is inside with Eddie Guidry, Bobby Chagnon, and those other assholes. This is the bench where he and Kristie talked together for a world-record six straight hours the night before she left. She is the only girl he's ever talked to for more than three seconds in his life. Theron sees a black dog in front of the lounge, lifting its leg and pissing in the doorway. He whistles, calls to it. Blackie, he says. Satan. Duke. Come here, boy. He pours a little puddle of beer on the sidewalk. The dog licks it up. He tells the dog about Kristie, about her eyes, you wouldn't believe how blue, about how she smiled more on the one side of her mouth than the other. He tells the dog how in four years, when he and Kristie are eighteen, they would be getting married and moving to California.

California is Kristie's idea. The dog rests its chin on the bench and looks up at Theron. Theron scratches the dog's head. He says, We were talking about it on the phone tonight. When he and the dog finish their beer, Theron tosses the can over his head into the park. The dog fetches it and brings it back. You booze hound, Theron says.

Theron stops at the Dixie Dandy for a Mr. Pibb and an Abba-Zaba. He tells the dog to sit. He pats the dog's head, scratches his chin. Good boy, Rex! I'll be back in a sec. Stay! The dog sits, cocks his head, watches Theron. Theron sees a woman in black jeans and a black tank top making a phone call at the pay phone by the ice merchandiser. Her left eye is bruised, her left cheekbone swollen. The tattoo on her arm says "Free Bird." She sniffles, wipes her nose with the heel of her hand. She pats her pockets, but can't find a match.

Theron tells her he doesn't smoke. Sorry. You okay? She tells him she walked into a glass door. Theron checks on Bandit and goes into the store. The woman lets the phone dangle from its braided metal leash, runs to the guy pumping gas. He gives her a book of matches and tells her to keep them. Motel matches, she notices. The Evangeline—*Enjoy the pleasures of Acadiana.*

Back at the phone, the woman leans against the plate-glass window, lights her cigarette. She says, Precious, you need to come and fetch me. She sees the man pumping gas watching her. She smiles and turns away. Because you're my fucking sister, that's why. She sees the boy at the register fishing through his pockets for change. She tells Precious that Randy promised to God he'd keep his hands to himself. She nods. I know, she says. I know. She cries. I can't resist him, Precious. Sometimes it's just his smell.

The man at the pump gets into his car. Theron comes out of the store and breaks off a piece of candy for the dog. The man pokes his head out the car window and asks Theron if there's a decent restaurant in town. There's a woman in a red dress with the man. Yes, sir, Theron says. There's Johnson's Grocery for boudin, but they might be closed. The woman says, A sit-down restaurant. Theron says, Yes, ma'am. If you like seafood. She does. He says, You'll want Skipper's then. Just follow them signs to Opelousas. Be on your right. The man thanks Theron, says, Nice dog. What's his name? T-Bone, Theron says.

The woman in the red dress watches the woman in black hang up the phone, check the coin return slot for change, and slump against the Dixie Dandy window. The sign above her

head reads HUNTERS' SPECIAL!!! CASE OF PBR LONGNECKS $12!!!
The woman in red says, Bert, you need to call her. His wife,
she means. Bert says he will. I told you I would. Tonight. When
we get to the motel. He squeezes her hand and smiles. I love
you, Zera, he says. Zera says, Tell her I don't make a habit of
dating married men. Bert's glad she made an exception in his
case, but doesn't say so. When he tells Zera that Marlene doesn't
know anything about them, Zera says, Every woman knows.
And then they're quiet until they reach Skipper's.

Zera asks Jason the waiter to take her dish away and bring
her another Bloody Mary. Bert says sure, why not, he'll have
another martini. We only live once. Zera says the smell of the
boiled shrimp is making her sick for some reason. Bert takes
her hand and smiles. He lifts an eyebrow, says, Maybe you're
. . . and he doesn't say the word "pregnant," doesn't need to.
Zera tells him not even to joke about it. He gives her a peck
on the cheek. Bert stares at the print of six sailors in white
Dixie cup hats sending him a semaphore signal that he can't
read. Zera says, You're not just a husband, Bert. You're a
daddy. He knows that. Your children, she says. Bert says he'll
deal with his children. She says, They'll think this mess is all
their fault. Bert thanks Jason for the drinks. He tells Zera the
children will come to understand in time, see that it was all
for the best. She says, They'll blame me. They'll hate me. Bert
puts his arm around her shoulder, pulls her toward him. He
hugs her, kisses her hair. We'll be okay, he says, you and I.
Zera excuses herself. She has to go to the ladies'. She stands.
Bert says, You knew what you were getting into. Yes, she did.
But, she says, did you know what you were getting out of?

Bert watches her walk away. He sips his martini, takes out

his cell phone. Eleven messages from Marlene. He puts the phone back in his pocket. What a day this has been. First his cowardly message on the answering machine. Not something he's proud of, but he had to do it that way, or it could never have been done. Now that the ball is rolling, things'll go easier. He certainly can't go home again after such cruelty. And then their meandering drive south without a destination, letting the whimsy of the road signs lead them to Eros and Dry Prong, to Lonepine and Mamou. You may not have a destination, but you arrive at one anyway. You stop, and there you are. And here they are at this terrific little restaurant in Eunice. And that makes Bert think about the boy at the Dixie Dandy.

Theron and the dog walk along the railroad tracks toward the Val-Court Trailer Park and home. Theron takes the pistol from his belt and aims at a telephone pole. He figures he could hit it easy, but doesn't want to scare King away, or whatever the hell his name is. King, he says to the dog. Baron? The dog watches him. Theron coaxes the beer can out of the dog's mouth. Okay, boy, go fetch, he says, and he tosses it ahead onto the tracks. But the dog picks up a scent. Woofs. Theron aims the pistol at the dog's flank. The dog scoots off into the pigweed, his muzzle to the ground. He's gone. Raccoon, Theron thinks. Possum maybe.

Theron imagines that Kristie is watching him, that somehow this is possible. She saw how he lowered the gun, spared the dog. She knew he wouldn't shoot, knows the bullet's a charm, not a missile. Of course, if someone were to start something . . . A year ago Theron saw Alvin Straughter's Catahoula hound get snapped in half by a Winnebago out on 13. The old man driving didn't even slow down. If that happened right here, right now, this minute, Theron would make his one shot count, that's for sure. And Kristie knows this, too. Theron tucks the pistol into his belt.

Everything he does now, he does for Kristie. He whistles, kicks a stone, combs his fingers through his hair the way the boy in the jeans ad does. He smiles at nothing. He walks a little slower, like a man with plenty on his mind, a man with dreams. He sees himself as Kristie sees him, like from a distance. He's outside himself. And then it's the future. He and Kristie are on their back porch in California and she's telling him what made her fall in love with him a long time ago. His quietness, sweetness, his kindness. And his cuteness. The way he was always thinking. She could just tell, she is saying, could tell on that very first night how he was no sorry-ass swine like the boys who only want you for the one thing, how he was husband material.

BERT STEPS OUT of the motel room to call his wife. He sits in a metal tulip chair by a round concrete table. He shuts his eyes to steel himself. He sees his children's lovely faces, blank as ponds. He hears the *gick gick gick* of the cricket frogs and the muffled laughter from the TV in Unit 8. He tries to imagine Marlene in the house somewhere, but can't place her. He takes a deep breath, inhales the cloying sweetness of honeysuckle, and punches in the house number on speed dial.

Marlene is standing in the middle of the kitchen, holding a glass vase of lilies and asters that Tracy brought over when she came by to pick up the kids. Marlene can't remember where she was going with the flowers. She's staring at the ceiling light trying to retrace her steps, summon her thoughts. She's standing there, and then she's somewhere else, someplace she's never been to before where there's nothing to see, really, nothing to understand. And she's grateful for the provident analgesia of not remembering. She shuts her swollen eyes and exhales. When the phone rings, her whole body jerks. She drops the vase, and it shatters on the tile floor. She clutches her head in her hands and screams. She answers, but all she can do is cry into the phone. Cry and choke and try to catch her breath. She slumps to the floor, leans back against the fridge. She tries to say her husband's name.

Marlene rehearsed what she would say to him when he called, but now she can't compose herself enough to reason, to charm, to soothe, to argue, to flatter, to warn, to forgive, to ask to be forgiven. When she thinks that her uncontrollable tears might be angering Bert, she cries even more. She apologizes between gasps for breath. She says, I'm . . . I'm . . . I'm . . . I'm, but that's as much as she can manage. Finally, when she can speak, she says, I need you, Bert. You can't just walk out on ten years of marriage. She doesn't give Bert a chance to answer, to say that certainly he can and is, in fact, doing just that. She says, Everything I do I do for you. She says, You can't do this to your children. And then she listens to Bert's reasonable voice, but will not hear what he is telling her. She says, We need to talk. Not like this, not on the phone. She sobs. She says, Is she listening to you right now, Bert? Is she standing there beside you?

Marlene looks at the strewn flowers and snapped stems by

her feet, at the shards of glass glistening like ice in the pud-
dled water, and it looks to her like someone has wandered into
this garden of the dead and vandalized a grave site. She sees
that her ankle is bleeding, and this calms her. She says, Don't
expect your Jezebel to hang around for long, Bert. They never
do. And then she tells him that she gets it now, that she
understands why he called, not out of concern for her or for
his children, but to mollify his little missy, to ease her guilty
conscience. Bert says she's wrong about that, dead wrong.
When she tells him that he might as well kill her as leave her
like this, he tells her to pull herself together, please. She says,
What am I supposed to do, Bert? And why am I supposed to
do it? Answer me. Marlene knows that the only thing she cannot do is let Bert hang up. Without the tether of his voice,
she'll float away. She wants to know how long this infidelity
has been going on, but Bert doesn't want to talk about that
now. He wants to say good night to the kids. The kids aren't
here, she says. Tell me what you're doing.

You're in Eunice? That's her name? Marlene says. Yes, I
know, Bert. It was a joke, and she laughs because she remembers the motel family standing in the express checkout line at
Safeway, and the girl telling her mom that she would never let
a boy touch her down there, and when the mom said she
would hope not, the girl said, Not down there in Eunice, and
Marlene is tickled by the hilarity of this coincidence and by
the delicious image of fastidious Bert and his tenable darling
trying to sustain what they would call their passion in some
dim and dingy motel room, pretending they aren't offended
by the brittle wafer of hand soap, by the threadbare towels, the

knobby mattress, the must and the mold, the dispiriting land-scape painting—*Peaceful Sunset*—over the bed. Marlene looks at herself in a crescent of broken vase. She says, I'm all nose and lips. I fit in the palm of your hand. I *am* making sense, Bert. I *am* pulled together.

BREAKING IT DOWN FOR YOU

I UNDERSTAND CONSEQUENCES, CAPTAIN. I KNOW what dying means. Means you're always gone. Your troubles are over. If you've been weak, now you're strong. If you've been scorned, now you're beloved. Means my baby's in heaven. Gone to Jesus. Praise God! There's worse things in life than death. Am I right about that? Choirs of angels singing my baby to sleep. You know the hymn that goes "How gracious are thy mercies, Lord; they hallow all my days"? The Lord is a merciful God. I didn't mean what I did to my little girl. I love Kiesha, and I want her to forgive me for what I did to her.

If I tell you what happened can I have a McDonald's?

All right then, here's the true facts of what happened. I planned to eat those breakfast sausages with my grits and eggs. You see how it is. I was—whatyoucallit—was provoked. Always provoked. Sausages, soiled drawers, spilled root beer, whineyness, sass, lost toys. Always something. You have children, Captain? Then you know what I'm talking about. I know you do.

I know what type of baby I have. She get up all types of nights to eat up food, everything. What kind of two-year-old do that? Ate the sausages uncooked. Made her sick. Maybe if I could have said something. Words leave you when you're mad, like they're afraid or something. If I had the words, I think I would not have done it. I lost my temper for the first time. I fit my hand over her tiny face, and I slammed her head against the 'frigerator, against the wall, on the floor where she was sick. She screamed bloody murder. Her mama said, "Kiesha, honey, you're getting a beating on account of you got inside the 'frigerator and got sick on the linoleum." That way Kiesha sees the connection between my beating and her badness.

No sir, her momma and I ain't married. I can't be tied down, you know what I'm saying?

Then I spanked Kiesha with the plastic hairbrush. Just all over. I shook her a bit, squeezed her stomach. I guess I squeezed too hard. She stopped crying. Just stared at me. I can't help thinking if she had just eaten all her potatoes at supper, she wouldn't have been hungry. She's stubborn about potatoes. If the welfare had taken her away last time. A lot of *ifs*. I'm a good person, Captain. I have a good personality. You can see that. I just lost my mind.

CLOSE BY ME FOREVER

AT SEVENTEEN, VIVIEN POWERS LOVED PATSY Fantasia, a boy with black curls, amber skin, and alarming blue eyes, loved him even before she knew him. His solitary image intruded on her every thought. She felt tremors when he walked by and would have to calm herself. Even now when she thinks of him, Vivien wonders what it was about Patsy—his beauty or his mystery—that drew her love to him and marvels at what little thought or effort was involved.

Vivien sets the table for two with the holiday dishes, the cloth napkins, the good flatware. She arranges sprigs of holly around the Santa candle. She sits a minute, smooths the wrinkles on the snowflake tablecloth, and recalls the Christmas when she was a girl in winter and Patsy walked her home from midnight Mass in the snow. At her front porch he gave her a gift, an orange box of Tangee face powder. Then he took off his hat and kissed her. Vivien hears the horn from the Sheridan Street drawbridge and checks the clock over the stove. She wonders how Patsy is now, where he might be. Does he ever think of her? She wishes she could know that.

At twenty-one, Vivien married Jackie Paradise. He was a sweet boy, shy, attentive, handsome. A boy with a reliable future, her father said. They dated for two years and married without really deciding to. A wedding was simply the next logical and natural step. What else were they to do with their lives? Vivien walks into the living room. Jackie's asleep, sitting up on the sofa. She brushes his gray hair with her fingers, says, "Jackie, where have you gone?" She puts an album of carols on the hi-fi, calls the Chinese takeout to have supper delivered. She fishes in her purse for money and recalls, for some reason, her childhood maroon and silver bicycle with the wire basket and the streamers on the handlebars, sees it clearly, watches herself pedal down Grafton Street to Iandoli's Market. She's fallen for it again, this annual trick the holidays perform of making *now* disappear and pulling *then* out of thin air.

Vivien and Jackie had the one child, Margaret Mary, who lived for ninety-seven minutes. The boy, Henry, was nineteen when he died in Vietnam. Vivien recalls how relieved she and Jackie had been when Henry first got drafted. At least now he'd be off drugs; he'd get a haircut, start looking like a human being again. That's Henry in his uniform in the photo on the end table. The girl in the other photo is the baby of the family, Noelle. It's her community college graduation picture. Noelle still lives up north. Vivien hoped that Noelle, Dave, and the kids could visit for the holidays. She told Noelle on the phone, "This could be your father's last Christmas." Noelle said, "Geez, Ma, don't be so morbid. Anyway, we can't swing it this year. Besides, what's Christmas without snow?"

Now Vivien's sitting on the sofa with Jackie. She's holding his hand, folding the cuff on the reindeer sweater she knitted him. She looks at his face, tries to see the Jackie she married. Vivien wants him to sing along to "O Little Town of Bethlehem," but he won't. He can't. He says, "I want my bird."

"Your what?"

Jackie taps his trousers pocket. His bird. He folds his hands like he's praying, opens them, closes them, shows Vivien what he means. Why can't she understand? "My bird."

"Your wallet, you mean."

"Yes." Finally.

"It's on your dresser. You don't need your wallet tonight, dear."

But he does need it, though he doesn't know why. He stands but seems to lose his sense of direction. Vivien holds his shoulders, sits him down, fetches his wallet. She puts it on the arm of the sofa. Jackie peeks at her out the corner of his eye, but he won't turn his head. He hasn't been himself lately.

Vivien's not sure when this—what to call it?—this *mutation* began. First, Jackie forgot his glasses, his keys. That's normal enough. Then he forgot to lock the doors at night. Then he began to forget words in the middle of sentences. He'd forget to pay the bills, to turn off the stove. She'd tell him, "It's easy. When the timer dings, take the food out of the oven." "Sure," he'd say, "if I can remember the food is *in* the oven." And when he did remember, he'd burn his hands trying to remove the roast without pot holders. Used to be he liked to watch the Dolphins on TV, enjoyed a round of golf with Lefty and Mac at Orangebrook. Now he just sits here, moans, drops things. He doesn't read his mystery novels anymore. He's mostly unaware of the present, doesn't anticipate the future, and he's losing his grip on his past. She's not sure what he understands anymore, if anything. Vivien quit her part-time job at Burdines to stay with him.

And that's when she started finding maps he'd drawn and

bits of scribbled notepaper all over the house, telling himself how to get to Publix or to the bank, the parking lot, the dry cleaner's. She found his dentures between the mattresses on her side of the bed. Sometimes he thought he was in the old house in Massachusetts. She'd find him standing at the wall where he thought the door to the bedroom should be. This morning, Jackie looked at her, and she could tell from his hollow stare that he didn't know who she was. He's called her Grace (his older sister's name), and Emma (a cousin), and Margo. Today he called her Jeannie. He doesn't recognize old friends, people in the building. Someday, Vivien worries, he'll call her Mom because his mother will be the only person left in his mind.

She can fool herself sometimes, think this is a phase, something he'll get over, or at least he won't get any worse. But when she's awake in the middle of the night, and it's perfectly dark and Jackie's snoring like a baby, and she gets out of bed and walks to the parlor, well, there's no escaping what has always been right there for both of them—the unknowing, the unfeeling, the dreary end of possibility. How can love lead to this? And in the dark and in the silence, she feels the shame of losing her children, of planning a life without Jackie. She can open the blinds and let in the light from North Ocean Drive, and that helps. She'll hear traffic—the people speeding along as if nothing's happening, as if the world is not shattered.

This is Vivien and Jackie's forty-ninth Christmas together, their twelfth in Florida. Vivien wants this Christmas to be special. And so she's bought a small artificial tree and braided it with a garland of blinking white bulbs. She's set out ribbon candy and Christmas cards, hung a wreath on the door, and Advent calendar on the fridge, and arranged a crèche on top of the TV—angel hair, straw, and everything. The Magi are chipped, but serviceable. She looks at the figurines, sees wisdom paying homage to innocence, logic to faith. Or is it hope? Maybe faith *is* hope, she thinks. She'll tell him, "Jackie, you have memories to remember." If she can get him to recall Christmases past, she might reawaken the joy they once felt together, the joy that has seemed to leak from Jackie's life. In this way, Vivien believes, something can be born for them tonight.

The phone rings. It's Noelle. Vivien talks to the grandchildren. Paige babbles about Buzz Somebodyorother who's a spaceman, and Randy says he got a wicked cool skateboard. "Here," Vivien says, "talk to Grandpa." She hands the phone to Jackie and goes to the kitchen for eggnog. When she returns, the phone is hung up. Wrong number, Jackie says. The boy from Five Chinese Brothers arrives with the lotus prawns and Happy Family. Vivien tips him generously, wishes him a Merry Christmas, invites him in for a cup of cheer. "Thanks, but no thanks. Busy tonight." The legend on the paper sleeve for the chopsticks says *Happiness, Salary, Longevity, Pleasure.*

After supper, Vivien undoes the Velcro snap on Jackie's blue bib, wipes the pearly rice off his chin. She guides him to the sofa. They sit. She leans into him, puts her head on his shoulder. He does not wrap his arm around her. She listens to the music. "Away in a Manger." She takes his hand, holds it on her lap. "You know this one, Jackie. Sing it with me." And she begins to sing along. "Be near me, dah-dee-dah, I ask thee to stay . . ." She puts his fingers to her lips so he can feel the words. "Close by me forever, and love me, I pray." Jackie presses her mouth closed. "I'm tired, Viv."

She presents him with his gift, opens it for him. It's a photo he doesn't recognize of their Christmas forty-four years ago. She wants to remind him who he is and what he's relinquishing with his collapse into oblivion. And she's doing this for herself, too, driven by the absence of any love she can feel, dazed by his recent indifference. She needs him back. After all, who is Vivien without Jackie? She points at the boy in pajamas. "That's Henry," she says. "There's Noelle on my lap. Just six days old." Jackie stares at the photo. He knows this has meaning, but he's not sure what it is, like when someone comes in from the cold and you can smell the outside all around them. Well, he can smell the outside but doesn't know who carried it to him. This is Jackie's dilemma: He's losing his past but is trapped inside it. He's trying to be here, but he's there. The past is his home, but the rooms are empty.

If he can't remember what happened, then Vivien wants him to imagine it. "Can you do that, Jackie?" she says. He thinks he can. "Picture this," she says. And she tells him the story of their fifth Christmas, the one in the photo, when she was just home from the hospital with the baby, and they were in the living room of that little apartment over the Five & Dime. She tells him about the tree, how they strung it with popcorn and cranberries, hooked candy canes on the branches, how the stockings were hung from the windowsill, how Henry was wild about his new electric train. "And when the kids were settled into bed," she tells him, "we both wore our gifts—my charm bracelet, your flannel robe—and we cuddled on the sofa. We had music on, just like now. Snow drifted by the streetlight and you whispered in my ear and said, 'Viv, I've never been so happy,' and you kissed my forehead, my lips, my left eye, my right eye, and I knew then that love is hard to stop once you get it going, and I knew we would always be happy together."

Jackie says, "The radiator clanged."

Vivien looks at him and smiles. "That's right."

"We slept all night on the sofa."

"We did." Vivien laughs, kisses Jackie on the cheek, snuggles against his chest. He understands, she thinks. Yes. Jackie touches her face and rests his hand in her hair. This is his gift, she knows, this touch. Memory is only one way to authenticate your life, love is another. Love that has a future, he's saying to her, you need to work at. Even if the future's indifferent, unmerciful, it's still embraceable. Remembering is a gesture of the brain; love a gesture of the heart. She tells him, "We did. We slept until five when the baby woke us up." Vivien's story of Christmas past comes to a finish, but life is the story that doesn't end. Things will go on, she thinks. They must.

Vivien tucks Jackie into bed and kisses him on the forehead. His skin is damp and cool. She straightens the jewelry boxes and photographs on the dresser, smooths the wrinkles in the lace doily. When she hears Jackie snore, she showers and dresses for sleep. She carries the blanket and pillow to the living room. She takes down one of her new Harlequins from the bookshelf. *A Ghost of a Chance*. She puts on her half-glasses and reads the back cover. "He's a man from her past; she's a woman of the present. Together they have no future!" Yes, they do, Vivien knows. She switches on the reading lamp, kicks off her mules, and settles on the sofa. She tucks her legs under her, wets her finger, turns to page one. *The man with the eyepatch stepped onto the elevator behind her.* Vivien enjoys romance novels because she knows that in the end, the heroine—Jocelyn in this book—will get what she wants—the family castle that is her rightful inheritance—and find true love as well—in this case with Sebastian. There's already enough despair in the world that you don't need to go looking for it in books. The first time that Jocelyn meets Sebastian Furlong, she understands—and so does Vivien—that he is her one and only, and Vivien knows as well that he will never be unfaithful to Jocelyn, even though he might seem to be, and he will never abandon her, though all of her friends are certain that he will.

Vivien comes to the point in the novel where Jocelyn learns that Sebastian's ex-wife, Tophelia, has been committed to a very pastoral and posh asylum in the north country and that dear, sweet, forgiving Sebastian, in order to provide for her inordinately expensive care, has reluctantly accepted an executive position with Solomon Howell and Associates without knowing that Solomon Howell is Jocelyn's first cousin and the very man who would rob her of her legitimate legacy. This is the start of the fifty or so pages that Vivien thinks of as the inevitable dark days of the romance, the storm before the calm. She yawns, rubs her eyes, stretches, and sees him sitting there in the armchair. "Jackie, what on earth are you doing out of bed?"

He looks up from his crossword puzzle, and Vivien sees that it's not Jackie at all. She closes her eyes and massages her temples. When she opens her eyes, the man is still there, and he's smiling at her. He wants to know if she needs anything. She says yes, she needs to know who he is and how did he get into her house. He seems to slump into the chair. She wonders why she's not frightened. Because this can't be happening. Because she's dreaming, of course. She's fallen asleep while reading. And then she recognizes those alarming blue eyes. She says, "Patsy Fantasia, what are you doing here?"

He says, "When you fell asleep on the sofa, I thought for sure you'd be out for the night."

It makes perfect sense that she'd dream about Patsy—the Christmas memory and the novel about an old admirer returning. She looks at her book and sees the letters on the page, but can't read the words. See, it *is* a dream.

Patsy says, "All the excitement's worn you out."

"Excitement?"

"The kids, the grandkids."

"What do you know about Jackie's grandchildren?"

Patsy stands. He rubs his left knee, flexes it. "We've been over this and over this, Viv." He picks up the photo on the end table and shows it to her. "Jackie Paradise. The two of you were engaged."

"That's my son Henry."

"We have three daughters: Diane, Carolyn, and Theresa."

"We have nothing of the kind."

"Jackie was killed in Korea."

Vivien shakes her head. "I'm just going to wake up now and end this nonsense."

"Come on, I'll put you to bed. You'll feel better in the morning."

"Jackie's in bed."

"I'll show you he's not."

Vivien needs to ground herself. She stares at the crèche on the TV. Just where she'd arranged it. "It's Christmas."

"You remember!"

"Of course I remember what day it is."

Patsy sits beside Vivien, straightens his left leg. He's smiling and crying at the same time.

Vivien says, "What's wrong with you?"

"The Cognex is helping. I knew it would. You're getting better, Viv. You are." He takes her hands in his hands, kisses them.

Vivien wonders if you can do that in a dream—feel the pressure of lips like that.

Patsy says, "I want you to try to remember our honeymoon for me."

"We didn't have a honeymoon, Patsy Fantasia. And I'm so sorry you ended up as a lunatic."

"We took the train to Boston. We stayed at the Essex. Room 312."

Something about the name, the Essex, rings a distant bell with Vivien. But didn't she and Jackie honeymoon in New York City? Still, it's like she can see the name in gold Old English letters on a black awning over the hotel's front entrance and a doorman in a red Beefeater's uniform, standing inside the doors, keeping out of the drizzle.

"We saw Frank Fontaine at the Old Howard in Scollay Square. After the show, we had hot dogs and beers at Joe & Nemo's. The next afternoon we rode the swan boats."

When Vivien closes her eyes, she can see the glare of the bright sun in the silver water, the Canada geese paddling along in the boat's wake, the daylilies growing along the shore. She squeezes Patsy's hand as she must have done on that afternoon boat ride. She does remember, she does. "We walked along the Charles, didn't we?"

"For hours."

"How could I have forgotten, Patsy? Even for a second? What's wrong with me?"

"Nothing we can't handle."

"I thought you were gone forever."

"I've been right here all along." He kisses her eyes and her forehead. "And I'm not going anywhere."

"Oh, Patsy, you were always my Harlequin, my good-looking boy, my one and only love." Vivien hugs Patsy and cries into his shoulder. He rocks her and hums "Away in a Manger."

For now, Vivien lets go of her past and forgets her future. She's a woman of the present. She says, "I can't explain it, Patsy, but it's like I've lived, like I'm living, two lives. What a precious gift."

DIED AND GONE TO HEAVEN

WHEN DOYLE AUGARDE'S MOTHER EULA PASSED away of natural causes in the locked bedroom of her camel-back house on Black Bayou Road, a house that she had shared with Doyle and with Doyle's smutty wife Golden for a year, with Doyle alone for twenty-three years, with Doyle and his daddy Pierre for twenty-seven years, and with her old maid aunts for six years before that, when she died from the bacterial complications caused by a backed-up colostomy bag, from that and from a lack of food or liquid, from stubbornness, you might say—she was just so determined to make Doyle and his suck-egg wife apologize for eating the last of the Little Debbies, eating them out of spite (they know she favors a pecan spinwheel before bedtime, a spinwheel, a glass of buttermilk, and *The 700 Club*), that she got all in a swivet and locked herself in the room and waited for Doyle to knock *shave-and-a-haircut* like he does, to tell her how truly sorry he was, to beg her to come out please and join him and the penitent Golden, and promised herself she would not leave the room until he did just that, and when he didn't, she first swooned and slept and then lapsed in and out of "hallucinations," we would call them, "visions" is how she thought of them, in which she and the Lord wrestled on the bed, and each time she thought she had Him pinned, He turned into a different animal, like a weasel or a nutria or a water moccasin, or the Lord appeared to her as a Realtor in a handsome seersucker suit and with a prep-school haircut and brought along photos of possible homes for her in heaven, one more lovely than the last, and she told Him she just wanted to be as far away from Pierre as possible, and didn't she and Jesus laugh at that one, and then she lost consciousness completely after six days, so that she no longer heard the televison droning day and night, no longer suffered the stab of Doyle's laughter, the abrasion of Golden's shrill and grating voice, and all her dreams were dreams of setting off for church but never getting there, getting lost instead in woods that were never there before, or forgetting her hat and having to go home to get it, or falling down and getting up and falling down again, or waiting at the crossing for the westbound train to pass and counting the cars until the whistle faded into oblivion, and when at last Doyle was roused from a dead sleep by that smell and followed his nose to the bedroom, and when his knock went unanswered, he broke down the door and wished he hadn't because it stank so like hell in there that even the vermin were trying to escape, then he and Golden put on their Y2K gas masks, latex gloves, and disposable coveralls, wrapped the body in the bedsheets, and dumped it in the drainage ditch along Blessing the Cattle Road, and everything would have been hunky-dory had not Tommy Ray Wilcoxen gone out teal hunting—out of season, mind you—over to Frenchman's Brake and come across the squad of feasting turkey vultures.

Tommy Ray got close enough to see that this roadside carrion was no deer, close enough to set the vultures to hopping and hissing. He raised his shotgun, aimed at the red-faced boss bird, the one displaying his wings and staring down his long hooked bill into the barrel of the shotgun, and fired, killing the vainglorious son of a bitch, and scaring the bejesus out of the others, who lifted off the body with a ruffle and clatter of wings and flew to a nearby stand of oaks and took their roost. Tommy Ray could then see that this unfortunate meal was Miss Eula Augarde, not from her eyeless and lipless face, which was, in fact, unrecognizable as even human, and not from the punctured colostomy bag, which until that moment had been her secret from the town, but from the brace on her left leg (cerebral palsy). He kicked at the dead vulture, nudged it with his foot onto the road. Normally he'd have taken the bird home and cooked up a fricassee, but you don't eat something that's been eating your neighbor. That's where you draw the line. He looked up at the preening vultures, down at the body, up at the preening vultures. He ran practically all the way to Forrest Behlin's house and called the police.

When Officer Gethern Kincaid arrived at the scene, there stood Tommy Ray with his shotgun shouldered, and there was the body in the ditch. Gethern unholstered his service revolver, crouched behind the opened door of his cruiser, aimed the pistol at Tommy Ray, told Tommy Ray to lay down his weapon, and called for backup. Tommy Ray tried to explain that he was the guy who called the police and all he was doing was keeping yonder vultures at bay.

"Put the weapon down! Now!"

"You'll shoot me if I do."

"Shoot you if you don't."

Tommy Ray pointed to the corpse with his shotgun. "Eula Augarde."

Gethern said, "You're beginning to piss me off, sir." He knew you don't shoot a man who's not threatening you, and it was clear from the smell that this was no fresh kill in the ditch, and clear, too, that this old boy was not about to start trouble. Still, Gethern wondered, now that he had committed himself to disarming the suspect, how could he back down and save face, both? "I'm asking you nicely to lay down your weapon." Might as well be talking to that dead and gone vulture.

"They say her husband was a kneewalking drunk. Took her leg brace with him when he went out carousing. Beat her with it, too, they say. And now this. That ain't no kind of proper life."

You see, this was exactly what Gethern didn't like about police work, the thuggery of it, the intimidation. He prefered persuasion to threats. If he had wanted to be a bully he would have become a schoolteacher. His dream assignment with the force would be as a hostage negotiator, a man a perp could trust, not fear. He heard the approaching siren.

Tommy Ray stared up at the set of wheeling vultures soaring on the updraft. "Handsome at a distance, ain't they?"

Gethern couldn't understand why he didn't command respect. Here he stood, belted and badged, in his starched uniform, his polished tactical boots, his Stetson, and he was pointing a gun at a man who was completely ignoring him. This sort of embarrassment and disrespect could lead to rash behavior and catastrophe one day.

Officer Danny Falconetti stepped out of his cruiser, put on

his hat, tucked his thumbs into his belt, said, "Tommy Ray, what you up to?"

"Not teal hunting."

Danny motioned for Gethern to holster his revolver. "Let's take a look-see." He and Gethern approached the picked-over corpse.

Tommy Ray said, "I suspect foul play."

"No time for jokes," Danny said.

"What?"

Gethern gagged, held his hand over his mouth, retched, stumbled back to the cruiser. Danny told him he ought get a hold of the medical examiner and have the EMTs come on out. "How's your daddy, Tommy Ray?"

"Fair to middling. Now that he's got the Oldtimer's he don't remember he's got the slow-eating cancer."

"We count our mercies."

"I suspect Doyle's behind this."

"Just out walking your shotgun, were you?"

"God bless the NRA."

GETHERN WIPED DOWN the kitchen table with a gritty dishrag and washed his hands with dishwashing detergent at the pitted sink. He shook them dry, wiped them on his pant legs. He took a deep breath at the open window. The stink of decay lingered in the house something awful. He sat at the table and took notes on what they were calling the crime scene while Danny interviewed the Augardes across the room. Doyle and Golden sat on the brown and yellow plaid couch holding hands; Danny sat in the matching armchair. Gethern noted the smallish Coldspot fridge with the broken handle. The fridge had been painted a flat white at least once with a brush. On top of the fridge, a banjo-playing coconut monkey wearing a straw hat. A four-burner Caloric gas range. An open can of bacon drippings on the counter beside a plastic mixing bowl of used scouring pads. A dented aluminum measuring cup between the bowl and the Sunbeam Mixmaster. A wall shelf with four tin canisters on it and a box of wooden matches. Above the shelf, a paint-by-number *Last Supper*. No clock, he noted. No calendar. A bare lightbulb in the middle of the ceiling. A mocha wall phone with a rotary dial. No coffeepot.

Doyle said, "Well, I wouldn't use the word 'dumped' myself, Officer. We set her down real gentle."

"Doyle even said a prayer over the body," Golden said.

Danny steepled his fingers and rested his chin on them. "You've committed a felony, Mr. and Mrs. Augarde."

"I told you she was dead when we found her," Doyle said.

"And you didn't call an ambulance, did you?"

"Like I said, she was dead already."

"Nothing they could do for her at a hospital," Golden said.

Danny leaned forward. "You don't get to determine who's dead. You a doctor?"

"Could have been," Doyle said.

"You should see how smart he is at *Jeopardy*."

"Is there something wrong with you two?"

"My prostrate kicks up couple of times a year. Happen to you?"

Danny said, "My pros*tate*'s just fine."

"Like getting stabbed up the you-know-what. Set you walking on your tiptoes."

Danny said, "A person's dead when a physician says she's dead. And you cannot dispose of the body until a physician signs a death certificate."

"Pardon me, but you don't need to be a doctor to know a person's passed, Officer. If there ain't no breath and there ain't no heartbeat, if her smell could knock a buzzard off a shit wagon, if her skin's green and blistered and her tongue's swollen out her mouth, and her nose and ears are dripping a stinky fluid, she's dead."

Gethern saw a photo album up with the chipped dishes in the cabinet over the sink. He took it down. Some of the photos had come loose of their corner mounts and slipped out of the book. He picked them up and carried it all to the table. Lots of pictures of Doyle as a child. Doyle with his six-shooters; Doyle in a Confederate battle cap; Doyle riding the back of a big old golden retriever; Doyle asleep beside a four-foot catfish in the bed of a pickup.

Danny said, "Why didn't you call Mulhearn's Funeral Home?"

"Now we're talking money, which we ain't got much of."

"Even a burial in the backyard would have been a more decent response to her death, don't you think?"

"She hated the idea of burial."

Golden said, "She was closetrophobic. Hated tight places."

Danny shook his head, sat back in the chair. "Why am I trying to reason with the pair of you?"

Doyle smiled. "You're a reasonable man is why. Am I right?"

Danny said, "According to the medical examiner, your mother was dead at least a week when we found her."

"About right," Doyle said.

"So what you're telling me is that your mother was dead for several days in that room right there, and the two of you didn't know it. Complete surprise."

"She was a woman who liked her privacy, and we tried to respect that," Doyle said.

"There was no reason for her to die."

"Does death need a reason, Officer?" Doyle said.

"You could have saved her life."

Golden said, "When the Lord calls you, there's nothing you or I or any of us can do."

"Well, you see right there you committed another felony—abuse of a senior citizen."

"You making that one up?" Doyle said.

"Hell no."

"Back up a car length, Officer. I'll tell you who's abusive," Golden said. "Eula Augarde, that's who. Lord have mercy on her spiteful soul."

And she cried and Doyle rubbed her shoulder and looked at Danny and said, "She's been through a lot."

"That woman hated me from day one. She did all she could do to drive a wedge between Doyle and me." She kissed Doyle's hand.

Danny said, "Did either of you ever consider that maybe Miss Eula was jealous of Golden? That she'd had Doyle to herself all these years and now here comes this intruder that she'll have to share her boy with?"

Doyle said, "No, I never did."

Golden said, "Sounds like she had some growing up to do."

Gethern saw a photograph of a sweet young woman with

long dark braids and a handsome young man in a checkered suit sitting in what looked to be a Ferris wheel carriage.

Golden said, "When you look at what we did right now, it does seem we acted kind of rash. We panicked maybe, but we just knew we had to get the putrid carcass out the house."

Doyle said, "I don't like other people doing my dirty work for me. Wouldn't been fair to Benton Mulhearn to walk in on misery like that."

Gethern showed the picture to Doyle.

"That's Mother at the state fair in Shreveport," Doyle said.

"And that's your daddy?"

"Don't know who that is."

Gethern looked at the photo, at Doyle, at the photo.

"She kept her past private," Doyle said.

"Did you love your momma?" Danny said.

"She was my mother."

"That's not an answer."

"Well, I can't say we were close exactly. Not so close as I'd have a reason to kill her, desecrate her body or anything."

Danny said, "Was your daddy good to her?"

"Daddy was a cocksucker."

Golden said, "Why, Doyle Augarde—"

"A son of a bitch, plain and simple, Officer."

"He beat her, did he?" Danny said.

"Beat her, beat me, beat the dog."

"How'd he die?"

"Fell asleep on the railroad tracks down to Elysian Fields."

Gethern said, "I don't understand, Mr. Augarde, why you aren't grieving for your loss."

"Because she's in a better place."

"The Kingdom of Heaven is like unto treasure hid in a field," Golden said.

Gethern asked if he could keep the photo awhile.

Doyle said, "You can take the whole album for as long as you want. I don't live in the past."

"Just the photo, thanks."

Golden said, "Why do you want it?"

"I see this handsome, happy young woman at the fair, and today I saw what came of her life. Just trying to reconcile the two images."

"You're like the Profiler on the TV," Golden said.

"That what police do with our tax dollars now?" Doyle said. "Reconcile?"

Danny said, "We arrest malefactors, Doyle. And we'll be back for you. Don't go nowhere."

GETHERN SAT IN a booth at the Mohawk Tavern, nursing a drink and studying the photograph of Miss Eula at the state fair. Miss Eula and her escort. They looked to be about sixteen. When Gethern was sixteen, he took Chalice Whitley to the Neville High School junior prom. Somewhere in the house he has a photo of him and Chalice slow dancing, smiling brightly into the camera. Chalice married Porter Allgood and moved to Fort Worth. Just because you're happy and in love at sixteen or you're upbeat and ambitious at twenty-five, which is what Gethern was, that's no guarantee you won't arrive eventually at wretchedness and desolation. Gethern wondered if Miss Eula took the photo down on occasion, looked into her past right there in her hands, and remembered this day in Shreveport with her beau, remembered what he said just after the picture was taken, how he touched her hand at the top of the ride, and when she looked at this young couple she was half of, did she feel the ache of lost love, did it fill her with regret, or did she embrace the exhilarating knowledge that once she was loved and once there was promise?

"Where did you come across a picture of Waymore Claxton?" Tommy Ray leaned over the table and squinted. He had two PBR longnecks in his right hand.

"You about scared the life out of me," Gethern said.

Tommy Ray handed Gethern a bottle and sat down across from him. "Second time this week."

"You know this guy?"

"Don't know the gal with him."

"Eula Augarde."

"Nuh-uh!" Tommy Ray took the photo and turned it to the light from the bar. "Doyle killed her."

"Not according to the medical examiner."

"There are many ways to kill a person."

"His name's Claxton?"

Tommy Ray told Gethern that Waymore's daddy used to own the paper mill. Waymore himself went to college back East, lived in New York City, wrote a book about Monroe, only he called it Madison, and when his daddy died, Waymore moved back to town, sold the mill, and settled into a life of luxury. Lives on the Northside. Clips coupons, listens to opera, hosts little dinner parties.

"Did you read his book?"

"Nor anyone else's." Tommy pulled a toothpick out of his shirt pocket and worked it between his teeth. "You ever tasted pan-seared teal breast?"

GETHERN'S PREFERRED READING ran to biography and true crime, but he did enjoy the heck out of Waymore Claxton's *Just Like You Only Different*. The book was a well-written, intelligent, and compelling coming-of-age story. He couldn't put it down; read it in the cruiser, at meals, in line at Albertson's, at bedtime. He finished in two days. Yes, Waymore had changed the name of the town, but he had changed nothing in the town. Part of Gethern's pleasure came from reading about places that he knew. Like the Mohawk. Like the Dinner Bell, where he ordered the catfish basket and read Chapter Ten, in which the young hero, Wade, takes his sweetheart, Ila, to the Dinner Bell on their first really formal date, and she tells him that she has never in her life been inside a restaurant, and he thinks she must be joking.

Some of the businesses in the book were gone now, but Gethern remembered them from his childhood: Spatafora the Cobbler, with the Cat's Paw sign in the window and the boots on the shelves behind the counter; Bevo Smitz Typewriter Repair on North Sixth at Louisville; the Coney Dog Hut on Grand. Gethern's mother took him for coneys and Dr Pepper every Saturday afternoon. They'd sit outside at a picnic table and watch the river slide by. When Gethern's mother died, she was loony as a betsey bug and didn't know her own boy from Adam's off-ox. So loony that she made herself a Clorox milkshake, and it looked like she'd finished most of it before she died.

. . .

GETHERN CALLED ON Waymore Claxton. They sat out on the patio by the pool and drank bottled springwater with lemon wedges. Waymore had short feathered white hair and thick black eyebrows. He was lean as a mink, looked like he hadn't gained a pound in fifty years. He wore a starched blue-striped Oxford shirt with a monogrammed left cuff, wheat-colored corduroys, deck shoes, no socks. He asked Gethern which Kincaids were his people. Gethern said the First Baptist Kincaids. "Lamar was your daddy?"

"My uncle. Davis was my father."

Waymore advised Gethern to drink at least eight glasses of water a day to flush out the impurities. He said he normally ate only boiled, skinless chicken and green vegetables, but not string beans. "You'd have to be criminally reckless to eat beef anymore." He smiled. "Speaking of crime, am I under arrest, Officer?"

Gethern laughed and explained that no, this was a social call, said that he'd just finished the novel and wanted to say how much he liked it. Waymore thanked him. Gethern asked him why he hadn't written another.

"I had one story to tell, and I told it."

Gethern handed Waymore the state fair photograph.

Waymore put on his reading glasses. "God, I remember that suit. What was I thinking?" He smiled at the photo, shook his head. "You're here about Eula."

"Trying to make some sense of her life, I guess."

"We don't make sense, we make love," Waymore said. "And we make art; we make conversation."

"In your novel, Ila is Eula."

"And Wade is I."

"You and Eula Augarde!"

"Eula Rankin back then. God rest her soul."

"The book ends with Wade leaving Madison."

"After he's told Ila he's homosexual."

"After his affair with the attorney."

"Vocations were changed to protect the guilty." Waymore dabbed at his eyes with a napkin. "Allergies."

"Did you know Eula's husband?"

"Pierre the squidgereen. Short, nasty, and brutish. He'd been in our class until he dropped out of school. Dumb as nails and crazy as a shithouse rat."

"He beat her."

"So I was told."

"Why do you suppose she married the man?"

"She was a Christian woman."

"And?"

Waymore crossed his legs, leaned forward, clasped his hands over his knee. "When I left for Princeton, Eula didn't know it, but she was pregnant."

"With your child?"

"I'll deny it."

"Doyle Augarde is your flesh and blood."

Waymore closed his eyes and said, "But he is not my son."

"We could prove that he was."

"But why would you?"

"Why didn't Eula call you when she found out?"

"She was horrified by my sin, as she called it, my abomination. And, I suppose, by what she saw as my betrayal. I had defiled her and then abandoned her. So she found a willing man, bedded him, told him she was with his child, and forced him to marry her."

GETHERN HAD GUESSED right. There had been an investigation into the death of Pierre Augarde in July 1981. Gethern retrieved the file. Pierre Augarde, a forty-six-year-old male Caucasian, had a history of arrests and convictions for public drunkenness, loitering, and lewd conduct. A charge of assault against a liquor store clerk had been dismissed. The subject's upper body had been found 150 yards from the tracks behind the abandoned Color Tile outlet. The rest of him landed in a patch of cogon grass close by the rails. The likely scenario was that Pierre was stumbling drunk, wandered to the tracks, tripped on the rail, fell, and passed out cold. There were, however, some indications that the death may not have been quite so accidental. Photos of footprints at the scene indicated an unusual amount of pedestrian traffic in the vicinity of impact. A piece of pink and yellow strawberries-and-daisies-print gingham cloth was found caught on an exposed nail of a busted-up fruit crate in the lot beside Color Tile. Looked to Gethern that it might have been torn from a housedress. He found two notes in the file. The first, written in pencil on the back of a Spat's Pharmacy receipt, was found at the scene and read: "mr. I have put up with u and ur cruelty 4 2 long. I hope u rot in hell." The other note, addressed to Police Chief Lonnie Sims, was typed on Claxton Paper Mill stationery and signed by Castor Claxton. Mr. Claxton respectfully suggested that the time had come to close the ill-advised investigation into the death of the "reprobate Augarde." A derelict who brutalized his family was mercifully dead. "Lonnie, do we really care to know how the beast died?"

GETHERN STOPPED BY Doyle's and asked if he might see the family Bible. On the records page, he saw the entry for Doyle's birth. "This here your momma's handwriting?" Doyle said it was. Gethern closed the Bible and handed Doyle the state fair photograph and told him the boy with his mother was Waymore Claxton.

Doyle stared at the TV. "That old fairy?"

"You know him?"

"We've howdied, but we ain't shook."

Golden looked at the photo, then back at the TV, where a fisherman standing on a bass boat was casting his line into a bed of water lilies. She examined the photo again, raised her eyebrows, and nodded. "You can tell from his posture he's light in his loafers. See how he holds himself so prissified. And that suit! You can always tell. Take Mr. Henry Perch over to Perch's House of Dolls and Gifts. He's not fooling a soul, is he? Not for one skinny minute."

Doyle said, "Mother had a homosexual friend. Gives me the heebie-jeebies just thinking about it." And his whole bodied shivered.

Gethern told the couple he guessed they'd avoid prison time despite Doyle's rather extensive criminal record.

"Youthful indiscretions," Doyle said.

"Possession of cocaine, DUI, grand theft."

"When I was young and foolish, I was young and foolish."

Gethern figured they'd get a fine was all. The TV fisherman landed a four-pound bass, kissed it, held it for the camera, and tossed it back in the lake. What the hell was the point of that? Gethern wondered.

Doyle claimed they couldn't pay a fine. "Can't suck blood from a stone."

Gethern said, "You might could try working."

"I have."

Golden said she was applying for a job at the new Red Lobster out to the mall. "I would enjoy being a hostess, but like Doyle says, the real money is in waitressing. And with a personality like mine, the sky's the limit."

That's when Gethern noticed it, hanging on the broken handle of the fridge—a pink and yellow strawberries-and-daisies-print gingham apron. He walked to the fridge and felt the threadbare cloth. "Your mother's?"

Doyle said, "She's had that forever. Made it herself."

Gethern said, "Do you remember much about the day your daddy died?"

"I remember that he was drunk, locked Mother in her room, made me drive him to the Club Elite. When I got back, Mother had snuck out her window. Don't know how she did it with the leg and all. Went to the drugstore for headache powders."

"Folks, would you all mind turning off the TV for just a second?"

Golden hit the *Off* button on the remote, stood, tugged at her shorts. "I'm going to leave you boys to chat while I soak in the tub." And she excused herself.

Gethern sat in the armchair. "Doyle, I want you to know this conversation is off the record, so to speak."

"I've got nothing to hide." Doyle tucked a pinch of snuff between his cheek and gum.

"How did you feel when your daddy locked your mother in her bedroom?"

"I hated her. Hated that she put up with the beatings and all, that she didn't fight back, that she never up and left the sorry son of a bitch and took me with her. She left me here to be treated like dirt and beat like a rug."

"Are you saying you didn't hate him?"

"I didn't care about him enough to hate him. I pitied him, I suppose."

"Because?"

"I feel like he might not have been a rabid dog if he hadn't been with her." Doyle pounded the arm of the couch with his fist. "Sometimes she made me so goddam mad, I hit her, too—knuckles on top of her head, just to say, 'Wake the fuck up, would you!'" Doyle spit into his dip cup. "If Daddy had met a woman like Golden, a woman with some fire, a woman he could love and respect, then maybe he would have lived a sober life, been a successful man. Life is all about chance, isn't it? You come to a fork in the road, and you flip a coin. And everything that ever happens in your life results from the bounce of that coin."

"Or you make a choice."

"Your fate is sealed."

"He beat her, you said."

"He liked to grab her titties and squeeze and twist them till she screamed and then he'd twist harder till she stopped screaming. Slam her head against the wall. Kick her in the crotch. Lift her off the floor and heave her into furniture."

"Jesus Christ."

"Every day of her life."

"And you never stopped him?"

"When I tried, he beat her worse."

"Call the cops?"

"Said he'd kill her before the cops arrived."

"Your mother lived in hell."

"For twenty-seven years."

"And you didn't have the decency to bury her properly."

"'Let the dead bury the dead.'"

"You acted disgracefully."

"That's not how I see it."

"Let me ask you point-blank. Did you kill your daddy?"

"Many times. In my dreams."

S O M E H O W   G E T H E R N wasn't surprised to see Tommy Ray waiting for him on the front step when he got home. Tommy Ray stood and held up a plastic sack. "Brought you some teal breasts."

"How'd you know where I lived? Law enforcement officers have unlisted addresses."

"You ain't hard to find." He handed Gethern the sack. "You're welcome."

"Thank you. Come on in."

Inside the door, Gethern asked Tommy Ray to leave his boots on the rug.

"You serious?"

"As an overdue mortgage."

Tommy Ray sniffed the air. "Still got that new-modular-home smell."

"Get you a drink?"

"I think it's the chemicals they put in the paneling."

"Beer?"

"Twist my arm."

"I'll put the teal in the fridge."

"Live here alone?"

"I do."

"No pets even?"

"I've got tropical fish on my screensaver." He handed Tommy Ray a bottle.

"Arrest Doyle yet?"

"Falconetti's on his way right now."

They sat at the kitchen table. Gethern gave Tommy Ray a coaster for his bottle.

Tommy Ray said, "Murder One?"

"Improper disposal of a body."

"That's it?"

"That's what we can prove."

Tommy Ray whistled, shook his head. "Where's the justice?"

"In the sky, by and by."

"One time I heard Doyle tell some knuckle-walking friend of his that he'd held his momma's arms while his daddy beat her head with a skillet."

"When was this?"

"We were maybe fourteen. Standing in line for the wrestling matches at the Sugar Theater."

Gethern thought, Is he going to have to deal with this kind

of cowardly and loathsome behavior all his life now? Will it harden and embitter him? Will he become cynical, someone he wouldn't like to know?

Tommy Ray said, "A boy in his forties still living with his momma. That's peculiar."

"He told me he was a homebody."

"Him with a wife and all."

"Said his mother depended on him."

"I tried married, but it didn't take."

"I'm sorry."

"My wife, she was backward coming forward, you see. Shy. With me. In the bedroom. Something like that will scrape your nerves raw. So now I live with my brother Troy."

"Let me get you another beer." Gethern rinsed the bottle in the sink and dropped it in the recycling bin. "You're the first guest I've had to the house."

"Thank you." Tommy Ray took the bottle. "You ever get married?"

"Never did."

"Think you might?"

"I would like to."

"Got a girl?"

"No one steady."

"Step number one."

"I had a lavaliered sweetheart one time. Had a diamond solitaire engagement ring on layaway at Friedman's."

"You got to get back up on the horse, son."

"Why don't I cook us that teal?"

"Got Tabasco?"

. . .

GETHERN FOUND THE photo of him and Chalice in a speckled file box on the shelf in his bedroom closet. He sat on the edge of his bed and looked at it. You can't see it in the photo, but Gethern remembered the corsage of pink spray roses on her left wrist and the gold crucifix ring on her third finger. At the prom, they left the dance for a walk out on the golf course. They stood beneath the pines holding hands and smiling at each other. Chalice laid her head on his shoulder, and he thought he'd died and gone to heaven. He felt unworthy of such bliss. He embraced Chalice and they kissed. He heard the band faintly playing "Desperado," and he thought what a wonderful life this is. Happiness is so easy. And so fleeting. How did he become this twenty-five-year-old bachelor who only ever had the one true love? Keeping the photograph around was probably not a good idea, but tossing it out was a worse one. One day he called Chalice at their usual time, and she did not answer the phone. And then she was busy after school. She wasn't at the library. And then she showed up at his door with a carton of the gifts he had given her and was sorry to have to tell him that, well, Gethern, I'm sorry, but I've found someone new. Gethern sat at the edge of the bed and closed his eyes. The ceiling fan clicked and clicked.

On his drive over to Waymore Claxton's house, Gethern stopped at Elysian Fields to look around some. He parked in front of the burned-out shell of the Club Elite, saw from a torn poster on the plywood over the busted-out window that Tremaine Davis and His Pleasure Kings were playing or had played at Simmie's Diddy wah Diddy. Someone had drawn a mustache on Tremaine's face and horns on his head. Gethern thought maybe if he walked around the area, he might be able to picture what really happened that night. He didn't believe in vibes—it wasn't that—but perhaps he'd notice something that others had missed. The abandoned Color Tile was now a Salvation Army Thrift Store, a rack of frayed and soiled winter jackets on the sidewalk out front. The cogon grass had been paved over. He could see that if Pierre had been about to haul his drunken ass home that night, he was heading in the wrong direction. Crossing the tracks here meant stumbling into a notoriously nasty and drug-infested neighborhood. It did not seem likely that Pierre was on his way to score heroin.

Gethern knew that the cloth found at the scene matched the apron in Eula's kitchen. He did not believe in coincidence. The handwriting on the pharmacy-receipt note matched the handwriting in the family Bible. Eula was here when Pierre died, and probably not as a witness to an accident. Gethern did not believe in prescience. Eula had the motive to murder her despicable husband, certainly. She had the opportunity— her son said so. But did she have the means? She could not have overpowered Pierre, could not have dragged him or his body to the tracks. Gethern wanted to believe that the easiest explanation was the best explanation. Pierre was an accident waiting to happen.

GETHERN SAT DOWN, laid the file folder between himself and Waymore on the couch, and looked at the framed photograph on the coffee table.

Waymore said, "That's Wylie—Wylie Arceneaux—and I in Patmos. At Theo's Restaurant, enjoying our moussaka and retsina." Waymore sipped his port. "Wylie wanted to die in the birthplace of Western civilization. We rented a cozy little house overlooking Vagia Beach. At night I read to him. The local bestsellers: *The Iliad, The Odyssey, Revelation.* He lived for seven months there. I scattered his ashes in the Aegean. All very romantic, very tragic, very difficult to talk about. I stayed for two years because I couldn't bear to leave him."

"You're a fortunate man."

Waymore slapped his knees. "Indeed! And you've arrested the unfortunate Doyle Augarde."

"And the missis."

"Eula has been avenged."

"For the second time."

"How so?"

"Eula murdered Pierre."

"Don't be silly. Drunks fall onto railroad tracks and die all the time."

"Six times in the last ten years in Ouachita Parish."

"There you go."

"We have a note in her handwriting found at the scene. We have a piece of her dress found at the scene. We have photographs of footprints at the scene."

"There were lots of footprints."

"Were there?"

"I would imagine."

"Prints that matched her braced shoe." Gethern opened

the file and showed Waymore the photos. "What bothers me, what I can't figure out, is why take such desperate measures to solve a problem? Why do the worst thing possible? Why commit murder? Why not run away, call the authorities, get professional help?"

Waymore filled his port glass. "Why are you so dogged and bothered by Eula's dismal life, Mr. Kincaid?"

"She made a choice to stay with the man who was battering her, an irrational choice."

"We don't all or always act logically, I'm afraid. We don't always do what is in our best interest."

"And I think you helped her."

Waymore sat back and smiled. "Kill the husband?"

"I can give you my theory, but I'd rather hear your story."

Waymore cleared his throat and nodded. "At first she tried to pacify him."

"How do you know this?"

"She wrote to me over the years. She said that he was going to kill her and kill 'our son.'"

"He didn't want to kill her. He'd have no one left to damage."

"He might have killed her accidently just the same."

"Why didn't she leave him?"

"Every beating made her more helpless."

"A helpless woman doesn't commit murder."

"Exactly."

"Unless she has help."

"When she couldn't pacify Pierre, she grew passive herself, figuring if she did nothing, he'd have no reason to hit her. So he hit her for doing nothing, hit her because his eggs were cold or the carpet was soiled. There's evil in this world, Kincaid."

"What went wrong in Pierre's life, do you think, to make him so vicious?"

"There's folks will tell you he was possessed by the devil."

"Which lets him off the hook."

"Eula didn't kill him, by the way. I did."

"What happened?"

"Long story short. I was in town visiting my ailing father."

"And she was locked in her bedroom."

"Where she'd hidden a key. She let herself out and called me. I drove her to Elysian Fields, parked behind the old Color Tile. Real dark back there. Eula waited on the sidewalk across from the club. When Pierre saw her he bellowed some obscenity and stumbled after her. She limped as fast as she could toward the tracks. She snagged her dress, and he nearly caught her, but he tripped and fell. I stomped the accelerator. He stood. I ran him down. Bounced him clear over the roof of the car. We dragged his body to the tracks. End of story."

"Why?"

"He needed killing."

"No one's above the law."

"We both know you can't prove it."

"I have a duty."

"So did I. You do what you have to do, Kincaid."

GETHERN LET HIMSELF into the Augardes' empty house. He switched on the light. The television was tuned to some ranting talk show. He opened the photo album and took the state fair photograph, saw the two smiling kids, squinting into the dazzling sun. The man on TV said he wished it were the Wild West again, and if it were, he'd gun down whatever liberal writer he was talking about. Put a bullet between his eyes. Gethern slipped the photograph into the family Bible. He rolled up the apron and stuffed it in his pocket. He looked over to the couch and pictured Doyle and Golden in their inevitable postures, slumped into the cushions, blunt-eyed and slack-jawed, their spellbound and spongy faces locked on to the TV screen. Gethern walked over to the TV, sat in the armchair, braced himself, and kicked in the screen with the heel of his boot. He tore his pants and sliced his leg behind the knee. His pants were soaking up the blood. He took the Bible and walked to the bayou. He cut his pant leg with his jackknife and dunked the leg in the water. He washed the leg, wrapped the apron over the gash, and opened the Bible to *Revelation.* He read about all those angels coming down from heaven, sounding their trumpets, warning us all about the murderers and whoremongers at the gates of the city, about those who loveth and maketh a lie. And he looked up into the clear night, saw the Milky Way splashed across the sky, and realized how everything in the universe was so far away, and was, he knew, speeding away from everything else in the universe, speeding away from him, from this place, this earth, this small patch of bottomland where he sat bleeding and remembering, getting smaller and smaller. He sank his hands into the soft clay of the bayou bank, shut his eyes, and held on.

LEFTY

IT'S FIVE YEARS FROM NOW, AND CINDY AND I ARE
living in a log home in Wyoming. She's sleeping. I'm in our
cozy living room, reading in front of the fire, when, just out
of nowhere, I remember today, Christmas 1999, in West
Virginia, and my walk in the woods, and how the cold and the
litter of oak leaves and the lichen-carpeted rocks reminded me
of my childhood in New England—acorn fights, horse cob-
blers on strings, football in the schoolyard, trash burning in
rusted oil barrels. I close my book, fold it on my lap—I'm
reading about how to build a concrete smokehouse, wondering where in Sublette County I can find an iron door—and
I'm seized by loneliness because my son is nineteen, and he
has left me—he's in college in Florida or he's waiting tables
in L.A. or he's leading eco-tourists through the Amazon. He's
home for the holidays and he's lying on the floor. On the
mantel over the fireplace is the warbler's nest I found on my
walk that Christmas and a framed photo of Tristan at six
months. I ask him about the movie he's making, *Iglesia Vida
Loca,* or about the play he's writing, *Tristan Shout,* or about the
band he plays in, Linoleum Blownaparte. I don't usually talk
about my writing, but tonight I want to. I tell Tristan I'm writing a story called "Lying in Bed," and I'm stuck on a scene. I
say let's go for a walk, and we do.

We live on Fremont Lake, and the wind is howling down the Wind River Range. We bundle up. We crunch and trudge along the snowy road to Pinedale. Tristan wears the cowboy hat I bought him. I tell him I've got this character who has something important to say, but can't find the words. Tristan says, Do you know *why* he can't say whatever it is to whomever it is? I suddenly want to leap on my son, wrestle him down, roll us around in the snow. I say, *He's afraid.* Of? *Of losing everything he has: his family, his talent, his touch, his friends, his memory, his self.* What has he done to earn such fear? *Committed the sin of solitude.* He sounds melodramatic, and anyway, not talking won't keep it all from going away. *You're right about that.*

We see the lights of town. When we get there, we can warm ourselves at the Jim Bridger Tavern. We'll sit at the bar, have a drink, talk about Tristan's future, his plans for now. I'll want to know when he thinks he can come back for a visit. His mother misses him. I'll talk about my old man, Tristan's pépère, Lefty, who was recruited by Jesse Burkett to pitch in the Boston Braves organization. This was after the war, after seasons in semi-pro, and his wife was pregnant with me and refused to live in Evansville, Indiana. The man worked fifty years for the power company stoking coal, driving a backhoe, and went to work every day whether he was sick or tired or hung over, and when he retired, they gave him a table lamp made from a service meter, and he went blind within a year.

Lefty's grandfather abandoned his family when my grandfather was born, took his name, Burt Ash, and his heritage and vanished. And Lefty's been trying to find old Burt all his life. He has the idea we're Irish and not French. By now we'll be on our second cognacs, and I'll tell Tristan how Lefty and I once went to Arkansas so he could have these acupuncture treatments on those eyes, and how every morning and every night he prayed the rosary, prayed for his vision, for the chance to drive again, to see his great-grandchildren, to be independent. I tell Tristan that he and I and Lefty ought to make a trip to Hot Springs for the races in March. We'll go to Oaklawn, to Doe's for steaks, to the Ohio Club for cocktails. We'll take in the baths, treat ourselves like kings. We'll stay at the Arlington. How about that? What do you say?

But, of course, it's five years from now, and Lefty's Parkinson's keeps him tethered to the house these days, two thousand miles from me. I look across the bar into the mirror, into my face as dingy as an old sheet, and I feel ludicrous. What am I thinking of, for God's sake? And that's when my son— who's sleeping now in the cabin in the West Virginia woods— blesses me. After the races, he says, we'll drive to Monroe. I want to show Pépère where I was born. Or he says, I'll be home for your birthday next month. Or he says, I hear you.

Murder Your Darlings

MY HONEY ANNICK HAD BEEN AFTER ME TO write a thriller, a potboiler, a beach and airplane paperback, a page-turner, a murder mystery, a sizzling suspense novel, a *read*, as opposed to a book. She thought it was time I had a savings account, a 401(k), and decent health insurance. She said every writer in South Florida writes thrillers, and they all make money. "What makes you so special?"

"I make money."

"Real money," she said. "Just write one thriller."

"They don't let you write just one."

"And then you can go back to the squalid and the quirky. You have to kill someone, Johnny."

I said, "What kind of pillow talk is this?" We were in bed, and I was feeling frisky. I'd been trying to get Annick to take off her 10 MOST WANTED SQUIRRELS T-shirt. Annick smelled like patchouli and soil.

Then this woman who loved me said, "Why don't you want to write a book that someone would like to read?"

This was not the foreplay I'd been expecting. My new novel, *The Bright Sun Will Bring It All to Light*, was about to be published, and I was anxious about its critical reception. I needed a snuggle and squeeze. I was off on a promotional book tour in a few days and was frazzled just thinking about it.

Spot sneezed. He was in the closet, spying on us through the slats in the folding door.

Annick thought I was being irresponsible. She thought I was afraid to fail, and that's why I wouldn't tackle a thriller. I told her every story's a failure. She rolled her eyes.

She said, "It's not a sin to write for money."

I nuzzled my face into her neck.

"Writing for your art doesn't make you a saint."

"I write for the reader."

"Write for an audience."

"I don't have an audience. I'm not the Pope."

"You are so Catholic."

"Lapsed."

"The worst kind," she said. "You think you're holier than the Church."

Annick had found "The Lester Dent Pulp Paper Master Fiction Plot" on the Internet and printed it out for me. She said, "Just follow the directions."

"That's not writing."

"Johnny, you know plots give you trouble."

She gave me Raymond Chandler's "Ten Commandments for the Detective Novel." Number Five: "It must have enough essential simplicity to be explained easily when the time comes."

"Annick, I write what I have to write."

Spot pushed open the closet door, walked to the bed, laid

his muzzle on the mattress, snorted, sighed. I said, "Are we keeping you up?" He put his paw on the mattress. I warned him. "Spot, you know the rules." He scratched my arm.

Annick said, "Maybe he needs to go o-u-t."

Spot woofed that he did. Then he bounded out of the room. I got out of bed, slipped on a T-shirt and shorts. "You're not going to fall asleep, are you?"

Annick smiled, yawned theatrically, pulled the sheet to her chin. Spot pranced back to the room with the leash in his mouth. I told him, "We're only going as far as the Llinases' house." He dropped the leash, sat, stared at me. "Okay, we'll go to Mr. Parkyn's, but that's it. Capisce?" Spot turned to dash out of the room and smacked his head against the doorjamb.

When we got back, Annick wanted to talk. I nestled against her. She had come up with a story that I could write about a private investigator. "He used to be a hairstylist and makeup artist. He's a master of disguises. And, yes, he's gay. Right off, you've got yourself a niche market."

"I'm listening." I slid the sheet down to Annick's waist.

"Mostly he spies on spouses, handles some insurance fraud cases."

"But then he gets his big break."

"He's also a dresser at the opera. Opera's his passion. And the extra income doesn't hurt."

"He's supporting his ailing mother."

"The night before the opening of *La Bohème* at the Center for the Performing Arts, the renowned but thoroughly obnoxious tenor is murdered at a supper club in Wilton Manors. In a very gruesome way."

"His understudy did it!"

"Everyone has a motive. This particular Rodolfo was an odious and despicable human being."

I heard Spot lapping the water in his bowl. When he gulps like he was then, he ends up pushing the bowl with his muzzle, and he has to keep walking after it as it scrapes across the terrazzo floor.

"Eamon Ruiz."

"Pardon me?"

"Our hero."

I kissed her nose. Then I kissed Sammy Seeds and Frankie the Feeder. Annick pulled the T-shirt over her head. I kissed her belly. Then we heard someone singing, "It wouldn't be so bad if it hadn't been so good." Spot must have stepped on the TV remote and turned on CMT.

In a Volatile State

Annick sat in the living room watching the news, drinking her first cup of coffee. She was talking to the TV, which meant she was talking to me. She didn't want to disturb me while I wrote, but she did want me to know that she was distressed and angry about the five hundred children in Florida's welfare system who've gone missing, and why wasn't I out there on the couch with her and Spot, venting my outrage? Why wasn't I composing scathing letters to the editor of the *Sun-Sentinel*?

Florida is a dangerous place for children. Part of the reason for the disappearance of the five hundred children might be that the state hired 183 convicted felons (yes, that includes child molesters) as child-care workers. One of the nonfelonious workers recently passed out drunk in her car with an infant strapped in the back seat. The worker had been unconscious, snoring and drooling, for nine hours when the cops found her and the dehydrated baby.

Babies get lost here, and they get pummeled, get dropped in Dumpsters, tossed out apartment windows, thrown from highway overpasses. They are stolen from hospitals, sold for drugs, kidnapped off the streets, murdered by boyfriends because they soiled their diapers, or murdered by dads because they wouldn't stop crying. A Seminole father drowned his two sons on the reservation to get back at his ex-wife. The tribe refused to prosecute him. A mom drove her car into a canal, killing herself and her three babies, so that the welfare workers wouldn't take them away. A dad sodomized his three-month-old son while Mom was off at work.

Babies are left home while moms go to bingo. Or they are suffocated in locked cars while dads run into the bar for a drink. Children are gunned down in drive-by shootings, are struck by hit-and-run drivers, are raped by teachers, by priests, by coaches, by counselors. They are allowed to live in filth and to starve. They are scalded with boiling water. Their bones are broken, their skulls fractured, their teeth shattered. Their skin is burned with cigarettes. Their bodies are stuffed into backpacks and buried in shallow graves. Annick says we only have one job to do, and that's to protect and care for our children, and we don't have the will to do it.

Florida's not only a harrowing place for kids, it's tough on fiction writers. How do you compete with daily life here? Right now a hospital is accusing labor organizers of using

voodoo to frighten the workers into voting for union repre-
sentation. A recent Miami city manager was arrested for steal-
ing money from the "Do the Right Thing Foundation" so he
could buy tickets to sporting events and nights out with his
mistress. In Hialeah Gardens, the "Mini-skirt Mayor" was
convicted of hiring a hit man to kill her husband. Her husband testified on her behalf. A county commissioner went to
jail for voter fraud. His wife was having an affair with his
lawyer. He appealed his conviction. He also said, "If you've
been here long enough, you know that nobody gives a flying
fuck if you ran a clean campaign. Nobody gives a shit if you're
involved in absentee ballot fraud or what have you. The
bottom line is that you won." Crazy Eddie and the Z-man
squared off in the Miami mayoral race which Z apparently
won until they tallied up the number of dead people who
voted for him, some, apparently, more than once. Z showed
up in the middle of the night in his robe at a woman's house
carrying a gun and wanting to know why she didn't vote for
him. Crazy Eddie was arrested for throwing a statue of St.
Barbara at his wife in a domestic disturbance. At a County
Commission meeting Chairwoman Marge Gwinn tried to cut
off Commissioner Eleana Mazpul, and Mazpul responded
with, "You're going to leave here in a body bag if you keep this
up." After corporate raider Chick Kachedorian was convicted
of securities fraud, he built a $10 million, 36,000-square-foot
house with twenty-one bathrooms and a basketball court, hid
his money in his own Spirit of Love Foundation, and declared
bankruptcy, owing creditors $200 million. He coaches Little
League. The president of the Miami-Dade County teachers
union was convicted of embezzlement. The president of the

Broward County teachers union was convicted of child pornography. It goes on and on.

You might wonder why we have so many political and corporate reprobates living down here. We have a Homestead Exemption Law, which, among other things, ensures that no matter what crime you've committed, no matter whose money you've stolen, no one can seize the house you live in. And so the stock swindlers buy some land, pump their cash into multimillion-dollar mansions, and all their wealth is safe. That's why everyone from Al Capone to the Salvadoran generals who ran the death squads moves to the Sunshine State. It used to be patriotism, but now it's Florida that is the last refuge of the scoundrel.

I heard Annick use the words "electric chair." I put down my pen.

In a Delicate Way

Annick said, "Guess what I am."

"You're a set designer."

"That's what I *do*. What *am* I?"

We were on the beach promenade walking to Angelo's for pizza. "You're hungry."

"Guess what *we* are."

I watched a man on Rollerblades with a python around his neck and a tattoo of a flaming Sacred Heart over his heart weave between pedestrians. I said, "In love."

"We're pregnant."

I stopped walking, took her hand, and gave her a second to burst out laughing at her joke.

"According to the Pregnosis test."

"Holy shit." I shook my head and smiled. "You need to see a doctor."

"I've got an appointment with Khani in the morning."

So just when we were sure that Annick would never get pregnant, she got pregnant. Just when I had resigned myself to fatherlessness, I was becoming a father. And just when it had become conspicuously apparent that Florida was hazardous to children's health, we were having a kid.

Annick said she couldn't eat cheese and couldn't even look at anything fried, so she ordered linguini with oil and garlic. I ordered beer with my pizza. I said we should probably get married, make it all official, and we should sell one of our houses or maybe both and move somewhere else. Somewhere safe and sane.

She said, "Whoa, Johnny. A pregnancy at forty-two is more problematic than a pregnancy for a younger woman. Let's not get ahead of ourselves."

I tried to imagine this new baby. He was wearing, or she was, I couldn't tell, a cloth cap at a rakish angle. She had violet eyes and flushed cheeks. The middle of her upper lip was pointy like a beak. Over the sound system, Rosemary Clooney sang "Mambo Italiano." The talk at the next table seemed to be about nihility, nonexistence, and I thought we're getting a more philosophical class of tourist than we used to, but then I heard the woman repeat "facility" and understood her to mean the ladies' room. Next door at the ice-cream shop a mother shook her crying child, telling him, Stop it right now, you hear me? A chevron of pelicans glided over the surf. In the dusky light, the first twinkle of gambling ships on the horizon. I squeezed Annick's hand.

Annick was five weeks pregnant, we found out. We were to keep an eye on her blood pressure. We bought a blood pressure cuff and monitor and a stethoscope. Dr. Trask, the obstetrician, said we should consider an alpha feto-protein test to check for spina bifida and Down syndrome. And what if we found out in the affirmative? What then? Well, we chose not to think about that until and if we needed to. If Annick found herself getting fatigued or achy, she was to get rest immediately. Everything looks great, Dr. Trask said. We bought zinc, folic acid, and multivitamins. We bought leafy green vegetables, multigrain cereals, Evian water, and Toll-House cookies.

I bought a used walnut cradle at Babycakes—we were going to be needing it anyway—and an incredibly lifelike vinyl "So Truly Real" baby doll. I wrapped the doll in her receiving blanket, laid her in the cradle, and put the cradle by the bed. I called Spot. He moseyed in and stopped when he saw the cradle. He sniffed it, backed up, and barked. I told him, No! He stuck his nose through the slats and woofed. He put his paws up on the cradle and when he tried to stand, the cradle rocked and he smacked his chin on the top bar. This was going to take a while. When I picked up the doll, Spot leaped at it. I slapped his nose. He sneezed. Twenty minutes later I had Spot licking the doll's arm. Licking and growling, I'll admit, but more licking. Whenever he stealthily opened his mouth, I said, Tut! and he stopped. Good boy, Spot! But then he grabbed the doll's arm in his teeth and took off for the kitchen. Better, I thought, he gets this out of his system now.

Dog Mental

Spot likes to pad around the house, following his nose from room to room, sniffing about to see that all is well. What he's really doing is he's looking for trouble. Like maybe there's a line of white-footed ants crawling out of an electrical outlet, and he can bark at them. Or there's a scrub lizard loose in the house that he can scare up and chase behind the furniture. I eased the bedroom door shut—just the slightest snick as the latch bolt slipped into the well of the strike plate. But that was like a gunshot to Spot the Vigilant. He scratched at the door. When he heard the purr of the zipper on my roll-on luggage bag, he woofed and dug at the floor. I put the luggage back into the closet, the socks back into the drawer, and opened the door. I said, "How's my sweetie pie?"

Spot sniffed the floor, the bed, under the bed, under the cradle. He walked into the closet and barked at the luggage. I told him, Okay, you caught me, but I was only packing for our sleepover at Annick's. I couldn't tell him the truth—not yet—that I was off on a two-week book tour. Spot can't handle the truth. The phone rang. Annick asked me if she could buy a small BB gun. I said, "Annick, listen to yourself."

"But the friggin' squirrels are driving me crazy. And the raccoons are worse. It's not fair."

Annick's preferences in wildlife ran to the winged and the colorful. Annick had planted milkweed, verbena, and shrimp plants to attract butterflies, and soon the yard was busy with metalmarks, zebra longwings, American ladies, and red admirals. She put up feeders to attract birds. She imagined a little paradise of hummingbirds, painted buntings, and palm warblers. What she got were grackles, mourning doves, and blue jays, and the jays quickly developed a taste for red admirals. Eventually, a pair of cardinals arrived, and then a northern parula, and the occasional monk parakeet. Annick was in heaven.

When the squirrels began raiding the feeders, Annick set out ears of corn and Squirola cakes. And that worked until the raccoons appeared—a mom and her three adorable and ravenous kits. Annick was briefly charmed by the babies, even put out puppy chow and unsalted peanuts for them. They ate the chow, the nuts, the corn, and the cakes. They climbed the banana tree and ate the fruit. The squirrels returned to the feeders. The birds vanished. Annick ordered quart jars of fox and coyote urine and broadcast the pellets along the perimeter of the yard. The urine had no deleterious affect on the raccoons and squirrels, but did seem to attract possums and the occasional iguana.

"One of the raccoons came after me this morning with his teeth bared. He was hissing."

"Annick, you can't buy a gun. It's illegal to fire a weapon in the city limits. This isn't Hialeah."

"Jimmy Spillane shot the coconuts out of his tree."

"Jimmy Spillane is psychotic."

"I saw a marsh rat and a squirrel fighting over birdseed this morning and I was rooting for the rat."

"We'll be over after I take Spot to therapy."

See Spot Run

When Spot disrupted a canine wedding ceremony (between Casimir, a Lithuanian hound, and Bijou, a rat terrier) at Bark Park, he was given a choice: sixty hours of community service or permanent banishment from the park. (This was not his first offense.) When I suggested to the pigtailed park ranger that sixty hours seemed excessive, she told me that she considered the attempted rape of the bride at the altar a particularly shameful crime. I said, "Spot's fixed. There was no ravish in his rapture."

She took the citation book out of her breast pocket. "How do you think poor Casimir must feel right now? His little jewel defiled."

I said, "Spot's mount was not Vesuvian."

She asked me for my identification.

"His rapier has been dulled. There's no starch in his noodle. Bijou remains Casimir's exquisite and chaste trinket."

She said, "Can we please talk like adults?"

I registered Spot as a therapy dog at the Prince of Peace Nursing Home in Hollywood. His affability and charm were meant to "bring sparkle to a sterile day." Spot was a natural. He likes everyone, is completely indiscriminate in his relationships. His community service should have been a breeze.

On our first visit, Spot pranced into the lounge like he owned the joint, saw all the new, if not especially bright, faces, and wagged his mighty tail at the prospect of all the delectable petting he was in for. The errant tail swept a water glass off

Mr. Torrey's tray. Stefan, the aide, went for a mop, a broom, and a dustpan.

Stefan said how Spot was maybe a little too rambunctious for this kind of work. Mrs. Agajanian yelled, "Bad dog," at Spot, and Spot barked at her, one of those get-out-of-your-wheelchair-and-we'll-see-who's-a-bad-dog kind of barks. Stefan said he wouldn't tolerate any more of this disruptive behavior.

Mr. Ujjalroop wanted Spot to do some tricks. I explained how we weren't entertainers, just visitors. He waved us away. I introduced Spot to Mrs. Borzilleri. He sweetly laid his paw on her knee. She screamed bloody murder. Stefan said, "A polite dog does not touch a person unless invited."

On our next visit, the residents were celebrating Mr. Reyes's ninety-first birthday. Spot got a pointy party hat and a dish of Neapolitan ice cream and angel food cake. He was so wired he couldn't sit during the balloon volleyball game. Just as Mr. Ujjalroop, one hand on his turban, reached to swat the balloon, Spot leaped and struck the balloon with his nose. Then he ran under the net, muscled Mrs. Borzilleri out of the way, and punched at the balloon. When it popped, a startled Mrs. Fangboner fell to the floor and broke her delicate wrist.

So now Spot was on both probation and a short leash. When we got to the lounge, Elvis was there. Elvis Nguyen is a Vietnamese nail tech who spends an afternoon a week doing manicures and pedicures at the home. Turns out the residents had taken a bus to Broward General for their flu shots, so we were alone. Elvis did Spot's nails a light shade of orchid.

Elvis and I sat on the couch. On the television, a young

woman in a red camisole sat up in bed weeping. The man she was with buttoned his shirt and examined himself in the mirror. I wondered if Telemundo was tackling Chekhov. The woman said, *"Por que, Enrique? Por que?"* Elvis wanted to know how come I didn't have a job. I told him I wrote stories and mentioned the new book. He said, "Would I like your book?"

"Tell me what you like to read."

"Louis L'Amour. Everyone in Xa Vo Dat read L'Amour. It's how we learned English, pardner. L'Amour is America's Shakespeare."

We agreed to exchange books—*The Bright Sun . . .* for *Last of the Breed*. Elvis told me he wanted to move out West, and he was saving every penny he made to "get out of Dodge." He said, "I want to be able to look all around me and see the horizon. I want to look for miles in all directions and see that I'm the only person there."

Wild Kingdom

When Spot and I arrived, Annick was sitting at the kitchen table drinking herbal tea, eating yogurt and wheat germ, reading a cookbook. Spot blasted through the door, ran to Annick, and sat pretty beside her. He licked Annick's face and slobbered on her neck while she hugged him, called him her beauty Spot, her prettiest baby. "Yes, he is!"

I poured myself a cup of coffee, kissed Annick, and sat at the table. Spot went to his toy box, slid the cover off with his nose, took out his jollyball and doggie donut and dropped them to the floor. He took out his plush, grunting mallard, gave it a shake, and tossed it over his shoulder. He stuck his nose back into the box and came out with his boingo bunny, which no longer boings. He carried the bunny to the rug and lay down.

Annick said, "How does this sound? Cajun squirrel ravioli?"

"Annick, you didn't kill a squirrel?"

"Not yet."

I looked at the cookbooks on the table. *Wok on the Wild Side* and *Game Time.*

She said, "Did you see the paper this morning?" She took the local section out of the pile and passed it over.

A mother and her boyfriend locked her seven-year-old daughter in a room for ten months and gave her so little food she weighed twenty-five pounds when she was rescued. She was made to use a closet as her toilet. The boyfriend also punished the child by biting her on the back.

Annick said, "If you wrote a thriller, we could move away."

The squirrels were running across the window screens in the Florida room and leaping from the screens to the bird feeders. It was like they were at an amusement park. Annick opened the door, and Spot ran out, and the squirrels dove for the mangroves, where they sat, flipped their tails, and barked at Spot.

I said, "They sent trappers into the mangroves."

Annick's face brightened. "For the squirrels?"

"For the monkeys."

Five days earlier at dawn, a man driving along Dania Beach Boulevard struck and killed a monkey who'd been crossing the road with a coconut. When the man got out of his car to move the body, a troop of monkeys leaped from the trees and charged him. "They were shrieking," he said. "Baring their fangs. I just made it to the car. One of them had his tail straight up in the air and a stick in his hand." Well, that was enough to get the lawsuit-shy city attorneys on the case. They hired a couple of Seminoles to go in and catch every fringe-faced vervet they could find. The trappers stood to clear $800 for each monkey they delivered to a health lab.

In the morning we told Spot we'd be right back. We were running to Petsmart for dog chow and we needed him to stay here and keep the squirrels off the screens. Annick put out a bowl of Spot's favorite meal, baked kibbee. She and I drove to my place, where I packed my bags and stored So Truly Real on my closet shelf. Annick dropped me at the airport. I told her, Yes, I'll think about the thriller. You take care of our babies.

On the Road Again

The tour began in New Orleans. I picked up a rental car. (I may or may not have had money on my credit card when I showed up. I held my breath, listened for the whirr of the blessed approval machine. I'd sent the payment in at the last minute.) I'd be driving through Louisiana and Mississippi to Memphis. Redbuds in bloom all the way. I somehow lucked out and got upgraded to a top-floor suite at the Sheraton on Canal. Before bed, I headed down to the Pelican Bar and learned that the American Academy of Dermatologists were convening here. I eavesdropped on conversations about surgical hair restoration and skin lesions. (You don't want to know.) I made some notes toward my thriller:

Eamon Ruiz is out line dancing at Longhorns. He's in the middle of a Walk Across Texas when his cell phone vibrates. He checks the caller ID, sees it's Bronwyn Barnett, his boss, the artistic director of the South Florida Opera. Eamon takes off his cowboy hat, shouts into Orson's ear that he'll be back shortly. He goes upstairs to the Black Stallion Saloon where he can hear himself think. Bronwyn tells him that Aldo Tripodi—their Rodolpho—has been murdered behind the Casablanca Supper Club. Eamon tells her to call the cops. She has. She says, We need your help.

Why?

We need to keep this as low profile as possible. It could ruin the Opera.

Eamon says, Listen to yourself, Bronwyn. You sound like you're in some pulp fiction novel.

Someone stuck a hose in Aldo's mouth and poured sulfuric acid down his throat.

Ouch.

Someone with issues.

And thick rubber gloves.

There may have been some hanky-panky going on.

Hanky-panky?

Mifky-pifky, Eamon. Aldo's pants were down to his ankles and so were his satin panties.

Not a pretty picture.

Why are tenors always so goddamn brainsick?

Meet you at the Casablanca in twenty minutes.

Hector gave the corpse an Italian bath and a trouser adjustment before the police arrived.

Not a wise thing to do, Bronwyn.

Eamon punches Off. His hunch is that the murderer is trying to frame the understudy. The understudy is the killer's real target, and poor randy, great-bellied Aldo was merely a pawn in the killer's game. But then Eamon wonders if he isn't getting ahead of himself.

Back in the room, I called Annick. She and Spot were up watching a pet psychic on Animal Planet. Apparently, this toy poodle named Belmondo was channeling Cromwell, a greyhound who had lived with James II. Annick said she was learning a lot about the Restoration. She said she'd gone to Home Depot, bought a Hav-a-Heart trap, baited it with canned mackerel, and set it out in the yard by the heliconia. Within twenty minutes she'd caught the Harrisons' cat, Malvolio. I said, Try peanuts. She told me she felt fine—some cramps, a little nausea.

I stuffed plugs into my ears, put on my eyeshade, fell asleep, dreamed of Annick in a red camisole. She was studying her round belly in the mirror. She said, Why, Johnny? Why? So Truly Real fussed in her cradle. I told Annick, I think she's hungry. At three A.M. I got blasted out of sleep by a furious party in the adjoining suite. People banged into my door; women screeched in the hallway. Then the music got louder. I called security. In five minutes, everything stopped, like that! I slept again until six when I got a series of hang-up phone calls from, I imagine, a frustrated cosmetic dermatologist. I'd spoiled his annual dalliance with a perky drug rep, and now he was going back to Decatur unfulfilled. I got a note in the morning from Billy Shelby, security supervisor, thanking me for "taking the time to inform us about the noise issue."

I SHOWED UP for my two o'clock signing at the Booketeria in Gretna. This was a Saturday, and the warehouse was nearly empty. The assistant manager I was to meet had taken the day off to go fishing. A young sales associate, who'd been dusting books, was assigned to help. She announced over the loud-speaker that I was here to sign my new book, *The Bright Sun Will Bring Us All Some Light*. Close enough. She pointed me to my table. I bought a coffee from a kid who told me he read graphic novels, sat at a table with my stacked pyramid of books, and waited. A woman approached and asked if I'd written any books she's read. I said, Tell me what you've read. She thought about that, then she said, Well, what's this book about?—a legitimate question, of course, but an impossible one to answer. So I said, It's about love and death. She cocked her head, lifted an eyebrow. Was I trying to be cute or something? I knew what she wanted. It's not a romance, I said. Not a mystery. It's not a thriller. She walked away. I was alone again at the launch of my grand book tour. The kid at the café turned away when I caught him pitying me.

I found a book on childbirth and took it to my table. I saw that a fetus at six weeks looks not unlike a seahorse with fingers. I took out my notebook and got to work on the thriller. *Eamon arrives at the Casablanca and sees that the deputy in charge of the crime scene is an old beau, Randy Eversole. I think,*

Well, this could be interesting. Randy becomes Eamon's adversary, an obstacle in Eamon's solving the case. But why would he? *Randy has a wife and two teenage boys. So maybe he's ashamed of his fling with Eamon. Or resentful. Or maybe he's still in love with Eamon.* That's when I realized that a gentleman in a running suit was standing at the table. He introduced himself—Crumpton Murray. We shook hands. Said he was here to buy my book. I said, Let me buy you a coffee. He said, I got to run. He told me to sign the book for Crumpton and Quennelle, and he spelled the names for me. Crumpton said, Don't feel bad. You wrote a book; the folks who ain't here did not.

Meanwhile the corpse is lying in the alley, covered by a blanket. *Eamon notices Bronwyn eyeing Randy. Eamon says, Randy, would you mind if I took a peek at the tenor? Randy says, Step away from the body, sir.*

Two Thumbs Down

Annick called me at seven on Sunday morning.

I said, "How were the reviews?"

"The guys from Little Rock and Houston think you're a genius."

"The *Times*?"

"Seemed like he praised it in spite of himself."

"And the bad news is?"

"A couple of people didn't like it, really didn't like it."

I asked Annick to fax the reviews to me at the hotel. She said wasn't I going to ask about Spot.

"How's Spot?"

"He misses you. He's restless, has toys scattered all over the house. He'll play with his fleecy bone for five minutes and then drop it."

"How are you feeling?"

"I've got an appointment with the doctor. Spotting a little. Just want to be safe."

I told Annick that people who read potboilers want to be spoon-fed. She said they read more than anyone else and buy books like crazy. They keep the book business afloat and subsidize writers like you. I said, Thanks, honey. She said, It goes like this: A murder happens and many people are suspected. All but one of these suspects—the murderer—are somehow eliminated. The murderer is arrested or is killed.

I STOPPED AT Bo's Café in Ferriday for breakfast and read the *Natchez Democrat*. I saw that a local man decapitated his pit bull and kept its head, wrapped in foil, in his freezer. Pit bull's name had been Manson, and he wouldn't listen to reason, the owner/killer said. I took out my scissors and clipped out the article. Why does he keep the head? I finished my grits, ordered more coffee, and then I read the reviews.

The first reviewer wrote that my characters (my darlings) were "one-dimensional" and "neither memorable nor deserving of the reader's sympathy." Yikes! They were "blurry repositories of clichéd feelings." And then he got nasty. He was so flustered he misspelled my name throughout the review. The second reviewer found my characters "offputting" [sic] and "superficial," and objected to what she saw as my "cheap shots at contemporary fiction."

The two bad reviews I'd gotten were both written by citizens of Iowa City. I figured these dogs in the manger were students at the famous writers school. Annick must have noticed the coincidence, too. She sent along a Web page of Iowa facts. Iowa is the thirtieth state in population, the twenty-third in land area, and ninety percent of that land is under cultivation. It's first in pork production, first in corn production, and second in soybean production. It's the eleventh smartest state. And here are the top ten fun things to do in Iowa: 10. View the Herbert Hoover birth cottage in West Branch. 9. Eat as much as you want for free at Pancake Day in Centerville. 8. See the country's largest collection of cotton balls in Waverly. 7. Visit the National Rotisserie Chicken Museum in Sigourney. 6. Attend the Donna Reed Festival in Denison. 5. Tour the American Eraser Factory in Des Moines and receive an eraser in the shape of Iowa. 4. Participate in National Tractor Safety Day, statewide. 3. Visit the Nail Clipper Shrine in Cascade. 2. Play mini-golf at the largest mini-golf course in the world in Dubuque. 1. Visit the Iowa 80 Truck Stop and order a Chubby Burger—two and a half pounds of meat!

This was like a message from above. Move to Iowa, son! Jell-O salads, amber waves of grain, unlocked front doors, 4-H Clubs, the State Fair, sober politicians, Scandanavian Days, balloon festivals, living history farms, scenic byways, American Gothic, wholesome after-school activities, the Music Man, halfway to everywhere, Quaker Oats, and John Wayne.

IN MONROE I checked into the Palms Motel, called my friend Kebo, and asked him to meet me at Enoch's in thirty minutes. Then I called Annick. I asked her would she want to move to Iowa.

"Do they have squirrels?"

Annick got a clean bill of health from the doctor. She's a little weak; she should rest. She bought a book of baby names. She bought a stuffed bunny. Spot thinks it's for him.

My friend Kebo is a character in *The Bright Sun, etc.* He can't understand why I make things up about him when his own life is so profoundly and flamboyantly troubled. I told him his troubles had no shape, and his problems never ended.

He said, "Romeo Pargoud's dead."

"Does that cancel your debt?"

"Far as I'm concerned."

"You have anything to do with his demise?"

"I won't dignify your insinuendo with an answer."

Kebo's a big boy, about 320 pounds. He's been a professional boxer, a chef, a repo man, a lawyer, an inmate, a bouncer, a home builder, a bodyguard for the Dalai Lama, a water-ski instructor, and the automobile mechanic that he currently was.

He said, "I want to be a private investigator."

"In Monroe?"

"In your next book."

"You been talking to Annick?"

"I specialize in tabloid crimes. I scour the tabs for cases no one else will touch."

"I suppose you'll run into Elvis eventually."

"*Kebo and the King.*"

"You don't really think he's alive, do you?"

"I'd like to think so. White pompadour, thick spectacles. He's got a woman who loves him so much she bought him a gun cabinet for Valentine's Day."

"He's a lucky man."

"Think of the movie rights, Johnny. We'd be rich."

Evidence

The book tour was enjoyable most of the time (roasted calamari stuffed with chorizo and garlic chips in a lobster tomato reduction at Postrio in San Francisco), ludicrous some of the time (the two-minute *News at Noon* interview with the anchor who hadn't read my book, but could tell from the cover it was a hoot), and unpleasant on occasion (airports). I took notes as I traveled.

D.C.: *Annick calls and asks me to come home. No, she's not sick. She just thinks I should be there. I tell her I can't; this is a book tour; people are depending on me. She says, You can but you won't. I say if I come home now, then the book reviewers will have won. She doesn't laugh. She says, I've always supported you, but you can't be there for me the one time I ask, the one time I need you. Mr. Fiction can't be bothered, is that it? I ask her if she's been taking her vitamins. She says, Is this how you'll be as a father? She says, Maybe we should just call this off. Before I can ask her what "this" means, she hangs up. She calls back in twenty minutes to apologize. She's crying. She tells me it's her hormones driving her crazy. We kiss good-bye. She calls back in an hour to tell me that if I*

were at all sensitive I would know that it's not her hor-
mones at all. It's her fears. And she hangs up. I call back
and get her machine: You've reached Annick and Spot.
Today's words are chuff *and* fantod.

New York: *I ask my media escort if she's had to deal*
with any literary jerks. She sips her drink and tells me
about the writer who has two houses in two cities, one for
his wife, one for him. At a reception after a reading, said
writer hit on every girl under seventeen in the place and
took a blond high-school girl back to his hotel. The escort
said the writer was a pathetic predator (as well as a
pompous prig and ponderous prose stylist), but she wouldn't
tell me his name. I bought her another drink.

Cambridge: *In the atrium at Au Bon Pain, I sit beside*
a man wearing seven winter coats and carrying several
others. Evidently, he's looted the Salvation Army donation
box. The man beside him has several jackets stuffed inside
a plastic sack. Sparrows fly overhead, land on tables, peck
at croissant crumbs. A woman with a mat of gray hair
stands—she seems to have a single, knee-length dreadlock.
Everyone is more interesting than I am.

Portland: *A woman at the reading who plans on picking*
up my book at the library tells me she writes "goddess-
based, nude Buddhist guerrilla poetry."

Seattle: *I find an Internet café and check my predictably*
disappointing e-mail—all the usual penis enlargement

*and mortgage reduction opportunities. I write back to Dr.
Olofemi Okoye of the Central Bank of Nigeria and assure
him that I am down with sincerity of purpose, mutual
understanding, and utmost confidentiality, and if he will
just send me a cashier's check for the US $24.6 million,
we'll get the embezzlement ball rolling. I send an
"Expression of Love" bouquet to Annick. I walk to Pike
Place Market, buy a bowl of chowder, and watch the fer-
ries crisscross Elliott Bay. I think about life with baby, and
I see myself at my writing desk, the baby cooing in her
cradle beside the desk—I can rock her with my foot—and
Spot curled by the cradle, snoring and twitching in his
sleep. I'm writing about murder and mayhem. I call
Annick's cell and leave a message about how I love and
miss her. Annick's cell used to play "Ode to Joy." Now it
plays the Stones' "Satisfaction."*

San Francisco: *My driver/escort in San Francisco, Felix
Shorten, once took Jack Kerouac home to dinner at his
mom's in Jersey. Mom called Jack a bum, tossed him out.
Felix writes psychic novels and novelizations of movies, is
the lead vocalist in a performance poetry band, and is
married to Janis Joplin's ex-publicist. He likes being early
to our appointments. We're sitting at a sidewalk café in
Berkeley waiting to do an NPR show around the corner.
Felix tells me he's into media rights, and I'm not sure
what he means. He says he collects them, buys them on
the Internet. He's got twelve of them on his bookcase gath-
ering dust. I realize then that he means meteorites. He's
investing in meteorites. A woman, having an animated*

conversation with herself, walks toward us. I tell Felix
that delusional folks ought to be given fake cell phones, so
when they're babbling to no one, they look the same as all
the businessmen at airports. Felix seems a bit uncomfort-
able. I can tell I'd made a possibly non-PC joke in this
most PC of towns. (In Berkeley you can still smoke out-
side, but you have to keep moving.)

Harlan

Back at the hotel, I put the TV news on mute and called
Annick. She told me she'd been on the Internet all night looking at real estate in Iowa. "We could live like royalty."

On the news, a column of uniformed police officers and
citizen volunteers combed through an area of thick brush in
Golden Gate Park. Closed captioning told me that a boy had
blown off his index finger with an M-80, and the folks we saw
were searching for that missing digit.

Annick said, "I found this 120-year-old, two-story, 3/2, in
Harlan, porches front and back, three acres of land, cellar,
attic, and garage, asking $52,000. Can you believe it?"

"We can sell one house, keep the other, buy the Harlan
house—"

"Buy three. Invest in Harlan!"

"Live in Harlan for the summer and Florida in winter."

"You're forgetting about school."

"Home school?"

"West Ridge Elementary."

"How are you feeling?"

"I'm allergic to the iron supplements."

"What'll you do?"

"Eat more meat."

On TV a guy in a camouflage outfit pointed to where his dog had found the detonated finger. Had to slap the dog in the head to get him to give it up. As far as he could tell the finger was salvageable. Annick said, "You'll think about Iowa, then?"

"Nothing but."

I DECIDED TO write a thriller set in Iowa about a man named Harlan Audubon, a farmer who grew up in a quiet and unspectacular way out in the western part of the state. As a boy, Harlan rarely spoke up, rarely declared his needs and wants. He tried to please adults who, he hoped, might come to appreciate him. That meant being obedient, industrious, invisible, and God-fearing. He never had a close friend to speak of. Never had a proper girlfriend. Never stood out—just another stalk in an acre of corn. And then came the senior prom at Black Hawk High School, and it was arranged that he would escort Doris Breeding, whose parents owned Breeding's Rexall Drugs in town.

Harlan drove his father's Chevy pickup to the Grange Hall. He and Doris danced without enthusiasm or rhythm. They skipped the post-prom beer party at the cemetery, drove home in silence, and married two years later. Harlan's parents moved to town, into a front-gabled Craftsman with a spindlework porch, settled in to enjoy their retirement and await the arrival of their grandchildren. Harlan was to pay his father $300 a month until the mortgage on the farm was paid off. The children arrived, one-two-three. Girl-boy-girl. Eva-Ethan-Emma.

The novel begins with an accident. On their drive home from Eva's graduation party, Harlan's beloved daughters are killed when their pickup slams into a bridge abutment on Rock River Road. The girls had been speeding. Alcohol was involved. Doris was numb and desolate, was certain that she would have taken her own empty life had Ethan not been there for her. She quit going to church, told Harlan that the death of children was proof there was no God. Each Sunday morning, Harlan felt the shame of his family's absence at Shepherd of the Valley Methodist Church, felt the eyes of the congregation on him, felt the weight of their abominable pity. He reminded Doris that he'd been against letting the girls attend a party where there was bound to be drinking going on. If he had been obeyed, the girls would be alive today.

Doris screamed, picked up her coffee mug, and struck Harlan on the side of his face. He didn't mean to, but he did, he punched her, dislocated her jaw it turned out. He apologized immediately and profusely. He was bleeding at the eye, soaked with coffee. Doris fled to her parents, who took her to Mercy Hospital. A sheriff's deputy paid Harlan a visit, but charges were not filed. This was an aberration, wasn't it? Harlan said it was. Doris came home after weeks of entreaty and moved into the girls' old room. She and Harlan were civil but not intimate, familiar but not friendly. When Harlan suggested they move away from Black Hawk, get a new start somewhere else, Doris told him Black Hawk was home. But Doris did leave. Not long after Ethan had moved to Des Moines to work at a public relations firm, she left Harlan and moved into town. She found herself a receptionist's job at Johannsen's Funeral Parlor and a cozy rent house on Walnut Street. So: Harlan goes after Doris, begs her to come home. He's desperate, and yet he doesn't say what he has never said—that he loves her. He says he'll have to sell the farm. Can't work it alone. She tells him to go right ahead. Knock yourself out.

The stillness in the house makes him jittery. When he eats, he eats frozen dinners, standing at the sink. He drinks instant coffee, sleeps in his clothes on the Barcalounger. One night Harlan drives into town for a meal at Lundgren's. He's got the radio on, and he hears himself singing along with Johnny Cash and realizes he's feeling lighter-hearted than he has in a dog's age. He rolls down the window and sings. "I've been everywhere, man. I've been everywhere." He calls Arthur at Nelson Realty on the cell and tells Arthur's machine that he's decided to auction off the equipment and sell the farm. Come by in the morning and we'll set the wheels in motion. He stops at Drucker's Five & Dime and buys a road atlas of the U.S. He's never owned a map before in his life.

They're out of lapskaus, but Astrid recommends the poached halibut. To die for, she says. Harlan sits at the counter, looks around, and tries to memorize the place, thinking he'll never be here again. He remembers eating here with the girls after the father-daughter dance at the middle school. That may have been the proudest night of his life. He opens the atlas. He wonders what state is the opposite of Iowa and fig-ures it must be Nevada, all mountains and desert. Shaped like a guillotine's blade. He'll move to Nevada. And that's when he hears her voice.

Harlan looks in the mirror and sees Doris behind him walking to a table with a man he doesn't recognize. Astrid brings the halibut and freshens the coffee. And then Doris is laughing at something the fellow has said. Harlan puts down his fork and wipes his lips with his napkin. He walks to Doris's table and says hi. He tells her about the sale of the farm and about Nevada and all. Doris says she's happy for him. Doris's friend introduces himself, holds out his hand. Harlan tells him, Why don't you shut your cake hole. I'm talking to my wife. The man stands. Harlan pushes him back down in his seat. The restaurant goes quiet. Astrid ducks into the kitchen. The man slaps away Harlan's hand. Harlan grabs the man's throat, but before the ruckus gets out of control, Donny Lundgren has his hands on Harlan's shoulder and leads him back to the counter. He says, We don't want trouble, Mr. Audubon.

Later that night Doris is found murdered, strangled in her house. Harlan is roused before dawn by a knocking at his door. He lets the deputies in. The younger, familiar-looking deputy notices the road atlas opened on the kitchen table. He says, Going to disappear, were you? Harlan is arrested. Open-and-shut case, the deputies figure. Harlan gets his one phone call. He calls the only man who can help him out, Elvis Nguyen, nail tech, cowboy, private investigator.

I put down my pen, massaged my hand. I wanted to call Annick, but it was three A.M. back East. I'd done it—I had my thriller. All I had to do now was write it.

Monkey Business

I threw my suitcase in the trunk, hopped into the car, and kissed Annick. She eased out into the airport traffic. I said, "Where's Spot?"

"Under the bed. He's afraid of the monkey."

"What monkey?"

"The one in the backyard."

I could see she wasn't kidding. "The trappers must have driven him out of the swamp."

"There's an injunction against the trapping."

"The monkeys went to court?"

"The PETA people did. The squirrels are gone."

"One consolation."

"I miss them."

On the drive home Annick told me how at first Spot thought the monkey wanted to play fetch. The monkey would toss a banana at Spot, and Spot would get it, bring it back to the tree, drop it, and bark at the monkey. Finally the exasperated monkey snapped at Spot, and Spot backed off. She told me what drove Spot under the bed was what the monkey did to the squirrel.

"THE SQUIRREL WITH the white ears—the cute one—jumped from the chiminaya to the fence. The monkey reached out and caught the poor little thing in midair. Caught it by the throat in one hand, held it above his head and examined it. The squirrel went limp. You should have seen the monkey's eyes. He looked like Klaus Kinski. The monkey scowled at the squirrel, then tossed him in the water. Spot saw the whole thing."

When we got home, Kinski was not in the yard. Annick prepared me a martini while I crawled under the bed to talk to Spot. He thumped his tail, whined, licked my face, but wouldn't come out, not even when I showed him the glow-in-the-dark fetch ball I'd bought him. I told him everything would be fine now that I was back. He woofed. I said I'd be in the parlor with Annick.

We toasted my return. I touched her belly and said, "How's our baby?"

"I thought I felt him kick yesterday, but I'm not sure."

I showed her the tie-dye T-shirt I bought for baby in the Haight.

"Can you believe she'll be this tiny?"

"And you?"

"I'm okay." She smiled.

"I think I've got the start of a thriller."

Annick said maybe I shouldn't be writing pulp fiction after all.

"I think I'll try it anyway."

"You'll do something to violate each of the commandments. I know you will."

"It's all about misdirection."

"Then it's just a trick?"

"It's magic if you do it right."

And that's when we heard what sounded like a gunshot out back. We ran out of the house, heard splashing in the canal, and looked over to see Kinski floating face down in the water.

I SAID, "Thank God I'm your alibi."

"Who would have done this?"

"He went after my cat."

"Jesus Christ, Jimmy, you scared the shit out of us."

Jimmy Spillane tipped his cap and apologized. "Sumbitch had Babytat in his mitts. I warned him off."

Fish roiled around the monkey carcass, nudging it out to deeper water.

Annick said, "You were protecting your own, Jimmy. No one can blame you."

"Clean shot. Got him right here." Jimmy pointed to his forehead. "Ran about ten yards with his brains all over the hibiscus."

I heard the cruisers on their way.

Jimmy wore a tiny black Speedo, flip-flops, and a too-small T-shirt that said BIG DICK'S HALFWAY INN and had a drawing of a smirking green fish with sunglasses. Jimmy had no place to hide a smoking pistol, or anything else, for that matter. I said, "Jimmy, why don't we go inside for a drink."

He said, "I want them to know I was stone sober when I shot."

Something large grabbed hold of Kinski's leg and pulled him slowly under the water.

"Reckon I'll turn myself in." Jimmy walked through the yard to the street and waved down the speeding cruiser. Unfortunately, he waved with the hand that held the gun. In the story I would write, Jimmy is mowed down in a hail of bullets. He dies in Annick's arms—a man, slightly loco, but good-hearted, a cat lover trying to do the right thing. In the story, Annick, Spot, and I move to Iowa after Jimmy's death. We buy that house in Harlan. There's no place to get arepas or empanadas. No media noches, but we adjust. Friendships are purposeful and productive. There's quite a bit of amiable pressure to join organizations, associations, and clubs. Annick, the baby, and I are visited by Optimists, Lions, Rotarians, Chamber Ambassadors, Foresters, Masons, Owls, Eagles, and Moose. Annick volunteers at Log Cabin Days, directs the play about the history of Harlan. (Many Indians die.) She volunteers at Kinderfarm preschool. I become a Friend of the Library and work the funnel cake booth at the Tiny Lund Festival. We buy Girl Scout cookies, Bible Bars, Christmas cards, magazine subscriptions, and raffle tickets from kids who come to our door. We go to church socials, pancake breakfasts, spaghetti suppers, rummage sales, tag sales, and bake sales. I write my Black Hawk thriller/suspense novel that is a big hit with all but two of the Iowa critics. I make a modest fortune. Meadowlarks perch on the telephone wires and sing.

In real life, Annick and I stay right where we are. I don't write the crime novel. I lose heart when I realize how Doris had suffered so much heartache, had endured so much coldness, and now she seemed happy for the first time in her life. In real life, the alarmed deputy drives his cruiser into a mahogany tree and is knocked out by the air bag. Jimmy pulls him to safety. In real life, Annick loses the baby.

The Night Is Dark; the Hours Slip By

Eleven weeks into Annick's pregnancy, as a result of some embryonic abnormality, perhaps, or an insufficiency in the placental bed or a fault of the uterine structure or a hormonal imbalance or an aberration in the inseminating sperm or some other triggering mischance, her womb expelled the fetus. Annick apologized again. I told her she had nothing to apologize for. We were sitting at a picnic bench along the Intracoastal, sipping Irish whiskey, watching the sun go down over the mangroves and the yachts cruise home to Fort Lauderdale: *Obsession; Liquid Assets; Yachta Yachta Yachta.* Spot was on medication to calm his monkey-rattled nerves, and he was so lethargic we had to tie his plushy SpongeBob around his neck so he wouldn't lose it. He was passed out on the grass by a grill.

Annick said she felt like she had the one purpose in life and that was to protect and care for this unborn child, and she couldn't do it. She told me she knew she should be over the loss, shouldn't be trying to hold on to what cannot be embraced. I held her, kissed her hair. She said she felt her boundless world had suddenly become circumscribed. "I'm so sad."

I saw the park ranger's pickup truck a little too late to hide the whiskey bottle. The truck stopped, shone its headlights on us. I raised my arms above my head like a foiled bandit in a western movie. I picked up the bottle and walked to the truck. "You got me."

He said, "You know better than to consume alcoholic beverages on county property." He shook his head and pulled a pen out of his shirt pocket. "I'll have to write you a citation, sir." He looked past me to Annick and could see, I guess, that she'd been crying. "Your wife all right?"

I explained about the recent miscarriage. He slid the pen back in his pocket and told me to forget what he said. He waved me away. No, he didn't want the bottle. He said the proper way to drink in public was to be discreet. I thanked him. He told me he was sorry, very sorry. And he drove away.

Spot stood, stretched, shook his head, yawned, sniffed SpongeBob, spotted a pelican waddling along the walkway by the water and woofed at it. He lay back down. I told Annick we'd just gotten lucky. We drank to our good fortune. Annick asked me to massage her hands. I did. Her neck. The park ranger returned, cut the lights on his truck, cut the engine, and walked our way carrying a grocery sack. He introduced himself. Carlos Chavez. We all shook hands. He told us that some folks down the way had been having a party. He took out a bottle of Merlot and a bottle of Beaujolais from the sack. And two round loaves of country bread. He pulled out his Swiss Army knife and opened the wine with the corkscrew. He took out plastic cups. He said he knew we wanted to be alone, but please, if we would share the bread and wine with him. Being alone is not good. Annick tore off a hunk of bread. Carlos poured two glasses of Merlot. I stuck with the whiskey. He told Annick how sorry he was. She thanked him.

Carlos said, "My son is dead." He looked at us, poured wine into his cup, and sipped. "Carlito has been dead for two months, and I haven't talked to anyone about it." He put his head into his hands.

Annick said, "We're listening."

Carlos wiped his eyes, put a hand to his mouth, and sniffled. "Nine years old." He breathed deeply. "He fell down roller-skating and broke his wrist. They fixed him up at the emergency ward and sent us home. He was so proud of his cast." Carlos cried. Annick reached across the table and put her hand on his. I squeezed Annick's other hand. Carlos shrugged away his sorrow for a moment. "That night he got a terrific headache. He woke up screaming. He had a high fever, so we rushed him back to Memorial. While we were standing there in the hallway with Carlito on the gurney, he went into seizures. He was dead two hours later."

Carlos and Annick cried. I filled our glasses. Spot walked to the table and sat near Carlos. Carlos said, "I had to tell someone about my beautiful boy. I'm sorry."

We soaked our bread in the wine and ate. We drank some more. And then Annick asked Carlos what was it that had killed Carlito.

"A rare form of streptococcus. Antibiotics can't touch it. It went toxic and ate its way through the tissues and organs. And there was nothing anyone could do." Carlos wiped his eyes. He said to Spot, "What's your name?"

I said, "Spot."

Carlos tapped his thigh, said, "*Mancha!*" Spot stepped closer to Carlos and let himself be petted. "*Buen perrito!*" Spot wagged his sluggish tail. Carlos said, "Death came to the wrong door." He told us about the funeral and all the weeping frightened children from Carlito's school and about Carlito's room and how he still can't bring himself to open the door. Carlos told us how he and his wife don't speak to each other, don't look at each other. "Too much grief in the house," he said. "It fills up all the space. We're all suffocating. My wife, my daughters, myself. And so I stay at work until they're asleep." Spot put his chin on Carlos's knee. Carlos smiled. "*Mancha, mi bebe, Carlito esta muerto.* That's how it is, boy. Carlito is gone. He never said good-bye to me. *El murio por ninguna razon.* No reason at all."

Please, Consider Me a Dream

I drowsed in bed with my eyeshade on and my earplugs in. It could have been five in the morning, could have been ten. I knew Annick was in there with me when she turned over and yanked the quilt to her side. She can be fierce in her defense of sleep. I like to spend time drifting in and out of reverie and dreams before the cold hand of sensibility slaps me straight and I have to get up and get on with it. I lay there remembering a telephone conversation I'd had with my cousin Fairly the night before, either in the living room or in a dream. No, not a dream; she called for real, yes, called to tell me her dad, my uncle Romulus, was in recovery. The stomach mass wasn't a tumor after all. For years, evidently, Romulus had been swallowing coins, 217 of them, as well as paper clips, pins, needles, necklaces, and his dead wife's amber rosary beads. I said, It's good to finally know what's wrong. She said, What's wrong is there's no spark in his plugs. The engine's on, but the wheels aren't turning. I told her about Annick's miscarriage. Fairly told me we were fortunate indeed. She'd just read a book—"a true book, not one of your stories"—in which a boy grew up to torture and kill his parents, hacked them to death with a machete. "It's just not worth the risk, having kids. They're little time bombs, and if you don't defuse them . . ." And then I slipped into a dream, and I'm in the yard with Annick, and she's gardening in a red camisole, and she's still pregnant, and I notice that when she touches a flower, her fingernails take on its color, and then my snoring woke me, and I wondered if

Babycakes would take back So Truly Real, puncture wounds and all, and then I noticed Eamon, Elvis, Doris, and Harlan, sitting beside each other on an empty stage, house lights up, and I realized they were here to audition for my next novel, and I tell them to put down the scripts, today we're flying by the seat of our pants, because that's how I think directors talk, and I say, "You're in the intensive care waiting room at Memorial. The doctor comes in, pulls down his surgical mask, and says, 'I'm sorry, we've done all that we could do.' Go with it." But not much happens, and the doctor keeps repeating his line, and I found myself distracted, awake, thinking about the child we didn't have and how we ought to try again, but Annick said the pregnancy was a fluke and the fluke fizzled, and we'll have to live with that, and I wondered what she was dreaming, and I had no idea. Annick never tells me her dreams unless they involve my leaving her, and then she wants an apology.

I lifted the eyeshade and peeked at Annick. She was awake and reading. She wore the flannel cowgirl pajamas I'd bought for her while on the book tour. Annie Oakley had her rifle aimed right at me. She shot the ashes off the Kaiser's cigarette, remember, so I didn't make any sudden moves. Annick handed me the local section and opened to the movie page. Spot was snoring over in his faux-fleece dog nest under the influence of the last of the doggie Prozac.

"Why don't you write a screenplay. I've always wanted to go to the Academy Awards. Write a movie about a crime novelist."

"With a handsome dog and a ravishing girlfriend?"

"Make the girlfriend the central character."

I read about a mother who left her two-year-old son and her infant daughter alone in a flooded apartment while she went out "looking for money." The state's child-care workers had been called in twice previously to investigate the woman, but they found no evidence of physical abuse. The children were discovered by firefighters in a locked bedroom. The two-year-old was strapped into a car seat on the bed, his left hand tied to a closet door. The ten-month-old was tied to the slats of her crib. The heat was on. The temperature in the apartment was 110 degrees. And I wasn't dreaming.

"Oh, my God, look!" Annick pointed out the bedroom window, where a dozen roseate spoonbills had just alighted in a mangrove tree. She said, "They take my breath away." She cried for several minutes as I held her. She wiped her eyes, and we stared at the brilliant and improbably pink and scarlet birds, hoping they would not be startled into flight, and suddenly there was only now, and this now, I knew, would always be— in ten thousand years we would be right here, nestled in this moment without memory or expectation, Annick and I, rapt by this merciless, this boundless beauty.